THE FRONTIERSMEN

CHARLES EGBERT CRADDOCK

THE FRONTIERSMEN

BY

CHARLES EGBERT CRADDOCK

Author of A Spectre of Power, The Prophet of
the Great Smoky Mountains, In the
Tennessee Mountains, etc.

CONTENTS

Mary Noailles Murfree (January 24, 1850 – July 31, 1922)

Was an American fiction writer of novels and short stories who wrote under the pen name Charles Egbert Craddock. She is considered by many to be Appalachia's first significant female writer and her work a necessity for the study of Appalachian literature, although a number of characters in her work reinforce negative stereotypes about the region. She has been favorably compared to Bret Harte and Sarah Orne Jewett, creating post-Civil War American local-color literature.

The town of Murfreesboro, Tennessee, is named after Murfree's great-grandfather Colonel Hardy Murfree, who fought in the Revolutionary War.Murfree was born on her family's cotton plantation, Grantland, near Murfreesboro, Tennessee, a location later celebrated in her novel, Where the Battle was Fought and in the town named after her great-grandfather, Colonel Hardy Murfree.[3] Her father was a successful lawyer of Nashville, and her youth was spent in both Murfreesboro and Nashville. From 1867 to 1869 she attended the Chegary Institute, a finishing school in Philadelphia.[citation needed] Murfree would spend her summers in Beersheba Springs. For a number of years after the Civil War the Murfree family lived in St. Louis, returning in 1890 to Murfreesboro, where she lived until her death.

Being lame from childhood, Murfree turned to reading the novels of Walter Scott and George Eliot. For fifteen successive summers the family stayed in Beersheba Springs in the Cumberland Mountains of Tennessee, giving her the opportunity to study the mountains and mountain people more closely.

By the 1870s she had begun writing stories for Appleton's Journal under the penname of "Charles Egbert Craddock" and by 1878 she was contributing to the Atlantic Monthly. It was not until seven years later, in May 1885, that Murfree divulged that she was Charles Egbert Craddock to Thomas Bailey Aldrich, an editor at the Atlantic Monthly.[citation needed] Murfree visited the Montvale Springs resort near Knoxville, from 1886. Although she became known for the realism of her accounts, in fact she was from a wealthy family and would have had little contact with the local people while staying at the resorts.

She is buried at Evergreen Cemetery in Murfreesboro

THE LINGUISTER

THE mental image of the world is of individ ual and varying compass. It may be likened to one of those curious Chinese balls of quaintly carved ivory, containing other balls, one within another, the proportions ever dwindling with each successive inclosure, yet each a more minute duplicate of the external sphere. This might seem the least world of all, — the restricted limits of the quadrangle of this primitive stockade, — but Peninnah Penelope Anne Mivane had known no other than such as this. It was large enough for her, for a fairy-like face, very fair, with golden brown hair, that seemed to have entangled the sunshine, and lustrous brown eyes, looked out of an em brasure (locally called "port-hole") of the blockhouse, more formidable than the swivel gun once mounted there, commanding the entrance to the stockade gate. Her aspect might have suggested that Titania herself had resorted to military methods and was

although in the lapse of time they have come to pose successfully in the dignified guise of the " wise patriots of the pioneer period." More than once when the station was at tacked and the women loaded the guns of the men to expedite the shooting, she kept stanchly at his elbow throughout the thun derous conflict, and charged and primed the alternate rifles which he fired. 1 Over the trig ger, in fact, the fateful word was spoken.

" Oh, Nan," he exclaimed, looking down at her while taking the weapon from her hand in the vague dusk where she knelt be side him,—he stood on the shelf that served as banquette to bring him within reach of the loophole, placed so high in the hope that a chance shot entering might range only among the rafters, — " How quick you are ! How you help me ! "

The thunderous crash of the double volley of the settlers firing twice, by the aid of their feminine auxiliaries, to every volley of the Indians, overwhelmed for the moment the tumult of the fiendish whoops in the wild darkness outside, and then the fusillade of the return fire, like leaden hail, rattled against the tough log walls of the station.

" Are you afraid, Nan ? " he asked, as he received again the loaded weapon from her hand.

" Afraid ? — No ! " exclaimed Peninnah Penelope Anne Mivane — hardly taller than the ramrod with which she was once more driving the charge home.

He saw her face, delicate and blonde, in the vivid white flare from the rifle as he thrust it through the loophole and fired. " You think I can take care of you ? " he demanded, while the echo died away, and a lull ensued.

"I know you can," she replied, adjust ing with the steady hand of an expert the patching over the muzzle of the discharged weapon in the semi-obscurity.

A blood-curdling shout came from the Cherokees in the woods with a deeper roar of musketry at closer quarters; and a hollow groan within the blockhouse, where there was a sudden commotion in the dim light, told that some bullet had found its billet.

" They are coming to the attack again — Hand me the rifle — quick—quick— Oh, Nan, how you help me ! How brave you are — I love you! I love you! "

" Look out now for a flash in the pan !" Peninnah Penelope Anne merely admon ished him.

Being susceptible to superstition and a ponderer on omens, Ralph Emsden often thought fretfully afterward on the double meaning of these words, and sought to dis place them in their possible evil influence on his future by some assurance more cheer ful and confident. With this view he often earnestly beset her, but could secure no thing more pleasing than a reference to the will of her grandfather and a protestation to abide by his decision in the matter.

Now Peninnah Penelope Anne's grand father was deaf. His was that hopeless vari ety of the infirmity which heard no more than he desired. His memory, however, was unimpaired, and it may be that certain recollections of his own experiences in the past remained with him, making him a fine judge of the signs of the present. Emsden, appalled by the necessity of shrieking out his love within the acute and well-applied hearing facilities of the families of some ten " stationers," to use the phrase of the day, diligently sought to decoy, on successive

occasions, Richard Mivane out to the com parative solitudes of the hunting, the fish ing, the cropping. In vain. Richard Mivane displayed sudden extreme prudential care against surprise and capture by Indians, when this was possible, and when impossible he developed unexpected and unexampled resources of protective rheumatism. The young lover was equally precluded from set ting forth the state of his affections and the prospects of his future in writing. Apart from the absurdity of thus approaching a man whom he saw twenty times a day, old Mivane would permit no such intimation of the extent of his affliction, — it being a point of pride with him that he was merely slightly hard of hearing, and suffered only from the indistinctness of the enunciation of people in general. And indeed, it was variously contended that he was so deaf that he could not hear a gun fired at his elbow; and yet that he heard all manner of secrets which chanced to be detailed in his pre sence, in inadvertent reliance on his inca pacity, and had not the smallest hesitation afterward in their disclosure, being entitled to them by right of discovery, as it were.

Emsden, in keen anxiety, doubtful if his suit were seriously disapproved, or if these demonstrations were only prompted by old Mivane's selfish aversion to give away his granddaughter, finally summoned all his courage, and in a stentorian roar proclaimed to the old gentleman his senti ments.

Richard Mi vane was a man of many punctilious habitudes, who wore cloth in stead of buckskin, however hard it might be to come by, and silver knee-buckles and well-knit hose on his still shapely calves, and a peruke carefully powdered and tended. He had a keen, wrinkled, bloodless face, discerning, clever, gray eyes, heavy, over hanging, grizzled eyebrows, and a gentle manly mouth of a diplomatic, well-bred, conservative expression.

It was said at Blue Lick Station that he had fled from his own country, the north of England, on account of an affair of honor, — a duel in early life, — and that however distasteful the hardships and comparative poverty of this new home, it was far safer for him than the land of his birth. His worldly position there gave him sundry claims

of superiority, for all of which his hardy pioneer son had had scant sympathy; and Ralph Emsden, in the difficult crisis of the disclosure of the state of his affections, heaved many a sigh for this simple manly soul's untimely fate.

The elder Mivane, with his head bent for ward, his hand behind his ear, sat in his arm-chair while he hearkened blandly to the sentimental statements which Emsden was obliged to shout forth twice. Then Richard Mivane cleared his throat with a sort of preliminary gentlemanly embarrassment, and went fluently on with that suave low voice so common to the very deaf. " Command me, sir, command me! It will give me much pleasure to use my influence on your behalf to obtain an ensigncy. I will myself write at the first opportunity, the first express, to Lieutenant-Governor Bull, who is acquainted with my family connections in England. It is very praiseworthy, very laudable indeed, that you should aspire to a commission in the military service, — the provincial forces. I honor you for your readiness to fight — although, to be sure, being Irish, you can't help it. Still, it is to your credit that you

are Irish. I am very partial to the Irish traits of character — was once in Ireland myself — visited an uncle there " — and so forth and so forth.

And thus poor Ralph Emsden, who was only Irish by descent, and could not have found

Ireland on the map were he to hang for his ignorance, and had been born and bred in the Royal province of South Caro lina, — which country he considered the crown and glory of the world, —was con strained to listen to all the doings and say ings of Richard Mivane in Ireland from the time that he embarked on the wild Irish Sea, which scrupled not to take unprecedented liberties with so untried a sailor, till the entrance of other pioneers cut short a be guiling account of his first meeting with potheen in its native haunts, and the bewil dering pranks that he and that tricksy sprite played together in those the irresponsible days of his youth.

Emsden told no one, not even Peninnah Penelope Anne, of his discomfiture; but alack, there were youngsters in the family of unaffected minds and unimpaired hear ing. This was made amply manifest a day

or so afterward, when he chanced to pause at the door of the log cabin and glance in, hoping that, perhaps, the queen of his dreams might materialize in this humble domicile.

The old gentleman slept in his chair, with dreams of his own, perchance, for his early life might have furnished a myriad gay fancies for his later years. The glare of noonday lay on the unshaded spaces of the quadrangle without; for all trees had been felled, even far around the inclosure, lest thence they might afford vantage and am bush for musketry fire or a flight of arrows into the stockade. Through rifts in the foli age at considerable distance one could see the dark mountain looming high above, and catch glimpses of the further reaches of the Great Smoky Range, blue and shim mering far away, and even distinguish the crest of " Big Injun Mountain " on the sky line. The several cabins, all connected by that row of protective palisades from one to another like a visible expression of the chord of sympathy and mutual helpful neighbor-liness, were quiet, their denizens dining within. At the blockhouse a guard was

mounted — doubtless a watchful and stanch lookout, but unconforming to military meth ods, for he sang, to speed the time, a met rical psalm of David's; the awkward collo cation of the words of this version would forever distort the royal poet's meaning if he had no other vehicle of his inspiration. There were long waits between the drowsy lines, and in the intervals certain callow voices, with the penetrating timbre of youth, came to Emsden's ear. His eyes followed the sound quickly.

The little sisters of Peninnah Penelope Anne were on the floor before a playhouse, outlined by stones and sticks, and with rapt faces and competent fancies, saw whatso ever they would. In these riches of imagi nation a little brother also partook. A stick, accoutred in such wise with scraps of buck skin as to imitate a gallant of the place and period, was bowing respectfully before an other stick, vested in the affabilities of age and the simulacrum of a dressing-gown.

" I love your granddaughter, sir, and wish to make her my wife," said the bowing stick.

" Command me, sir ; command me ! " suavely replied the stick stricken in years.

The scene had been an eye-opener to the tender youth of the little Mivanes; the pomp and circumstance of a sentimental dis closure they would never forget.

Emsden, as hardy a pioneer as ever drew a bead on a panther or an Indian, passed on, quaking at the thought of the wits of the Station as he had never yet feared man, and his respected Irish blood ran cold. And when it waxed warm with wrath once more it came to pass that to utter the simple phrase " Command me " was as much as a man's life was worth at Blue Lick Station.

Emsden thought ruefully of the girl's mother and wondered if her intercession would avail aught with the old autocrat. But he had not yet ventured upon this. There was nothing certain about Mrs. Mi-vane but her uncertainty. She never gave a positive opinion. Her attitude of mind was only to be divined by inference. She never gave a categorical answer. And indeed he would not have been encouraged to learn that Richard Mivane himself had already con sulted his daughter-in-law, as in this high handed evasion of any decision he felt the need of support. For once the old gentle-

man was not displeased with her reply, com prehensive, although glancing aside from the point. Since there were so many young men in the country, said Mrs. Mivane, she saw no reason for despair ! With this approval of his temporizing policy Richard Mivane left the matter to the development of the future.

Emsden's depression would have been more serious had he not fortunately sun dry tokens of the old man's favor to cher ish in his memory, which seemed to inti mate that this elusiveness was only a shrewd scheme to delay and thwart him rather than a positive and reasonable disposition to deny his suit. In short, Emsden began to realize that instead of a damsel of eighteen he had to court a coquette rising sixty, of the sterner sex, and deafer than an adder when he chose. His artful quirks were des tined to try the young lover's diplomacy to the utmost, and Emsden appreciated this, but he reassured himself with the reflection that it was better thus than if it were the girl who vacillated and delighted to torture him with all the arts of a first-class jilt. He was constantly in and out of the house

almost as familiarly as if he were already betrothed, for in the troublous period that seemed now closing, with its sudden flights, its panics, its desperate conflicts with the Indians, he had been able to give an almost filial aid to Richard Mivane in the stead of the son whom the old man had lost.

Richard Mivane had always felt himself an alien, a sojourner in this new land, and perchance he might not have been able even partially to reconcile himself to the ruder conditions of his later life if the bursting of a financial bubble had not swept away all hope of returning to the status of his earlier home in England when the tragedy of the duel had been sunk in oblivion. The frontier was a fine place to hide one's pov erty and fading graces, he had once re marked, and thereafter had seemed to resign himself to its hardships, —indeed, sometimes he consigned his negro body-servant, Csesar, to other duties than his exclusive attendance. He had even been known to breakfast with his head tied up in a handkerchief when some domestic crisis had supervened, such as the escape of all the horses from the pin fold, to call away his barber. As this func-

tionary was of an active temperament and not at all averse to the labor in the fields, he proved of more value thus utilized than in merely furnishing covert amusement to the stationers by his pompous duplication of his master's attitude of being too cultured, traveled, and polished for his surroundings. He was a trained valet, however, expert in all the details of dressing hair, powdering, curling, pomatuming, and other intricacies of the toilet of a man of fashion of that day. Caesar had many arts at command touching the burnishing of buckles and buttons, and

O 7

even in clear-starching steinkirks and the cambric ruffles of shirts. As he ploughed he was wont to tell of his wonderful ex periences while in his master's service in London (although he had never crossed the seas); and these being accepted with seem ing seriousness, he carried his travels a step farther and described the life he remem bered in the interior of Guinea (although he had never seen the shores of Africa). This life so closely resembled that of Lon don that it was often difficult to distinguish the locality of the incidents, an incongruity that enchanted the wags of the settlement,

who continually incited him to prodigies of narration. The hairbreadth escapes that he and his fellow-servants, as well as the white people, had had from the wrath of the Indians, whom the negroes feared beyond measure, and their swift flights from one stockade to another in those sudden panics during the troubled period preceding the Cherokee War, might have seemed more exciting material for romancing for a ven turesome Munchausen, but perhaps these realities were too stern to afford any interest in the present or glamour in the past.

It was somewhat as a prelude to the siege of Fort Loudon by the Cherokees in 1760 that they stormed and triumphantly carried several minor stations to the southeast. Although Blue Lick sustained the attack, still, in view of the loss of a number of its gallant defenders, the settlers retreated at the first opportunity to the more sheltered frontier beyond Fort Prince George, living from hand to mouth, some at Long Cane and some at Ninety - Six, through those years when first Montgomerie and then Grant made their furious forays through the Cherokee country. Emsden, having served in

the provincial regiment, eagerly coveted a commission, of which Richard Mivane had feigned to speak. Now that the Chero-kees were ostensibly pacified, — that is, ex hausted, decimated, their towns burned, their best and bravest slain, their hearts broken, — the fugitives from this settlement on the Eupharsee River, as the Hiwassee was then called, gathered their household gods and journeyed back to Blue Lick, to cry out in the wilderness that they were " home " once more, and clasp each other's hands in joyful gratulation to witness the roofs and stock ade rise again, rebuilt as of yore. Strangely enough, there were old Cherokee friends to greet them anew and to be welcomed into the stockade ; for even the rigid rule of war and hate must needs be proved by its excep tions. And there were one or two pensive philosophers among the English settlers vaguely sad to see all the Cherokee tradi tions and prestige, and remnants of prehis toric pseudo-civilization, shattered in the dust, and the tremulous, foreign, unaccus tomed effort—half-hearted, half-believing, half-understanding — to put on the habi tude of a new civilization.

" The white man's religion permits pov erty, but the Indian divides his store with the needy, and there are none suffered to be poor," said Atta-Kulla-Kulla, the famous chief. " The white men wrangle and quar rel together, even brother with brother ; with us the inner tribal peace is ever un broken. The white men slay and rob and oppress the poor, and with many cunning treaties take now our lands and now our lives; then they offer us their religion ; — why does it seem so like an empty bowl ? "

" Atta-Kulla-Kulla, you know that I am deaf," said Eichard Mivane, " and you ask me such hard questions that I am not able to hear them."

It is more than probable that these sta tioners in the vanguard of the irrepressible march of western emigration had been tres passers, and thus earned their misfortunes, in some sort, by their encroachment on In dian territory ; although since the war the Cherokee boundaries had become more vague than heretofore, it being considered that Grant's operations had extended the fron tier by some seventy miles. It may be, too, that the Blue Lick settlers held their own

by right of private purchase ; for the in hibition to the acquisition of land in this way from the Indians was not enacted till the following year, 1763, after the events to be herein detailed, and, indeed, such purchases even further west and of an earlier date are of record, albeit of doubtful legality.

Now that peace in whatever maimed sort had come to this stricken land and these adventurous settlers, who held their lives, their all, by such precarious tenure, internecine strife must needs arise among them; not the hand of brother against brother, — they were spared that grief,— but one tender, struggling community against another.

And it came about in this wise.

One day Peninnah Penelope Anne Mi-vane, watching from the " port-hole " of the blockhouse, where the muzzle of that dog of war the little swivel gun had once been wont to look forth, beheld Ralph Emsden ride out from the stockade gate for a week's absence with a party of hunters ; with bluff but tender assurance he waved his hat and hand to her in farewell.

" Before all the men ! " she said to her self, half in prudish dismay at his effrontery, and yet pleased that he did not sheepishly seek to conceal his preference. And al though the men (there were but two or three and not half the province, as her hor ror of this publicity would seem to imply) said with a grin " Command me ! " they said it sotto voce and only to each other.

Spring was once more afoot in the land. They daily marked her advance as they went. Halfway up the mountains she had climbed: for the maples were blooming in rich dark reds that made the nearer slopes even more splendid of garb than the velvet azure of the distant ranges, the elms had put forth delicate sprays of emerald tint, and the pines all bore great wax-like tapers amidst their evergreen boughs, as if ready for kindling for some great festival. It is a wonderful thing to hear a wind singing in myriads of their branches at once. The surging tones of this oratorio of nature re sounded for miles along the deep indented ravines and the rocky slopes of the Great Smoky Mountains. Now and again the flow of a torrent or the dash of a cataract added

fugue-like effects. The men were constantly impressed by these paeans of the forests; the tuft of violets abloom beneath a horse's hoofs might be crushed unnoticed, but the acoustic conditions of the air and the high floating of the tenuous white clouds against a dense blue sky, promising rain in due season, evoked a throb of satisfaction in the farmer's heart not less sincere because un-sesthetic. The farmer's toil had hardly yet begun, the winter's hunt being just con cluded, and each of the stationers with a string of led horses was bound for his camps and caches to bring in the skins that made the profit of the season.

One of this group of three was the psalm-singer of the blockhouse. His name was Xerxes Alexander Anxley, and he was un ceremoniously called by the community " X," and by Mi vane " the unknown quan tity," for he was something of an enigma, and his predilections provoked much specu lation. He was a religionist of ascetic, ex treme views, — a type rare in this region, — coming originally from the colony of the Salzburgers established in Georgia.

We are less disposed to be tolerant of individual persuasions which imply a per sonal and unpleasant reflection. Xerxes Alexander Anxley disapproved of dancing, and the community questioned his sanity; for these early pioneers in the region of the Great Smoky Range carried the rifle over one shoulder and the fiddle over the other. He disapproved of secular songs and idle stories, and the settlement questioned his taste; for it was the delight of the sta tioners, old and young, to gather around the hearth, and, while the chestnuts roasted in the fire for the juniors, and the jovial horn, as it was called, circulated among the elders, the oft-told story was rehearsed and the old song sung anew. He even disap proved of the jovial horn — and the set tlement questioned his sincerity.

This man Anxley looked his ascetic char acter. He had a hard pragmatic counte nance, and one of those noses which though large and bony come suddenly short and blunted. His eyes, small, gray, and inscru table, seemed unfriendly, so baffling, intro spective, unnoting was their inattentiveness. His hair was of a sort of carrot tint, which color was reproduced in paler guise in his

fringed buckskin shirt and leggings, worn on a sturdy and powerful frame. His mouth was shut hard and fast upon his convic tions, as if to denote that he could not be argued out of them, and when the lips parted its lines were scarcely more mobile, and his words were usually framed to doubt one's state of grace and to contravene one's tenets as to final salvation. He rode much of the tune with the reins loose on his horse's neck, and perhaps no man in the saddle had ever been so addicted to psalmody since the days of Cromwell's troopers. His theologi cal disputations grated peculiarly upon Ems-den's mood, and he always laid at his door the disaster that followed.

" If I had n't been so traveled that day, — dragged through hell and skirting of purgatory and knocking at the gates of heaven, — I would n't have lost my wits so suddenly when I came back to earth with a bounce," Emsden afterward declared.

For as the hunters were coming at a brisk trot in single file along the " old trading path," as it was called even then, the fleecy white clouds racing above in the dense blue of the sky, their violet shadows

fleeting as swift along the slopes of the velvet-soft azure mountains, and the wind far outstripping them in the vernal budding woods, a sudden stir near at hand caused Emsden to turn his head. Just above him, on a rugged slope where no trees grew save a scraggy cedar here and there amidst the shelving ledges of rock outcropping through the soft verdant turf, he saw a stealthy, fur tive shape ; he was aware of a hasty cowed glance over the shoulder, and then a stretch ing of supple limbs in flight. Before he himself hardly knew it the sharp crack of his rifle rang out, — the aim was almost instinctive.

And it was as true as instinct, — a large black wolf, his pelt glossy and fresh with the renewal of the season, lay stretched dead in an instant upon the slope. Emsden sprang from his horse, tossed the reins to " X," and, drawing his knife, ran up the steep ascent to secure the animal's skin.

Only vaguely, as in a dream, he heard a sudden deep roar, beheld a horned creature leaping heavily upon its fore quarters, toss ing its hind legs and tail into the air. Then an infuriated bull, breaking from the bushes,

charged fiercely down upon him. Emsden threw himself into a posture of defense as instantly as if he had been a trained bull fighter and the arena his wonted sphere, holding the knife close in front of him, presenting the blade with a quick keen cal culation for the animal's jugular. The knife was Emsden's only weapon, for his pistols were in the holster on the saddle, and his discharged rifle lay where he had flung it on the ground after firing. He had only time to wonder that his comrades vouch safed him no assistance in his extremity. Men of such accurate aim and constant practice could easily risk sending a rifle-ball past him to stop that furious career. He could see the pupil of the bull's wild dilated eyes, fiery as with a spark of actual flame. He could even feel the hot puffs of the creature's breath upon his cheeks, when all at once the horned head so close above his own swerved aside with a snort from the dead body of the wolf at his feet. The bull passed him like a thunderbolt, and he heard the infuriated stamping which fairly shook the ground in the thicket below, where this king of the herds paused to bellow and paw

the earth, throwing clods high above the environing copse.

The woods seemed full of maddened, frightened cattle, and Emsden's horse was frantically galloping after the cavalcade of hunters and their pack-train, all the ani mals more or less beyond the control of the men. He felt it an ill chance that left him thus alone and afoot in this dense wilder ness, several days' travel from the station. He was hardly sure that he would be missed

«/

by his comrades, themselves scattered, the pack-horses having broken from the path which they had traveled in single file, and now with their burdens of value all foolishly careering wildly through the woods. The first prudential care of the hunters he knew would be to recover them and re-align the train, lest some miscreant, encountering the animals, plunder the estrays of their loads of hard-won deerskins and furs.

The presence of cattle suggested to Ems-den the proximity of human dwellings, and yet this was problematic, for beyond brand ing and occasional saltings the herds ranged within large bounds on lands selected for their suitability as pasturage. The dwell-

ings of these pioneer herdsmen might be far away indeed, and in what direction he could not guess. Since the Cherokee War, and the obliteration of all previous marks of white settlements in this remote region, Emsden was unfamiliar with the more re cent location of " cow-pens," as the ranches were called, and was only approximately acquainted with the new site of the settlers' stations. Nothing so alters the face of a country as the moral and physical convul sion of war. Even many of the Indian towns were deserted and half charred, — burned by the orders of the British com manders. One such stood in a valley through which he passed on his homeward way ; the tender vernal aspect of this green cove, held in the solemn quiet of the encircling moun tains, might typify peace itself. Yet here the blue sky could be seen through the black skeleton rafters of the once pleasant homes; and there were other significant

' O

skeletons in the absolute solitude, — the great ribs of dead chargers, together with broken bits and bridles, and remnants of exploded hand-grenades, and a burst gun-barrel, all lying on the bank of a lovely

mountain stream at the point where he crossed it, as it flowed, crystal clear, through this sequestered bosky nook.

Something of a job this transit was, for with the spring freshets the water was high and the current strong, and he was compelled to use only one hand for swimming, the other holding high out of the water's reach his powder horn. For, despite any treaties of peace, this was no country for a man to traverse unarmed, and an encounter with an inimical wandering Indian might serve to make for his comrades' curiosity concerning his fate, when they should chance to have leisure to feel it, a perpetual conundrum.

He had never, however, made so lonely a journey. Not one human being did he meet — neither red man nor white — in all the long miles of the endless wilderness; naught astir save the sparse vernal shadows in the budding woods and the gentle spring zephyr swinging past and singing as it went. Now and again he noted how the sun slowly dropped down the skies that were so fine, so fair, so blue that it seemed loath to go and leave the majestic peace of the zenith. The stars scintillated in the dark night as

if a thousand bivouac fires were kindled in those far spaces of the heavens responsive to the fire which he kept aglow to cook the supper that his rifle fetched him and to ward off the approach of wolf or panther while he slept. He was doubtless in jeo pardy often enough, but chance befriended him and he encountered naught inimical till the fourth day when he came in at the gate of the station and met the partners of the hunt, themselves not long since arrived.

They waited for no reproaches for their desertion. They were quick to upbraid. As they hailed him in chorus he was bewildered for a moment, and stood in the gateway leaning on his rifle, his coonskin cap thrust back on his brown hair, his bright, steady gray eyes concentrated as he listened. His tall, lithe figure in his buckskin hunting shirt and leggings, the habitual garb of the frontiersmen, grew tense and gave an inti mation of gathering all its forces for the de fensive as he noted how the aspect of the station differed from its wonted guise. Every house of the assemblage of little log cabins stood open ; here and there in the misty air, for there had been a swift, short spring

shower, fires could be seen aglow on the hearths within ; the long slant of the red sunset rays fell athwart the gleaming wet roofs and barbed the pointed tops of the palisades with sharp glints of light, and a rainbow showed all the colors of the prism high against the azure mountain beyond, while a second arch below, a dim duplication, spanned the depths of a valley. The fron tiersmen were all in the open spaces of the square excitedly wrangling — and suddenly he became conscious of a girlish face at the embrasure for the cannon at the blockhouse, a face with golden brown hair above it, and a red hood that had evidently been in the rain. " Looking out for me, I wonder ? " he asked himself, and as this glow of agi tated speculation swept over him the men who plied him with questions angrily ad monished his silence.

" He has seen a wolf! He has seen a wolf! J T is plain ! " cried old Mivane, as he stood in his metropolitan costume among the buckskin-clad pioneers. " One would know that without being told ! "

" You shot the wolf and stampeded the cattle, and the herders at the cow-pens on the Keowee Eiver can't round them up again ! " cried one of the settlers.

" The cattle have run to the Congarees by this time!" declared another pessimis tically.

" And it was you that shot the wolf ! " cried " X " rancorously.

" The herders are holding us responsible and have sent an ambassador/' explained John Ronaekstone, anxiously knitting his brows, " to inform us that not a horse of the pack-train from Blue Lick Station shall pass down to Charlestown till we indemnify them for the loss of the cattle."

" Gadso ! they can't all be lost! " ex claimed old Mivane floutingly.

" No, no ! the herders go too far for damages — too far ! They are putting their coulter too deep ! " said a farmer fresh from the field. He had still a bag of seed-grain around his neck, and now and again he thrust in his hand and fingered the kernels.

" They declare they '11 seize our skins," cried another ambiguously, — then, con scious of this, he sought to amend the mat ter, — " Not the hides we wear," — this was no better, for they were all arrayed in hides,

save Richard Mivane. " Not the hides that we were born in, but our deerhides, our peltry, — they '11 seize the pack-train from Blue Lick, and they declare they '11 call on the commandant of Fort Prince George to oppose its passing with the king's troops."

An appalled silence fell on the quad rangle, — save for the fresh notes of a mock ingbird, perching in jaunty guise on the tower of the blockhouse, above which the rainbow glowed in the radiant splendors of a misty amber sky.

" The king's troops ? Would the com mandant respond?" anxiously speculated one of the settlers.

The little handful of pioneers, with their main possessions in the fate of the pack-train, looked at one another in dismay.

" And tell me, friend Feather-pate, why did it seem good to you to shoot a wolf in the midst of a herd of cattle ? " demanded Richard Mivane.

Ralph Emsden, bewildered by the results of this untoward chance, and the further catastrophe shadowed forth in the threat ened seizure of the train, rallied with all his faculties at the note of scorn from this quarter.

" Sir, I did not shoot the wolf among the cattle. There was not a horn nor a hoof to be seen when I fired."

Mivane turned to " X " with both hands outstretched as much as to say, " Take that for your quietus!" and shouldering his stick, which had an ivory head and a sword within, strode off after his jaunty fashion as if there were no more to be said.

It was now Alexander Anxley's turn to sustain the questioning clamor. " I will not deny " — " That is, I said " — " I meant to say," — but these qualifications were lost in the stress of Emsden's voice, once more rising stridently.

" Not a horn nor a hoof to be seen till after I had fired. I did n't know there were any cow-pens about — did n't use to be till after you had crossed the Keowee. But if there had been, is a man to see a wolf pull down a yearling, say, and not fire a rifle because Madam Cow will take the high-strikes or Cap'n Bull will go on the ram page ? Must I wait till I can make a leg," — he paused to execute an exaggerated obeisance, graceful enough despite its mockery, — " (Under your favor, Cap'n

Bull/ and (With your ladyship's permis sion/ before I kill the ravening brute, big enough to pull down a yearling? Don't talk to me ! Don't talk to me ! " He held out the palms of his hands toward them in interdiction, and made as if to go — yet went not!

For a reactionary sentiment toward him had set in, and there were those fair-minded enough, although with their little all at stake, to admit that he had acted with rea sonable prudence, and that it was only an unlucky chance which had sent the panic through the herds with such disastrous effect.

" The herders should not stop the pack-train, if I had my will/' declared one of the settlers with a belligerent note.

" No, no," proclaimed another; " not if it takes all the men at Blue Lick Station to escort it! "

" Those blistered redcoats at Fort Prince George are a deal too handy to be called on by such make-bates as the herders on the Keowee River."

" Fudge ! The commandant would never let a bayonet stir."

" Gad ! I 'd send an ambassador for an ambassador. Tit for tat," declared Ems-den. " I 'd ask 'em what's gone with all our horses, — last seen in those desolated cow-pens, — that the voice of mourning is now lifted about! "

There was a chuckle of sheer joy, so abrupt and unexpected that it rose with a clatter and a cackle of delight, and culmi nated in a yell of pleasurable derision.

Now everybody knew that the horses bought in that wild country would, unless restrained, return every spring to " their old grass," as it was called, — to the places where they had formerly lived. When this annual hegira took place in large numbers, some permanent losses were sure to ensue. The settlers at Blue Lick had experienced this disaster, and had accepted it as partly the result of their own lack of precaution during the homing fancy of the horses. But since the herders manifested so little of the suavity that graces commercial inter course, and as some of the horses had been seen in their cow-pens, it was a happy thought to feather the arrow with this taunt.

" And who do you suppose will promise to carry such a message to those desperate, misguided men, riding hither an' thither, searching this wild and woeful wilderness for hundreds o' head o' cattle lost like needles in a hayrick, and eat by wolves an' painters by this time ? " demanded " X " derisively.

" I promise, I promise ! — and with hearty good will, too! " declared Emsden. " And I '11 tell 'em that we are coming down soon armed to the teeth to guard our pack-train, and fight our way through any resistance to its passage through the coun try on the open trading-path. And I '11 acquaint the commandant of Fort Prince George of the threats of the herders against the Blue

Lick Stationers, and warn him how he attempts to interfere with the lib erties of the king's loyal subjects in their peaceful vocations."

Thus Emsden gayly volunteered for the mission.

The next morning old Richard Mivane, thinking of it, shook his head over the fire, — and not only once, but shook it again, which was a great deal of trouble for him

to take. Having thus exerted his altruistic interest to the utmost, Richard Mivane re lapsed into his normal placidity. He leaned back in his armchair, the only one at the station, fingering his gold-lined silver snuff box, with its chain and ladle, his eyes dwell ing calmly on the fire, and his thoughts busy with far away and long ago.

He was old enough now to enter into the past as a sort of heritage, a promised land which memory had glozed with a glamour that can never shine upon the uncertain aspects of the future. The burning sense of regret, the anguish of nostalgia, the re-linquishment of an .accustomed sphere, its prospects and ideals, the revolt against the uncouth and rude conditions of the new status, the gradual reluctant naturalization to a new world, — these were forgotten save as the picturesque elements of sorrow and despair that balanced the joys, the interest, the devil-may-care joviality, the adventure, the strange wild companionship, — all that made the tale worth rehearsing in the flare and the flicker of the fireside glow.

The rains had come. The dark slate-tinted clouds hung low over the station, but

every log house, freshly dight with white wash of the marly clay, after the Indian method, still shone in the shadow as if the sun were upon it. The turf was green, de spite the passing of many feet, and where a slight depression held water, a few ducks, Carolina bred, were quacking and paddling about; now and then these were counted with great interest, for they had a trick of taking to the woods with others of their kind, and relapsing to savagery, — truly distressing to the domestic poultry pros pects of the station. The doors of the Mi-vane cabin were all ajar, — the one at the rear opening into a shed-room, unfloored, which gave a vista into more sheds, merely roofed spaces, inclosed at either end. A loom was in the shed-room, and at it was seated on the bench in front, as a lady sits at an organ, the mistress of the house, fair but faded, in a cap and a short gown and red quilted petticoat, giving some instruc tion, touching an intricate weave, to a negro woman, neatly arrayed in homespun, with a gayly turbaned head, evidently an expert herself, from the bland and smiling manner

f O

and many self-sufficient and capable nods

with which she perceived and appropriated the knotty points of the discourse.

In the outer shed, Caesar, clad like the Indians and the pioneers in buckskin, was mending the plough-gear, and talking with great loquacity to another negro, of the type known then and later as " the new nigger," the target of the plantation jokes, because of his " greenness," being of a fresh impor tation. He possibly remembered much of Africa, but he accepted without demur and with admiring and submissive meekness stories of the great sights that Caesar pro tested he had seen there, — Vauxhall Gar dens and Temple Bar (which last Caesar thought in his simplicity was a bar for the refreshment of the inner man) and a certain resort indisputably for that purpose called White's Chocolate House, — all represented as pleasantly and salubriously situated in the interior of Guinea. But after all, if a story is well told, why carp at slight anacho-risms ?

Richard Mivane's attention had been di verted from the thread of his own reminis cences by the fact that the little flax-wheel of Peninnah Penelope Anne had ceased to

whirl, and the low musical monody of its whir that was wont to bear a pleasant ac companiment to the burden of his thoughts was suddenly silent. He lifted his eyes and saw that she was gazing dreamily into the flare of the great fire, the spinning-wheel still, the end of the thread motionless in her hand. The burnished waves of her golden brown hair were pushed a bit awry, and her face was so wan and thoughtful that even her dress of crimson wool did not lessen its pallor. The voices of the three children on the floor grated on the old man's mood as they were busied in defending a settler's fort, insecurely constructed of stones and sticks, and altogether roofless, garrisoned by a number of pebbles, while a poke full of wily Indian kernels of corn swarmed to the attack.

" Why is my pretty pet so idle ? " he asked, for while the wheel should whirl he could dream.

She made no answer, only turned her troubled, soft hazel eyes upon him.

" And have you seen a wolf, too, that you have lost your tongue ? "

At the word " wolf" she burst into

tears. And then, discarding all caution in the breaking down of her reserve, she sprang up, overturning the wheel and rushing to his chair.

Now Richard Mivane had never encour aged his grandchildren to clamber over his chair. He protested great fear of the sticky fingers of the more youthful in contact with his preternaturally fine clothes ; he declared they reminded him of squirrels, which he detested ; he was not sure they did not look like rats. All this was of great effect; for his many contemptuous whimsical prejudices were earnestly respected.

For instance, whenever 'possum was served at the pioneer board they who partook car ried their plates for the purpose to a side table. " The look of the animal's tail is enough for me — it curls," he would say.

" So does a pig's tail curl," his son used to remonstrate sensibly.

" Not having kept a straight course so long, — then twirling up deceitfully like a second thought. This fellow is a monstros ity, — and his wife has a pocket for a cradle, — and I don't know who they are nor where they came from, — they were left over from

before the Flood, perhaps, — they look somehow prehistoric to me. I am not ac quainted with the family."

And turning his head aside he would wave away the dainty, the delight of the pioneer epicure time out of mind.

The diplomatic reason, however, that Richard Mivane was wont to shove off his grandchildren from the arm of that stately chair was that here they got on his blind side, — his simple, grandfatherly, affectionate predilection. The touch of them, their scrambling, floundering, little bodies, their soft pink cheeks laid against his, their golden hair in his clever eyes, their bright glances at close range, — he was then like other men and could deny them nothing! His selfishness, his vanity, his idleness, his frippery were annulled in the instant. He was resolved into the simple constituent ele ments of a grandfather, one part doting folly, one part loving pride, and the rest leniency, and he was as wax in their hands.

None of them had so definitely realized this, accurately discriminating cause and effect, as Peninnah Penelope Anne. She felt safe the moment that she was perched

on the arm of her grandfather's chair, her soft clasp about his stiff old neck, her tears flowing over her cheeks, all pink anew, es caping upon his wrinkled, bloodless, pale visage and taking all the starch out of his old-fashioned steinkirk. He struggled fu-tilely once or twice, but she only hugged him the closer.

" Oh, don't let him go ! Oh, don't let him go ! " she cried.

" The wolf that we were talking about ? By no means ! Lovely creature that he is ! We '11 preserve, if you like, wolves instead of pheasants! • I remember a gentleman's estate in Northumberland — a little beyond the river " —

" Oh, grandfather, don't let him go ! " she sobbingly interrupted. " It was he who shot the wolf and stampeded the herds, and the cow-drivers will quarrel with him when they would not have angry words with an other ambassador. They will kill him! They will kill him ! "

" What for ? Poaching ? — shooting their wolf?"

" Any one else would be safe, grandfa ther— except poor Ralph ! "

" Go yourself then, May-day ! "

66 1 would, grandfather ! I would not be afraid ! " She put her soft little hand on his cheek to turn his head to look into her confident eyes.

" An able and worshipful ambassador ! " he said banteringly.

66 Oh, grandfather, this is no time to risk quarrels among the settlers, and bloodshed. Oh, the herders would kill him ! And the Injuns aU so unfriendly — they might take the chance to get on the war-path again when the settlers are busy kiUing each other — and oh, the cow-drivers will kill Kalph Emsden ! "

All this persuasion was of necessity in a distinct loud voice; unnoticed, however, for a crisis had supervened in the play of the children by the chimney-place settle, and the sanguinary struggles and scalping in the storming of the fort were blood-curd ling to behold to any one with enough im agination to discern a full-armed and fierce savage in a kernel of corn, and a stanch and patriotic Carolinian in a pebble. But when Peninnah Penelope Anne, all attuned to this high key, burst out weeping with

commensurate resonance, all the vocations of the household came to a standstill, and her mother appeared, surprised and reprov ing, in the doorway.

" Peninnah Penelope Anne," she said with her peculiar exact deliberation and gift of circumlocution, " it is better to go and sew your sampler than to tease your grandfather."

" She does not tease me — I have not shed a tear! That was not the sound of my weeping ! " he declared facetiously, one arm protectingly about the little sobbing figure.

" He does not like his grandchildren to climb about him like squirrels and wild cattle," the lady continued. Then irrele vantly, " Long stitches were always avoided in our family. The work you last did in your sampler has been taken out, child, and you can sew it again and to better advan tage."

" And earn your name of Penelope," said Richard Mivane.

But he was putting on his hat and evi dently had some effort in prospect, for how could he resist, — she looked so childish

and appealing as she sat before the fire, weeping those large tears, and absently preparing to sew her sampler anew.

While Richard Mivane, by virtue of his early culture, the scanty remains of his pro perty, his fine-gentleman habits and tra ditions, and the anomaly of his situation, was the figure of most mark at the station, its ruling spirit was of far alien character. This was John Ronackstone, a stanch In dian fighter; a far-seeing frontier politician; a man of excellent native faculties, all sharpened by active use and frequent emer gencies; skilled and experienced in devious pioneer craft; and withal infinitely stub born, glorying in the fact of the unchange-ableness of his opinions and his immutable abiding by his first statements. After one glance at his square countenance, his steady noncommittal black eyes, the upward bull dog cant of a somewhat massive nose, the firm compression of his long thin lips, one would no more expect him to depart from the conditions of a conclusion than that a signpost would enter into argument and in view of the fatigue of a traveler mitigate and recant its announcement.

Nevertheless Richard Mivane expected " some sense," as he phrased it, from this adamantine pioneer. Such a man naturally arrogated and obtained great weight among his fellows, and perhaps his lack of vacilla tion furthered this preeminence. He was a good man in the main as well as force ful, but an early and a very apt expression of the demagogue. And as he tolerated amongst his mental furniture no illusions and fostered no follies, his home life har bored no fripperies. His domicile was a contrast to the better ordered homes of the station, but here one might have meat and

' o

shelter, and what more should mortal ask of a house ! He often boasted that not an atom of iron entered into its structure more than into an Indian's wigwam. Even the clapboards were fastened on to the rafters with wooden pegs in lieu of nails, although nails were not difficult to procure. He had that antagonism to the mere conventions of civilization often manifested by those who have been irked by such fetters before finally casting them off. It was a whole some life and a free, and if the inmates of the house did not mind the scent of the

drying deerskins hanging from the beams, which made the nose of Richard Mivane very coy, the visitor saw no reason why they should not please themselves. The stone-flagged hearth extended half across the room, and sprawling upon it in frowsy disorder was a bevy of children of all ages, as fat as pigs and as happy-go-lucky. He had hardly seated himself, having stepped about carefully among their chubby fingers and toes lest a crushing disaster supervene, than he regretted his choice of a confidant. He had his own unsuspected sensitiveness, which was suddenly jarred when the wife in the corner, rocking the cradle with one foot while she turned a hoe-cake baking on the hearth with a dextrous flip of a knife, and feeling secure in his deafness, cast a witty fling at his fastidious apparel. With that frequent yet unexplained phenome non of acoustics, her voice was so strung that its vibrations reached his numb per ceptions as duly as if intended for his ears. He made no sign, in his pride and polite ness, both indigenous. But he said to him self, " I don't laugh at her gown, — it is what she likes and what she is accustomed

to wear. And why can't she let me dress in peace as I was early trained to do? God knows I feel myself better than nobody."

And he was sensible of his age, his in firmity, his isolation, and his jauntiness was eclipsed.

Thus he entered the race with a handi cap, and John Ronackstone would hear none of his reasons with grace. He could not and he would not consent to the nomina tion of an ambassador in the stead of Ems-den, who had volunteered for the service, which was the more appropriate since it was he who had shot the wolf and brought the stampede and its attendant difficulties upon the herders of the Keowee River, and this threat of retaliation upon the Blue Lick Stationers. If there were danger at hand, let a volunteer encounter it! In vain Mi-vane argued that there was danger to no one else. John Ronackstone, who found an added liberty of disputation in the emphasis imposed by the necessity of roaring out his immutable opinions in an exceeding loud voice, retorted that so far as he was informed the " cow-drivers" on the Keowee were not certain who it was that had committed

this atrocity, unless perhaps their messen ger during his sojourn at Blue Lick Sta tion had learned the name from " X." But this uncertainty, Mivane argued, was the very point of difficulty. It was the maddest folly to dispatch to angry men, smarting under a grievous injury, messages of taunt and defiance by the one person who in their opinion, perhaps, had carelessly or willfully wrought this wrong. His life would pay the forfeit of the folly of his fellow-sta tioners.

Mivane noted suddenly that the woman rocking the cradle was laughing with an ostentatious affectation of covert slyness, and a responsive twinkle gleamed in the eyes of John Konackstone. As he caught the grave and surprised glance of his visitor he made a point of dropping the air of a comment aside, which he, as well as she, had insistently brought to notice, and Mivane was aware that here was something which sought an opportunity of being revealed as if by necessity.

" Well, sir," Konackstone began in a tone of a quasi - apology, "we were just saying — that is, I sez to X, who was

in here a while ago, — I sez, e I '11 tell you what is goin' to happen/ — I sez, ' old Gentleman Rick/ — excuse the freedom, sir, — ' he '11 be wantin' to send somebody else in Ralph Emsden's place.' X, he see the p'int, just as you see it. He sez, ' Some body that won't be missed — somebody not genteel enough to play loo with him after supper/ sez X. < Or too religious/ sez I. ' Or can't sing a good song or tell a rousing tale/ sez X. ' Or listen an' laugh in the right places at the gentleman's old cracks about the great world/ sez I. ' He '11 never let Ralph Emsden go/ sez X. ' Jus' some poor body will do/ sez I. ' Jus' man enough to be scalped by the Injuns if the red sticks take after him/ sez X. ' Or have his throat cut if the cow-drivers feel rough yet/ sez I. ' Jus' such a one ez me/ sez X. 6 Or me/ sez I."

" Sir," said old Mivane, rising, and the impressive dignity of his port was such that the cradle stopped rocking as if a spell were upon it, and every child paused in its play, sprawling where it lay, " I am obliged to you for your polite expression of opinion of me, which I have never done aught to

justify. I have nothing more to urge upon the question of the details which brought me hither, but of one thing be certain, — if Emsden does not go upon this mission / shall be the ambassador. I apprehend no danger whatever to myself, and I wish you a very good day."

And he stepped forth with his wonted jaunty alacrity, leaving the man and his wife staring at each other with as much surprise as if the roof had fallen in.

A greater surprise awaited Mivane with out. The rain was falling anew. In vast transparent tissues it swept with the gusty wind over the nearest mountains of the Great Smoky Range, whose farther reaches were lost in fog. The slanting lines, vaguely discerned in the downpour, almost oblit erated the presence of the encompassing forests about the stockade. He noted how wildly the great trees were yet swaying, and he realized, for he could not have heard the blast, that a sudden severe wind-storm had passed over the settlement while he was within doors. The blockhouse, the tallest of the buildings, loomed up darkly amidst the gathering gray vapor, and through the

great gates of the stockade, which opened on the blank cloud, were coming at the moment several men bearing a rude litter, evidently hastily constructed. On this was stretched the insensible form of Ralph Ems-den, who had been stricken down in the woods with a dislocated shoulder and a broken arm by the falling of a branch of a great tree uprooted by the violence of the gusts. He had almost miraculously escaped being crushed, and was not fatally hurt, but examination disclosed that he was absolutely and hopelessly disabled for the time being, and Richard Mi vane realized that he him self was the duly accredited ambassador to the herders on the Keowee River.

He went home in a pettish fume. No sooner was he within and the door fast shut, that none might behold save only those of his own household, who were accustomed to the aberrations of his temper and who regarded them with blended awe and re spect, than he reft his cocked hat from his head and flung it upon the floor. Peninnah Penelope Anne sprang up so precipitately at the dread sight that she overturned her stool and drew a stitch awry in her sampler,

longer than the women of her family were accustomed to take. The children gazed spellbound. The weavers at the loom were petrified; even the creak of the treadle and the noisy thumping of the batten — those perennial sounds of a pioneer home — sunk into silence. The two nesrroes at the

o

end of the vista beyond the shed-room, with the ox-yoke and plough-gear which they were mending between them, opened wide mouths and became immovable save for the whites of astonished rolling eyes. Then, and this exceeded all precedent, Eichard Mivane clutched his valued peruke and, with an inward plaintive deprecation of the ex tremity of this act of desperation, he cast it upon the hat, and looked around, bald, despairing, furious, and piteous.

It was, however, past the fortitude of woman to behold without protest this des ecration of decoration. Peninnah Penelope Anne sprang forward, snatched the glossy locks from the puncheons, and with a ten der hand righted the structure, while the powder flew about in light puffs at her touch, readjusting a curl here and a clev erly wrought wave there. The valet's

pious aspiration from the doorway, " Bress de Lord! " betokened the acuteness of the danger over-past.

" Why, grandfather ! " the girl admon ished Mivane ; " your beautiful peruke ! — sure, sir, the loveliest curls in the world! And sets you like your own hair, — only that nobody could really have such very genteel curls to grow — Oh — oh — grand father ! "

She did not offer to return it, but stood with it poised on one hand, well out of harm's way, while she surveyed Mivane reproachfully yet with expectant sympathy.

Perhaps he himself was glad that he could wreak no further damage which he would later regret, and contented himself with furiously pounding his cane upon the pun cheon floor, a sturdy structure and well cal culated to bear the brunt of such expressions of pettish rage.

" Dolt, ass, fool, that I am ! " he cried. " That I should so far forget myself as to offer to go as an ambassador to the herders on the Keowee! ' And once more he banged the floor after a fashion that dis-

o

counted the thumping of the batten, and the room resounded with the thwacks.

An old dog, a favorite of yore, lying asleep on the hearth, only opened his eyes and wrinkled his brows to make sure, it would seem, who had the stick; then clos ing his lids peacefully snoozed away again, presently snoring in the fullness of his sense of security. But a late acquisition, a gaunt deerhound, after an earnest observation of his comrade's attitude, as if referring the crisis to his longer experience, scrutinized severally the faces of the members of the family, and, wincing at each resounding whack, finally gathered himself together apprehensively, as doubtful whose turn might come next, and discreetly slunk out unobserved by the back door.

Peninnah Penelope Anne rushed to the rescue.

" And why should you not be an ambas sador, sir ? " she demanded.

66 Why — why — because, girl, I am deafer than the devil's dam! I cannot fetch and carry messages of import. I could only give, occasion for ridicule and scorn in even offering to assume such an office."

Peninnah Penelope Anne had flushed with the keen sensitiveness of her pride.

She instantly appreciated the irking of the dilemma into which he had thrust himself forgetting his infirmity, and she could have smitten with hearty enmity and a heavy stick any lips which had dared to smile. She responded, however, with something of her mother's indirection.

" Under your favor, sir, you don't know how deaf the devil's dam may be — and it is not your wont to speak in that strain. I 'm sure it reminds me of that man they call ' X,' — a sort of churl person, — who talks of the devil and blue blazes and brim stone and hell as if — as if he were a na-tive."

This was a turning of the sword of the pious " X " upon himself with a vengeance, for he was prone in his spiritual disquisi tions to detail much of the discomfort of the future state that awaited his careless friends.

The allusion so far pleased old Mivane, who resented a suspected relegation of him self to a warm station in the schemes of " X," that, although his head was still bald and shining like a billiard ball, he suffered himself to drop into his chair, his stick rest-ing motionless on the long-suffering pun cheon floor.

" If I could only hear for a day I 'd for give twenty soundless years ! " he declared piteously, for he so deprecated the enforced withdrawal from the enterprise that he had heedlessly undertaken, and felt so keenly the reflections upon his sentiments and sin cerity surreptitiously canvassed between Ronackstone and " X," and then cavalierly rehearsed in his presence.

" You are only deaf to certain whanging voices in queer keys/' his granddaughter declared.

" And how do I know in what sort of key the herders on the Keowee talk ? They may ' moo' like the cow, or ' mew' like the cat! I should be in danger of losing half that was said. And that is what these varlets here in the station know right well. It must seem but a mere bit of bombast on my part. It could never be seriously coun tenanced — unless I had an interpreter. Stop me! but if you were a grandson instead of a granddaughter, I would not mind taking you with me to interpret for me, though, Gadzooks, I 'd be like a heathen red Injun with a linguister! "

" And why am I not as good as any grandson ? " demanded Pen inn ah Penelope Anne, with a spirited flash of her bright hazel eyes and great temerity of specula tion ; for be it remembered the days of the theories of woman's equality with man had not yet dawned. " Sure, sir, I can speak when I am spoken to. I understand the Engh'sh language ; and " — her voice rising into a liquid crescendo of delight — "I can wear my gray sergedusoy sack made over my carnation taffeta bodice and cashmere petticoat, all pranked out with bows of black velvet, most genteel, and my hat of quilled primrose sarcenet, grand father. I 'd take them in a bundle, for if we should have rain I would rather be in my old red hood and blue serge riding-coat on the way, grandfather."

And thus it was settled before she had fairly readjusted the peruke on his head as he sat in his great chair and she clambered on its arm.

She had not heard of the disaster that had befallen Ralph Emsden, and she turned rather pale and wistful when the news was communicated to her. Then realizing how opportune was the accident, how slight was its ultimate danger in comparison with the jeopardy of the mission from which he was rescued, she fairly gloated upon the chance which had conferred it upon her grand father, and made her an instrument in its execution.

It was a queerly assorted embassy that rode out of the gates of the stockade, the ambassador and his linffuister. Richard Mi-

o

vane was mounted upon a strong, sprightly horse, with Peninnah Penelope Anne behind him upon a pillion. Following them at a little distance came his body-servant, Caesar, more fitted by temperament than either to enjoy the change, the spirit of adventure, and reveling in a sense of importance which was scarcely diminished by the fact that it was vicarious. He rode a sturdy nag and had charge of a led horse, that bore a pack-saddle with a store of changes of raiment, of edible provisions, and tents to fend off the chances of inclement weather. They were to travel under the protection of a trader's pack-train, from a reestablished trading-house in the Overhill Towns of the Cherokees on the Tennessee River ; and so

accurately did they time their departure and the stages of their journey that they met this caravan just at the hour and place des ignated, and risked naught from the unset tled state of the country or an encounter with some ignorant or inimical savage, prone to wreak upon inoffensive units ven geance for wrongs, real or fancied, wrought by a nation.

The trader, being a man habituated by frequent sojourns in Charlestown to me tropolitan customs and a worldly trend of thought, instantly recognized the quality of Mi vane and his granddaughter, despite the old red hood and blue serge riding-coat and their residence here so far from all the graces that appertain to civilization ; though, to be sure, Richard Mivane, in his trim "Joseph," his head cowled in an appro priate "trotcozy," and his jaunty self-pos session quite restored by the cutting of the Gordian knot of his dilemma, demonstrating his capacity to duly perform all his under takings, bore himself in a manner calculated to enhance even the high estimation of his fellow-traveler. After the custom of a gen tleman, however, he was most augustly free

from unwarrantable self-assertion, but he could not have failed to be flattered by the phrase of the trader, could he have heard it, in delivering over his charge to the herd ers on the Keowee River. " Gadzooks, neighbors, but I should n't be a whit sur prised if that old party is a duke in dis guise ! "

But the cow-drivers heard him not! They hardly heeded the coming and the going of the pack-train and their gossips the pack men ! They cared naught for the news the caravan brought of the country-side far above, nor the commissions they were wont to give for the various settlements and the metropolis far below! For so featly came riding in to the humble prosaic precincts of the cow-pens and into their hearts the vernal beauty of Spring herself, the living Bloom of charm and love, all arrayed in delicate gray sergedusoy opening upon carnation taffeta, and crowned with sheer quillings of primrose sarcenet, with a cheek that repeated these roseate tints and a glint of golden brown tresses curling softly against a nape of pearl, that the ranchmen were bewitched and dazed, and knew no more of good common-

sense. Their equilibrium thus shaken, some busied themselves in what might be called " housewifely cares," that the dainty vis itant might be acceptably lodged and fed, and afterward they cursed their industry and hospitality that thus left her conversation and charming aspect to the shirks and drones, who languished about her, and af fected to seek her comfort and minister to her entertainment. For the cow-drivers, like the other pioneer settlers of that region and day, represented various states of society and degrees of refinement, and to those to whom she was not as a blissful reminiscence of long ago, she appeared as a revelation, new and straight from heaven, a fancy, a dream ! It seemed meet to them that she arrived in the illusory sunset of a sweet spring day, like some lovely forecast of the visions of the night.

With their artless bucolic ideals of enter tainment they invited her out to show her the new calves. One of these little creatures, being exquisitely white and eminently pleas ing to look upon, was straightway named, with her gracious permission, " Peninnah Penelope Anne," and she was assured that

because of this name its owner, a slim, sen timental, red-haired youth, would never part from it. And it may be presumed that he was sincere, and that at the time of this fer vent asseveration he had not realized the incongruity of living his life out in the con stant heed of the well-being and compan ionship of a large white cow of the name of " Peninnah Penelope Anne." A more interesting denizen of the pen was a fawn, a waif found there one morning, having prudently adopted as a mother a large red cow, and a heavy brindled calf as a foster-brother. The instant Peninnah admired this incongruous estray, bleating its queer alien note in resonant duet with the calf in the plea for supper, a cord was slipped about its neck and it was presented in due form. In order that she might not be harassed by its tendance, a gigantic Scotch herder, six feet six inches high and twenty-five years of age, showed how far involuntary inanity can coexist with presumptive sanity as he led it about, the creature holding back heavily at every step and now and again tangling itself, its cord, and its disconcerted bleats about its conductor's long and stalwart legs.

Another of the herders, — all of whom were hunters and explorers as well, — whose mind was of a topographical cast, introduced her to much fine and high company in the vari ous mountain peaks, gathered in solemn symposium dark and purple in the faintly tinted and opaline twilight. He repeated their Cherokee names and gave an Eng lish translation, and called her attention to marks of difference in their configuration which rendered them distinguishable at a dis tance; and when she lent some heed to this and noted on the horizon contours of the mountains about her home, faint and far in an elusive amethystine apotheosis against the red and flaming west, and called out her glad recognition in a voice as sweet as a thrush, his comrades waxed jealous, and contravened his statements and argued and wrangled upon landmarks to which they had never before given a second thought in all their mountaineering experience, so keenly they competed for her favor. It was her little day of triumph, and right royally she reigned in it and was wont to tell of it for forty years thereafter !

At last the dusk was slipping down ; the

mountains grew a shadowy gray far away and a looming black close at hand; a star palpitated in the colorless crystal-clear con cave of the fading skies ; the vernal stretch of the savannas, whose intense green was somehow asserted till the latest glimmer of light, ceased to resound with the voices of the herds ; only here and there a keen me tallic note of a bell clanked forth and was silent, and again the sound came from a farther pen like a belated echo; the fire flaring out from the open door of the near est hut of the ranchmen's little hamlet gave a pleasant sense of hospitality and homely hearth-side cheer, for it requires only a few nights under a tent or the open canopy of heaven to make a woman, always the most artificially disposed of all creatures, exceedingly respectful to a roof.

To be sure the interior of this roof was well garnished with cobwebs, and Peninnah Penelope Anne's mother was so notable a housekeeper and had inculcated such horror of these untoward drapings and festoons that the girl was compelled to look sedulously away from them to avoid staring in amaze ment at their morbid development and pro-

portions. The superintendent of the ranch

— being an establishment o£ magnitude it had several sub-agents also — was so occu pied in putting the best foot of his menage foremost, not being prepared for such com pany, that, like many a modern house keeper, he let the opportunity for pleasure slip. When he proffered tea — he had sent a negro servant all the way to Fort Prince George for the luxury, where it could be found among the hospital stores, for tea was too mild a tipple for the pioneer cow-drivers

— he suffered the egregious mortification of pouring out plain hot water, having forgotten to put in the tea leaves to steep. He looked very hot and ruefully distressed as he re paired his error, and would not, could not meet the laughing eyes of his comrades, nor yet the polite glances of his guests resolutely seeing naught amiss. He was op pressed with a sense of the number and pro minence of his dogs about the wide hearth of his cabin; when the animals were there fore vigorously kicked out to make more space, instead of retiring with the usual plaintive yelp of protest appropriate to such occasions they took advantage of the pre-

sence of guests of distinction and made the rafters ring" and resound with their ear-splitting shrieks, and it was even neces sary to chase them about the room before they could be ejected. Indeed, several with super-canine strategy succeeded in counter marching their tormentors and remained in the group about the fire, wearing that curiously attentive look peculiar to an intel ligent animal when animated conversation is in progress.

The blazing fire in the great chimney-place, that stretched almost half across one end of the herder's cabin, illumined the walls and showed the medley of articles sus pended upon them,— horns, whips, brand ing-irons, skins, cattle-bells, lariats, and such like appurtenances of the ranch. The little lady was seated in the centre of the group of ranchmen ranged in a wide semicircle about the hearth of flagstones; the ethereal tints of her shimmering attire showed all their high lights; her face and golden brown hair seemed particularly soft and delicate in contrast with the rough tousled heads and bearded countenances about her; here and there the muzzle of a great animal, the flash

of fangs and red glow of formidable jaws, were half discriminated amidst the alter nate flare of the flames and flicker of the shadows, — all might have suggested the " mystick Crew of Comus" to Richard Mivane, being the only person present who had ever heard of that motley company, had not his thoughts been otherwise en grossed. He meditatively cleared his throat, took a sip of brandy and water, for he had long ago lost his genteel affiliations with tea, and hopefully opened the subject of his mission.

A change fell upon the scene, instant, definite, complete. In the mere broaching of business it might seem that beauty and charm are but tenuous at best, and power less to subdue the fiercer nature of man when his acquisitive and aggressive com mercial instincts are aroused. One of the most devout admirers of Peninnah Penel ope Anne tossed his head with a very belli cose and bovine obduracy when he intimated an incredulity of the statement that the herd had been stampeded without an ulterior motive of malice or nefarious profit. The gentle soul who had assumed the tendance

and protection of the fawn held down as he listened a shaggy intent head, like that of a bull about to charge, at the mere men tion of the shooting of the wolf. In fact, the suggestion of shadowy monsters which the dusky flicker and evanescent flare of the fire fostered and which was intensified by the proximity of open jaws, sharp fangs, heavy muzzles, and standing bristles amongst them, owed much of its effect to the unani mous expression of truculent challenge and averse disfavor. There were frequent con firmatory emphatic nods of great disheveled heads, the scarlet flushing of angry faces, already florid, and now and again a violent descriptive gesture of a long brawny arm with a clenched fist at its extremity. Richard Mivane's well-rounded periods and gentle manly phrasings were like the educated thrusts and feints of an expert fencer who opposes his single rapier to the bludgeons and missiles of a furious mob. He saw in less than five minutes that the scheme of extenuation and conciliation was futile, that retort and retaliation would be returned in kind, that the stoppage of the pack-train from Blue Lick on the way to Charlestown was inevitable, and that the redcoats, in voked by both parties, would doubtless be come embroiled with one or the other, — in short, bloodshed was a foregone conclusion.

Much as this was to be deprecated in any event, it was suicidal amongst these infant settlements by reason of the vicinage and antagonism of the fierce and only half-sub dued Cherokees, sullenly nourishing schemes of revenge for their recent defeat and many woes. But when he urged this upon the at tention of the herders, the retort came quick and pointed: " We ain't talkin' 'bout no Injuns ! — the Cherokees never meddled with our cattle ! We '11 settle about the stampede first, an' 'tend to the Cherokees in good time — all in good time ! "

Richard Mi vane was not possessed of much affinity with the ruder primitive qual ities, the stalwart candor and uncultured forces of the natural man ; and never had these inherent elements appeared to less advantage in his mind than when he was brought into disastrous conflict with them. He only held his ground for form's sake, and often his voice was overborne by the clamors of many responsive tones, all blar-

ing and arguing together. Much that was said he could not hear, and refrained from speaking when he perceived from the loud contending faces that he was denied for the nonce a rejoinder. But ever and anon the silver vibrations of the little linguister's voice rose into the big bass tumult as she rehearsed what had been said for her grand father's benefit, and the angry rush of sound stopped with an abrupt recoil for a moment, then surged on as before.

She looked very mild and petite among them, q.uite like a sedate child, her cheeks pinker than any of the rose tints of her apparel that were her pride, her lips red and breathlessly parted, her eyes bright and very watchful, her golden brown hair all red gold in the flicker of the fire. There was one wild taunting threat that she did not repeat, as if she thought it of no con sequence, — the threat of personal violence against Ralph Emsden. They had found out his name patly enough from their own messenger to Blue Lick Station. They would take out their grudge against him on his hide, they averred, — if they had to go all the way to Blue Lick to get it!

Now and again they sufficiently remem bered that indeterminate quantum of cour tesy which they called their " manners" to interpolate " No offense to you, sir," or " Begging the lady's pardon." Throughout she preserved a cool, almost uncomprehend ing, passive manner ; and it was in one of the moments of a heady tumult of words, in which they sometimes involved them selves beyond ah 1 interpretation or distin-guishment, that she observed with a sort of childish inconsequence that they could get Kalph Emsden easily enough if they would go to Blue Lick Station, — he was there now, and his arm and shoulder were so hurt that he would not be able to make off, — they could get him easily enough, that is, if the French did not raze Blue Lick Station be fore the herders could reach there.

If a bomb had exploded in the midst of the hearthstone, the astonishment that en sued upon this simple statement could not have been greater. A sudden blank silence supervened. A dozen excited infuriated faces, the angry contortions of the previous moment still stark upon their features, were bent upon her while their eyes stared only limitless amazement.

" The French ! " the herders cried at last in chorus. " Blue Lick Station ! "

" It was razed once/' she said statisti cally, " to the ground. The Cherokees did it that time! "

Her grandfather, always averse to admit that he did not hear, noted the influx of excitement, and was fain to lean forward. He even placed his hand behind his ear.

" The French ! " bellowed out one of the cow-drivers in a voice that might have graced the king of the herds. " The French! Threatening Blue Lick Station ! "

The elderly gentleman drew back from the painful surcharged vibrations of sound arid the unseemly aspect of this interpreter, who was in good sooth like a bull in disguise. " To be sure — the French," Richard Mi-vane said in response, repeating the only words which he had heard. " Our nearest white neighbors —- the dangerous Alabama garrison ! "

A tumult of questions assailed the little linguister.

" Be they mightily troubled at Blue Lick Station ? " asked one sympathetically.

The little flower-like head was nodded

with meaning, deep and serious. " Ob, sure ! " she cried. " And having the Cow-pens against them too — 't is sad ! "

" Zooks ! " cried the bull in disguise, with a snort. " The Cow-pens ain't against 'em — when the French are coming ! "

"Why have n't they sent word to the soldiers?" demanded another of the cow-drivers suspiciously.

"The soldiers?" she exclaimed incredu lously. " Why — the Cow-pens sent word that the soldiers were against Blue Lick too, and were going to stop the station's pack-train. Maybe the stationers were afraid of the soldiers."

To a torrent of questions as to how the news had first come, how the menace low ered, what disposition for defense the sta tioners could make, the little girl seemed bewildered. She only answered definitely and very indifferently that they could easily get Kalph Emsden if they would go now to Blue Lick, and take his hide, — that is, if the French and their Choctaw Indians had not already possessed themselves of that val uable integument, — as if this were their primal object.

" Why, God-a-mercy, child," cried the superintendent of the ranch, " this news set tles all scores ; when it comes to a foreign foe the colonists are brothers."

" And besides/' admitted one of the most truculent of the cow-drivers, " the cattle are all pretty well rounded in again; I doubt if more are lost than the wolves would have pulled down anyhow."

" And the Blue Lick Stationers' horses can be herded easy enough, — they are all on their old grass, — and be driven up to the settlement."

A courier had been sent off full tilt to the commandant at Fort Prince George, and night though it was, a detail of mounted sol diers appeared presently with orders to es cort the ambassador and his linguister into the presence of that officer.

For this intelligence was esteemed serious indeed. Although hostilities had now prac tically ceased in America, the Seven Years' War being near its end, and peace negotia tions actually in progress, still the treaty had not been concluded. So far on the fron tier were such isolated garrisons as this of Fort Prince George, so imperfect and in-

frequent were their means of communicat ing with the outside world, that they were necessarily in ignorance of much that took place elsewhere, and a renewal of the conflict might have supervened long before their regular advices from headquarters could reach them. Even a chance rumor might bring them their first intimation of a matter

o

of such great import to them. Therefore the commandant attached much significance to this account of an alarm at Blue Lick Sta tion, because of a menace from the nearest French at Fort Toulouse, often called in that day, by reason of this propinquity, " the dangerous Alabama garrison."

For this reason, also, the hospitable hosts made no protest against the removal of the guests to Fort Prince George, although it might seem that the age of the one and the tender youth of the other ill fitted them to encounter this sudden transi tion from the cosy fireside to the raw vernal air on a misty midnight jaunt of a dozen miles through a primeval wilderness. And in truth the little lady seemed loath to leave the hearth; she visibly hesitated as she stood beside her chair with her hand on its

back, and looked out at the black night, and the vague vista which the ruddy flare, from the wide door, revealed amidst the dense darkness; at the vanishing point of this per spective stood a group of mounted soldiers, " in column of twos " with two led horses, the scarlet uniforms and burnished accoutre ments appearing and disappearing elusively as the flames rose and fell. The sounds of the champing of bits and the pawing of hoofs and the jingle of spurs were keenly clear on the chill rare air and seemed some how consonant with the frosty glitter of the stars, very high in the black concave of the moonless sky. The smell of the rich mould, permeated with its vernal growths; the cool, distinct, rarefied perfume of some early flower already abloom; the antiphonal chant of frogs roused in the marsh or stream hard by, so imbued her senses with the reali zation of the hour and season that she never afterward thought of the spring without a vivid renewal of these impressions.

Her grandfather also seemed vaguely to hold back, even while he slowly mounted his horse; yet aware that naught is so im perative as military authority, it was only

his inner consciousness that protested. Out wardly he professed alacrity, although in great surprise declaring that he could not imagine what the commandant could want with him. The little linguister, for her part, had no doubts. She was well aware indeed of the cause of the summons, and so dis mayed by the prospect was even her doughty heart that the swift ride through the black forest was less terrible to her than the thought of the ordeal of the arrival. But the march was not without its peculiar trials. She shrank in instinctive affright from the unaccustomed escort of a dragoon on either side of her, looming up in the darkness like some phantom of the midnight. Even her volition seemed wrested from her by reason of the military training of the troop-horse which she rode; — he whirled about at the command " right-wheel!" ringing out in the darkness in the crisp peremptory tones of the non-commissioned officer, and plunged forward at the words "trot, march !" and ad justed his muscles instantaneously to the ac celeration implied in " gallop! " and came to an abrupt and immovable pause at " halt! " — all with no more regard to her grasp on

the reins than if she had been a fly on the saddle. As they went the wind beset her with cool, damp buffets on chin and cheek; the overhanging budding boughs, all un seen, drenched her with perfumed dew as she was whisked through their midst; the pace was adopted rather with reference to military custom and the expectation of the waiting commandant than her convenience ; at every sudden whirl responsive to the word of com mand she was in momentary fear of being flung beneath the swiftly trampling hoofs of the horses on either side of her, and de spite her recoil from the bigness and bluff-ness and presumable bloody-mindedness of the two troopers beside her she was sensible of their sympathy as they took heed of the instability with which she bounced about, perched up side-wise on a military saddle. Indeed, one was moved to ask her if she would not prefer to be strapped on with a girth, and to offer his belt for the purpose ; and the other took the opportunity to gird at the forgetfulness of the cow-drivers to furnish her with her own pillion.

Nevertheless she dreaded the journey's end; and as they came out of the forests on the banks of the Keowee Kiver, and beheld the vague glimmers of the gray day slowly dawning, albeit night was yet in the woods, and the outline of the military works of Fort Prince George taking symmetry and wonted proportions against the dap pled eastern sky, all of blended roseate tints and thin nebulous grays, her heart so sank, she felt so tremulously guilty that had all the sixteen guns from the four bas tions opened fire upon her at once she would not have been surprised.

No such welcome, however, did the party encounter. The officer commanding it

o

stopped the ambassador and the linguister and let the soldiers go on at a round trot toward the great gate, which stood open, the bayonet on the musket of the sentry shining with an errant gleam of light like the sword of fire at the entrance of Paradise. For now the sun was up, the radiance suffus ing the blue and misty mountains and the seas of fog in the valleys. Albeit its dazzling focus was hardly visible above the eastern heights, it sent a red glow all along the parapet of the covered way and the slope beyond to the river bank, where only two

years before Captain Coytmore, then the commandant, had been murdered at a con ference by the treacherous Cherokees. The senior officer, Captain Howard, being ab sent on leave, the present commandant, a jaunty lieutenant, smart enough although in an undress uniform, was standing at the sally-port now, all bland and smiling, to receive the ambassador and his linguister. He perceived at once that the old gentleman was deaf beyond any save adroit and accus tomed communication. He looked puzzled for a moment, then spoke to the sergeant.

" And who is this pretty little girl ? " he asked.

The sergeant, who had heard of her prowess in the havoc of hearts among the herders at the ranch, looked bewildered, then desperate, saluted mechanically, and was circumspectly silent.

" I am not a little girl," said Peninnah Penelope Anne Mi vane with adult dignity.

" Ah, indeed," said the embarrassed and discomfited officer. Then, turning to lead the way, he added civilly, " Beg pardon, I 'm sure ! "

If the sight of the sixteen guns on the

four bastions of Fort Prince George had caused Peninnah Penelope Anne to shrink from her normal proportions, not too ex pansive at best, she dwindled visibly and continually when conducted within the pal isaded parapets, across the parade, past the barracks, built for a hundred men but now somewhat lacking their complement, and into the officers' quarters, where in a large mess-hall there sat all the commissioned offi cers at a table, near the foot of which the two strangers were accommodated with chairs. It had so much the air of a court-martial, despite their bland and reassuring suavity, that Peninnah Penelope Anne, albeit a free lance and serving under no banner but her own whim, had much ado to keep up her courage to face them. Naturally she was disposed to lean upon her grandfather, but he utterly failed her. She had never known him so deaf ! He could neither hear the officers nor her familiar voice. He would not even tell his name, although she had so often heard him voice it sonorously and in great pride, " Richard Mivane Huntley Mi-vane, youngest son of the late Sir Alexan der Mivane Huntley Mivane, of Mivane

Hall, Fenshire, Northumberland." Now he merely waved his hand to deputize her. In truth he shrank from rehearsing to these young men the reason of his flight from home, his duel and its fatal result, although his pride forbade him to suppress it. He had come to think the cause of quarrel a trifle, and the challenge a wicked folly. It was a bitter and remorseful recollection as his age came on, and its details were edifying in no sense. Hence, as Peninnah Penelope Anne knew naught of the story she could not tell it, and he escaped the distasteful pose of a merciless duelist.

She gave his name with much pride, not ing the respect with which the officers heard it. She accounted for the incongruities of his presence here as the result of a trip from England to the province, where, as she said, " he was detained by the snare of matrimony." It was his own phrase, for as a snare he regarded the holy estate ; but the younger of the officers were pleased to find it funny, and ventured to laugh ; whereat she grew red and silent, and they perforce became grave again that they might hear of the French. Here she was vague and discursive, and prone to detail at great length the feud between the Blue Lick Station ers and the " cow-drivers " on the Keowee, evidently hoping that it might lie within the latitude of the commandant's military authority to take some order with the herder gentry, — for which they would not have thanked her in the least! But the officers of the garrison of Fort Prince George had thought for naught but the French, and now and again conferred dubiously together on the unsatisfactory points of her evi dence.

" Do you suppose she really knows any thing about it ? " the commandant said aside to one of his advisers.

Suddenly, however, her grandfather's hearing improved, and they were able to elicit from him the reports which he had had at second hand from the cow-drivers themselves, in retailing which he honestly conceived that he was repeating genuine news, never dreaming that the information had blossomed forth from his own mission.

While less circumstantial and satisfactory than the commandant could have wished, the details were too significant and serious of import to be ignored, and therefore he acted upon his information as far as it was developed.

He ordered out a scouting party of ten men, and, that he might utilize Blue Lick Station as an outpost in some sort where they might find refuge and aid, he dispatched to the settlement a present of gunpowder to serve in the defense of the station, in case of attack by the French, and two of the small coehorns of that day, each of which could be carried between two men, to assist the little piece already at the station. In return for the prospective courtesy and shel ter to his troops, he wrote a very polite letter urging the settlers to hold out if practicable, relying on his succor with men, ammunition, and provisions; but if compelled to give way, assuring the stationers of a welcome at Fort Prince George.

The herders at the cow-pens on the Keo-wee had also determined to reinforce Blue Lick Station, and with a number of the run away horses of the settlers, rounded up and driven in strings, several of them set forth with the British soldiers from the fort. In this company Richard Mivane and his granddaughter also took their way to Blue Lick Station in lieu of waiting for a pack-train with provisions from Charlestown, as they had anticipated.

It was a merry camping party as they fared along through the wilderness, and she had occasion to make many sage observa tions on the inconsistency and the unwisdom of man ! That the prospect of killing some Frenchman, or being themselves cruelly killed, in a national quarrel which neither faction, the cow-drivers nor the Blue Lick Stationers, half understood, should so en dear men to each other was a sentiment into which she could not enter. It was better, after all, to be a woman, she said to herself, and sit soberly at home and sew the rational sampler, and let the world wag on as it would and the cutthroats work their wild will on each other. The least suggestion that brought the thought of the French to their minds was received with eyes alight, and nerves aquiver, and blood all in a rush. The favorite of the whole camp was a young fellow who had achieved that enviable sta tion by virtue of an inane yet inconceivably droll intonation of the phrase, " Bong chure " (Bon jour\ delivered at all man ner of unconformable times and in inappro priate connections, and invariably greeted with shouts of laughter. And when at last the party reached the vicinity of Blue Lick and the stationers swarmed out to meet them, taking the news of the French inva sion at second hand, each repeating it to the other, and variously recounting it back again, never dreaming that it was supposed to have originally issued from the station, she meditated much upon this temperamen tal savagery in man, and the difficulty it occasioned in conforming him to those sa gacious schemes for his benefit which she nourished in her inventive little pate. The antagonisms of the Blue Lick Stationers and the cow-drivers from the Keowee vanished like mist. On the one hand the stationers were assured that the stampede of the cattle was now regarded as inadvertent, and al though it had occasioned an immense deal of vexatious trouble to the ranchmen, all were now well rounded up and restored to the cow-pens as of yore. And the ranch men in turn received a thousand thanks for their neighborly kindness in the restoration

of the horses of the Blue Lick Stationers, who knew that the animals had not been decoyed off by the herders, as a malicious report sought to represent, but had merely returned to their " old grass," according to their homing propensities. And both par ties loved the British soldiers, who had re inforced them, and intended to go a-scout-ing with the military expedition ; and the soldiers earnestly reciprocated by assisting in the preparations for the defense of the station. Especially active and efficient was the only artilleryman among them, and the paradisaic peace amidst all the preparations for war was so complete that his acrid scorn of that pride of the settlement, the little swivel gun, and of the stationers' methods of handling it, occasioned not even a mur mur of resentment.

Peninnah Penelope Anne, although re stored to private life and the maternal do micile, having retired from statecraft and the functions of linguister to the embassy, did not altogether escape public utility in these bellicose preparations. The young gunner, who had had the opportunity of observing her during the march hither,

shortly applied to her for assistance in his professional devoir. He wanted a deft-handed young person to construct the car tridge-bags for the ammunition which he was fixing for the little piece and the two coehorns. And thus it chanced that she found herself in the blockhouse, cheek by jowl with the little cannon, its grisly muzzle now looking out of the embrasure where she herself had once been fond of taking observations of the stockade entrance ; the men came and went and speculated upon the chances of the scouting quest, now about to set forth, while spurs clanking, ramrods rattling down into gun-barrels, voices lifted in argument or joyous resonance, made the whitewashed walls ring anew. The gunner, seated at a table carefully and accurately measuring out the powder, now and again urged strict cautions against the lighting of pipes or striking of sparks from gun-flints. When he applied himself briskly to the cut ting out of more bags from flannel for his cartridges, he looked very harmless and do mestic in his solicitude to follow his wooden pattern, or " pathron "as he called it, for the creature was Irish, He gave minute

and scrupulous directions to Peninnah Pe nelope Anne to sew the cylinder with no more than twelve stitches to the inch, and to baste down the seams, " now, moind ye that! — ivery wan ! — that no powther might slip through beyant! "

In the pride of the expert he was chary of commendation and eyed critically the circular bottom of every bag before he filled it with powder.

" See that, now," he said, snipping briskly with the scissors; " that string of woolen yarn that yez left there, a-burnin' away outside, might burst the whole gun, an' ivery sowl in the blockhouse would be kilt intirely, — moind ye that, now ! — an' they would n't be the Frenchies, nayther ! " He gave her a keen warning glance at rather close range, then once more re newed his labors.

The mockingbirds were singing in the woods outside. The sun was in the trees. The leafage had progressed beyond the bourgeoning period and the branches flung broad green splendors of verdure to the breeze. The Great Smoky Mountains were hardly less blue than the sky as the distant

summits deployed against the fair horizon ; only the nearest, close at hand, were sombre, and showed dark luxuriant foliage and massive craggy steeps, and their austere, silent, magnificent domes looked over the scene with solemn uplifting meanings. Oh, life ! life was so sweet, and love and friend ship were so easy to come by and so hard to part withal, and glad, oh, glad was she that no men of the French nation or any other were on their march hitherward to be torn in cruel lacerations by those wicked cartridges, so cleverly and artfully and cheerfully constructed, — men with homes, wives, mothers, sisters, children, every sol dier representing to some anxious, tender heart a whole world, a microcosm of affec tion, all illuminated with hope and joy, or to be clouded with grief and terror and loss and despair, — oh, glad, glad was she that the French invasion was but a figment, — a tissue of misconceptions and vague innuendoes and groundless assumptions.

And yet she was sad and sorry and ashamed, because of the futile bustle and bluster and cheerful courageous activity about her. Not a cheek had blenched ; not

a hand had trembled ; not a voice had been lifted to protest or counsel surrender, de spite their meagre capacities for defense and their number, but a handful. What would these men say to her if they knew that their patriotism and their valor were expended in vain, — above all, their mutual cause of quarrel wasted! — as pretty a bit of neigh borhood spite as ever stopped a bullet- all foolishly and needlessly reconciled with out a blow! She had saved them from a bloody feud, the chances of which were terrifying to her for their own sakes. But what would they say when discovery should come!

Still, it might never come. And yet, should they patrol the woods in vain and at last disperse and return each to his own home, she had no placidity in prospect, — she was troubled and sad and her sorry heart was heavy. Her scheme had succeeded beyond her wildest hopes. Her beneficent artifice had fully worked its mission. And now, since there was no more to be done, she had time to repent her varied deceits. Was it right ? she asked herself in consci entious alarm, not the less sincere because

belated. Ought she to have interfered, with what forces it was possible for her limited capacity to wield ? Had they an inalienable right to cut each other's throats ? Should she have so presumed ? And now —

" Howly Moses! " a voice in shrill agi tation broke in upon her preoccupation. " An' is it sheddin' tears ye are upon the blessed gunpowther ? Sure the colleen 's crazed ! Millia Murther ! the beautiful ca'-tridges is ruint intoirely! Any man moight be proud an' plazed to be kilt by the loikes o' them ! How many o' them big wathery tears have yez been after sheddin' into aich o' them lovely ca'tridges ? "

He had risen; one hand was laid pro-tectingly upon the completed pile of fixed ammunition as if to ward off the damping influences of her woe, while he ruefully contemplated the suspected cartridge bags, all plump and tidy and workmanlike, save for their possible charge of tears. She made no answer, but sat quite motionless upon her low stool, a cartridge bag unfin ished in her lap, her golden brown curls against the cannon, still weeping her large tears and looking very small.

His clamors brought half the force to the scene of the disturbance. A keen ques tion here, an inference needfully taken there, and the situation was plain !

In the abrupt pause in this headlong ca reer it was difficult to sustain one's poise. Now and again, indeed, sheepish conscious glances were interchanged; for since the grievance of the cow-drivers had been pub licly annulled and the horses of the Blue Lick Stationers had been restored in pure neighborly good-will, a resumption of the quarrel on the old invalid scores was impos sible. Perhaps some token of their displea sure might have been visited upon her who had inaugurated so bold and extensive a wild goose chase, but she looked so small as she sat by the cannon weeping her large tears that she disarmed retaliation.

So small she looked, indeed, that certain of the young blades, who filed in to gaze upon her and filed out again, would not believe that she could have invented so large a French invasion, and for several days they futilely scouted the woods in search of some errant " parlez-vous," all of whom, however, were very discreetly tucked

away within the strong defenses of Fort Toulouse.

The young* gunner alone was implacable. He was the first of the returning force to reach Fort Prince George, and he carried with him all the powder that had been sent under mistake to the Blue Lick Station, together with the tear-shotted cartridges, whose problematic interior damage he ex plained to the amazed, chagrined, and non plussed commandant.

" Oh, sor," the gunner said in conclu sion, solemnly shaking his head, " that gurl, sor ! — she is a wily one ! An' I should n't be surprised, sor, if she is a dale taller than she looks !"

The Blue Lick Station in time recovered its equilibrium, and was afterward prone to protest that of all frontier communities it bore the palm for the efficiency of its " linguister."

A VICTOR AT CHUNGKE

A VICTOR AT CHUNGKE

AT Tennessee Town, on the Tennessee River, there used to be a great chungke-yard. It was laid off in a wide rectangular area nine hundred feet long, two feet lower than the surface of the ground, level as a floor, and covered with fine white sand. The ancient, curiously shaped chungke-stones, fashioned with much labor from the hardest rock, perfect despite imme morial use, kept with the strictest care, exempt by law from burial with the effects of the dead, were the property of this Cher okee town, and no more to be removed thence than the council-house, — the great rotunda at one side of the "beloved square," built upon a mound in the centre of the village.

Surely no spot could seem more felici tously chosen for the favorite Indian game. The ground rose about the chungke-yard like the walls of an amphitheatre, on every side save the slope toward the '* beloved

square " and the river, furnishing an ideal position of vantage for spectators were they even more numerous than the hundreds of Cherokees of all ages that had gathered on the steep acclivities to overlook the game — some ranged on the terrace or turfy ridge around the chungke-yard, formed by the earth thrown out when the depressed area was delved down long ago, others disposed beneath the spreading trees, others still, precariously perched on clifty promontories beetling out from the sharp ascent. Above all, Chilhowee Mountain, aflare with the scarlet glow of its autumnal woods, touched the blue sky. The river, of a kindred blue, with a transient steely change under the shadow of a cloud, showed flashes of white foam, for the winds were rushing down from the Great Smoky Mountains, which were revealed for an instant in a clear hard azure against the pearl-tinted horizon — then again only a mirage, an illusion, a dream of stupendous ranges in the shimmer ing mist.

In the idle, sylvan, tribal life of that date, one hundred and fifty years ago, it might seem that there was scant duty re-

cognized, imposing serious occupation, to debar the population of Tennessee Town from witnessing the long-drawn game, which was continued sometimes half the day by the same hardy young warriors, indefati gable despite the hot sun and the tense ex ercise, straining every muscle. A few old women, their minds intent upon the pre paration of dinner, a few of the very young children, relishing their own pottering de vices as of a finer flavor of sport, a few old men, like other old men elsewhere, with thoughts of the past so vivid that the present could show but a pallid aspect — these were absent, and were not missed. For the most part, however, the little dweUings were va cant. The usual groups of loungers had deserted the public buildings, which con sisted of a bark-and-log house of tbree rooms, or divisions, at each angle of the " beloved square," and in which were trans acted the business affairs of the town; -one, painted red, was the " war-cabin," whence arms, ammunition, etc., were distrib uted, the divisions implying distinctions as to rank among the warriors; another, painted white, was devoted to the priestcraft of the

" beloved men " — head men of note, con jurers, and prophets; the cabin of the aged councilors faced the setting sun. as an inti-

o *

mation that their wars were ended and their day done; and in the fourth cabin met the "second men/' as the traders called the subordinate authorities who conducted mu nicipal affairs, so to speak — the community labor of raising houses, and laying off and planting with maize and pompions the com mon fields to be tilled by the women, " who fret at the very shadow of a, crow," writes an old trader. All these cabins were now still and silent in the sun. The dome-shaped town-house, of a different style of archi tecture, plastered within and without with red clay, placed high on the artificial mound, and reached by an ascent of stairs which were cut in regular gradations in the earth, lacked its strange religious ceremo nies ; its secret colloguing council of chiefs with the two princes of the town ; its visit ors of distinction, ambassadors from other towns or Indian nations; its wreaths of tobacco sent forth from diplomatically smoked pipes; its strategic " talks; " its exchange of symbolic belts and strings of

wampum and of swans' wings — white, or painted red and black, as peace hovered or war impended — and other paraphernalia of the savage government. Even the trading-house showed a closed door, and the Eng lish trader, his pipe in his mouth, smoked with no latent significance, but merely to garner its nicotian solace, sat with a group of the elder braves and watched the barbaric sport with an interest as keen as if he had been born and bred an Indian instead of native to the far-away dales of Devonshire. Nay, he bet on the chances of the game with as reckless a nerve as a Cherokee, — always the perfect presentment of the gambler, — despite the thrift which characterized his transactions at the trading-house, where he was wont to drive a close bargain, and look with the discerning scrupulousness of an expert into the values of the dressing of a deerskin offered in barter. But the one pursuit was pleasure, and the other busi ness. The deerskins which he was wearing were of phenomenal softness and beauty of finish, for the spare, dapper man was ar rayed like the Indians, in fringed buckskin shirt and leggings ; but he was experiencing

a vague sentiment of contempt for his attire. He had been recently wearing a garb of good camlet-cloth and hose and a bravely cocked hat, for he was just returned from a journey to Charlestown, five hundred miles distant, where he had made a considerable stay, and his muscles and attitude were still ad justed to the pride of preferment and the consciousness of being unwontedly smart. Indeed, his pack-train, laden with powder and firearms, beads and cloth, cutlery and paints, for his traffic with the Indians under the license which he held from the British government, had but come in the previous day, and he had still the pulses of civiliza tion beating in his veins.

For this reason, perhaps, as he sat, one elbow on his knee, his chin in his hand, his sharp, commercially keen face softened by a thought not akin to trade, his eyes were darkened, while he gazed at one of the contestants, with a doubt that had little connection with the odds which he had of fered. He was troubled by a vague regret, a speculation of restless futility, for it con cerned a future so unusual that no detail could be predicted from the resources of

the present. And yet this sentiment was without the poignancy of personal grief — it was only a vicarious interest that animated him. For himself, despite the flattering, smooth reminiscence of the camlet-cloth yet lingering in the nerves of his finger-tips, the recent relapse into English speech, the interval spent once more among the stir of streets and shops, splendid indeed to an unwonted gaze, the commercial validities, which he so heartily appreciated, of the warehouses, and crowded wharves, and laden merchantmen swinging at anchor in the great harbor, he was satisfied. He was possessed by that extraordinary renuncia tion of civilization which now and again was manifested by white men thrown among the Cherokee tribe — sometimes, as in his instance, a trader, advanced in years, " his pile made," to use the phrase of to-day, the world before him where to choose a home; sometimes a deserter from the British or French military forces, according to the faction which the shifting Cherokees af fected at the time ; more than once a cap tive, spared for some whim, set at liberty, free to go where he would — all deliberately

and of choice cast their lot among the Cherokees; lived and died with the treach erous race. Whether the wild sylvan life had some peculiarly irresistible attraction; whether the world beyond held for them responsibilities and laborious vocations and irksome ties which they would fain evade ; whether they fell under the bewitchment of " Herbert's Spring/' named from an early commissioner of Indian affairs, after drink ing whereof one could not quit the region of the Great Smoky Mountains, but re mained in that enchanted country for seven years, fascinated, lapsed in perfect content — it is impossible to say. There is a tra dition that when the attraction of the world would begin to reassert its subtle reminis cent forces, these renegades of civilization were wont to repair anew to this fountain to quaff again of the ancient delirium and to revive its potent spell. Abram Varney had no such necessity in his own case; he only doubted the values of his choice as fitted for another.

Apart from this reflection, it was natural that his eyes should follow the contestant whom he had backed for a winner to the

tune of more silver bangles, and " ear-bobs/' and strings of " roanoke," and gunpowder, and red and white paint, than he was minded to lightly lose. He had laid his wagers with a keen calculation of the relative endow ments of the players, their dexterity, their experience, their endurance. He was not influenced by any pride of race in the fact that his champion was also a white man, who, indeed, carried a good share of the favor of the spectators.

A strange object was this champion, at once pathetic and splendid. No muscular development could have been finer, no ath letic grace more pronounced than his phy sique displayed. The wild life and training of the woods and the savage wars had brought out all the constitutional endur ance and strength inherited from his stanch English father and his hardy Scotch mother. Both had been murdered by the Cherokees in a frontier massacre, and as a boy of ten years of age, his life spared in some freak of the moment, he had been conveyed hither, exhorted to forget, adopted into the tribe, brought up with their peculiar kind ness in the rearing of children, taught all the

sylvan arts, and trained to the stern duties of war by the noted chief Colannah Giga-gei, himself, the Great Red Raven of Ten nessee Town (sometimes called Quorinnah, the name being a favorite war-title spe cially coveted). The youth had had his baptism of fire in the ceaseless wars which the Cherokees waged against the other In-

o o

dian tribes. He had already won the " war rior's crown " and his " war-name/' a title conferred only upon the bravest of the brave. He was now Otasite, the " Man-killer " of Tennessee Town. He was just twenty years of age, and Abram Varney, gazing at him, wondered what the people in Charlestown would think of him could they see him. For a few days, a week, perhaps, the trader would refer all his thoughts to this civilized standard.

Tall, alert as an Indian, supple too, but heavier and more muscular, Otasite was in stantly to be distinguished by his build from among the other young men, although, like the Indians, he wore a garb of dressed deerskin. His face, albeit no stranger to the use of their pigments and unguents, still showed fair and freckled. His hair bore

no resemblance to their lank black locks; of an auburn hue and resolutely curling, it defied the tonsure to which it had been for years subjected, coming out crisp and ring leted close to his head where he was de signed to be bald, and on the top, where the " war-lock" was permitted to grow, it floated backward in two long tangled red curls that gave the lie direct to the Indian similitude affected by the two surmounting tips of eagle feathers. He was arrayed in much splendor, according to aboriginal standards; the fringed seams of his hunt ing shirt and leggings, fashioned of fine white dressed doeskin, as pliable as " Can ton silk crape," were hung with fawns' trotters; his moccasins were white and streaked with parti-colored paint; he had a curious prickly belt of wolves' teeth, which intimated his moral courage as well as syl van prowess, for the slaying of these beasts was esteemed unlucky, and shooting at them calculated to spoil the aim of a gun; many glancing, glittering strings of " roanoke " swung around his neck.

Nothing could have been finer, athlet ically considered, than his attitude at this moment of the trader's speculative obser vation. The discoidal quartz chungke-stone 2 had been hurled with a tremendous fling along the smooth sandy stretch of the yard, its flat edge, two inches wide, and the cu riously exact equipoise of its fashioning causing it to bowl swiftly along a great distance, to fall only when the original im petus should fail; his competitor, Wyejah, a sinewy, powerful young brave, his buck skin garb steeped in some red dye that gave him the look when at full speed of the first flying leaf of the falling season, his ears split and barbarically distended on wire hoops 3 and hung with silver rings, his moc casins scarlet, his black hair decorated with cardinal wings, had just sent his heavy lance, twelve feet long, skimming through the air ; then Otasite, running swiftly but lightly abreast with him, launched his own long lance with such force and nicety of aim that its point struck the end of Wyejah's spear, still in flight in mid-air, deflecting its direction, and sending it far afield from the chungke-stone which it was designed in falling to touch. This fine cast counted one point in the game, which is of eleven

points, and the Indian braves among the spectators howled like civilized young men at a horse-race.

The sport was very keen, the contest being exceedingly close, for Wyejah had long needed only one additional point to make him a winner, and when Otasite had failed to score he had also failed. The swift motion, the graceful agility, the smiling face of Otasite, — for it was a matter of the extremest exaction in the Indian games that however strenuous the exertion and tense the strain upon the nerves and grievous the mischances of the sport, the utmost placidity of manner and temper must be preserved throughout, — all appealed freshly to the trader, although it was a long-accustomed sight.

" Many a man in Charlestown — a well-to-do man" (applying the commercial standard of value) — " would be proud to have such a son," he muttered, a trifle dismayed by the perverse incongruities of fate. " He would have sent the boy to school. If there was money enough he would have sent him to England to be educated — and none too good for him !"

The shadows of the two players, all foreshortened by the approach of noontide, bobbed about in dwarfish caricature along the smooth sandy stretch. The great chungke-pole, an obelisk forty feet high planted on a low mound in the centre of the chungke-yard, and with a target at its summit used for trials of skill in marksmanship, cast a diminished simulacrum on the ground at its base scarcely larger than the chungke-lances. Now and again these heavy projectiles flew through the air, impelled with an incredible force and a skill so accurate that it seemed impossible that both contestants should not excel. There was a moment, however, when Otasite might have made the decisive point to score eleven had not the chungke-stone slipped from the hand of Wyejah as he cast it, falling only a few yards distant. Otasite's lance, flung instantly, shot far beyond that missile, for which, had the stone been properly thrown, he should have aimed. Wyejah, disconcerted and shaken by the mischance, launching his lance at haphazard, almost mechanically, struck by obvious accident the flying lance of his adversary,

deflecting its course — the decisive cast, for which he had striven so long in vain, and which was now merely fortuitous.

The crowds of Indian gamblers, with much money and goods at hazard upon the event, some, indeed, having staked the clothes upon their backs, the rifles and powder for their winter hunt that should furnish them with food, were at once in a clamor of discussion as to the fair adjustment of the throw in the score. The backers of Wyejah claimed the accidental hit as genuine and closing the game. The backers of Otasite protested that it could not be thus held, since Wyejah's defective cast of the chungke-stone debarred their champion from the possibility of first scoring the eleventh point, which chance was his by right, it being his turn to play; they met the argument caviling at Otasite's lack of aim by the counter-argument that one does not aim at a moving object where it is at the moment, but with an intuitive calculation of distance and speed where it will be when reached by the projectile hurled after it, illustrating cleverly by the example of shooting with bow and arrow at a bird on the wing.

Otasite and Wyejah both preserved an appearance of joyous indifference. With their lances poised high in the right hand they were together running swiftly up the long alley again to the starting-point, Ota-site commenting on the evident lack of intention in Wyejah's lucky cast with a loud, jocosely satiric cry, " Hala ! Hala ! " (signifying, " You are too many for me ! ")

" Lord ! how the boy does yell! " Abram Varney exclaimed, a smile pervading the wrinkles wrought about his eyes by much pondering on the problems of the Indian trade, feeling incongruously a sort of elation in the youth's noisy shouts, which echoed blatantly from the rocky banks of the Tennessee River, and with reduced arrogance and in softer tones from the cliffs of towering Chilhowee.

A sympathetic sentiment glowed in the dark eyes of an Indian chief on the slope hard by, the great Colannah Gigagei. He was fast aging now; the difficulties of diplomacy constantly increasing in view of individual aggressions and encroachments of the Carolina colonists on the east, and the ever specious wiles and suave allure-

ments of the French on the west, to win the Cherokees from their British alliance; the impossibility, in the gentle patriarchal meth ods of the Cherokee government, to control the wild young men of the tribe, who, as the half-king, Atta-Kulla-Kulla said, " often acted like madmen rather than people of sense" (and it is respectfully submitted that this peculiarity has been observed in other young men elsewhere); the prophetic vision, doubtless, of the eventual crushing of his people in the collisions of the great international struggle of the Europeans for the possession of this country, —all fostered tokens of time in the face of Colannah, and bowed his straight back, and set an unwonted quiver in the nerves of his old hand that had been firm in his heyday, and strong and crafty and cruelly bloody. But his face now was softened with pleasure, and the pride it expressed was almost ten der.

" When a few years ago the Governor of South Carolina," he said majestically, speak ing in the Cherokee tongue but for the Eng lish names (he pronounced the title " Go-weno "), " offered to take some Cherokee

youths to train in his schools and make scholars of them, I thanked him with affec tion, for his thought was kind. But I told him that if he would send some South Carolina youths to the Cherokee nation to be trained, we would make men of them! "

His blanket, curiously woven of feathers and wild hemp, requiring years of labor in its intricate manufacture, fell away from one gaunt arm as he lifted it to point with a kingly gesture at the young white man as the illustration of his training. Every muscle of strength was on parade in the splendid pose of hurling the great chungke-spear through the air, as Otasite thus passed the interval while waiting the decision of the umpire of the game. Then, with a kugh, oddly blent of affection and pride, Colannah took his way down the slope and toward the council-house: the council sat there much in these days of 1753, clouded with smoke and perplexity.

Judging by this specimen of his athletic training to feats of prowess, Colannah Gi-gagei might boast to the " Goweno" of South Carolina. It was not, however, merely in muscle that the young captive excelled.

As Abram Varney thought of certain ster ling manly traits of the highest type which this poor waif had developed here in this in congruous environment, one might suppose from the sheer force of heredity, he shook his head silently, and his eyes clouded, the pulses of Charlestown still beating in his veins. For he was wont to leave for months the treasures of his trading-house, not merely a matter of trinkets and beads, but powder, lead, and firearms, sufficient for accoutring an expedition for the "war-path," and great store of cloths, cutlery, paints, in the charge of this valiant gamester of chungke, stanch alike against friend and foe, as safely as if its wealth were beneath his own eye. So in secure had become the Cherokee allegiance to the government that it was impossible now under its uncertain protection to retain white men from the colonies here in his em ploy as agents and under-traders, or, indeed, those whose interest and profits amounted to an ownership in a share of the stock. The earlier traders in neighboring towns one by one had gone, affecting a base sev eral hundred miles nearer the white settle ments. Some had shifted altogether from

the tribe, and secured a post among the Chickasaws, who were indubitably loyal to the British. While their withdrawal added to Varney's profits, — for each trader was allowed to hold at this time a license only for two Indian towns, it being before the date of the issuance of general licenses, and the custom which they had relinquished, the barter with the Cherokees for deerskins, now came from long distances, drawn as by a magnet to his trading-house at Tennessee Town, — it had resulted in his isolation, and for years he had been almost the only Brit ish subject west of the Great Smoky Moun tains. He had no fear of the Cherokees, however — not even should the political sky, always somewhat overcast, become yet more lowering. He had long been accustomed to these Indians, and he felt that he had fast friends among them. His sane mercantile judgment appraised and appreciated the added opportunities of his peculiar position, which he would not lightly throw away, and the development of Otasite's incongruous commercial values not only removed the possibility of loss during his absence, but added to his facilities in enabling him to

secure the fidelity of Indians as packmen, hitherto impracticable, but now rendered to Otasite as one of the tribe. He had recog nized with satisfaction, mingled with amuse ment, national traits in the boy, who, despite his Indian training, would not, like them, barter strings of wampum measuring " from elbow to wrist" without regard to the rela tive length of arm. Yet he had none of the Indian deceit and treachery. He was blunt, sincere, and bold. His alertness in compu tation gave Varney genuine pleasure, al though they wrangled much as to his method, for he used the Cherokee numeration, and it set the trader's mercantile teeth on edge to hear twenty called " tahre skoeh" — two tens.

" And why not ?" Otasite would demand, full of faith in his own education. "The Chickasaw will say 'pokoole toogalo ' — ten twos " — and he would smile superior. This was his world, and these his standards — the Cherokees and the Chickasaws!

He was not to be easily influenced or turned save by some spontaneous acquies cence of his own mind, and Varney found himself counting " skoeh chooke kaiere "

(the old one's hundred) before he ever in duced Otasite to say instead " one thou sand." "

The boy even ventured on censorship in his turn. " You say ' Cherokees' and ' Chick-asaws' when you speak of the Tsullakee and the Chickasaw; why don't you then say the English-es and the French-es ? " For the plural designation of these tribes was a co lonial invention.

His bulldog tenacity, his orderly instincts, his providence, so contrary to the methods of the wasteful Indian, his cheerful industry, his indomitable energy and perseverance, — all were so national that in days gone past Varney used now and again to clap him op the shoulder with a loud, careless vaunt, " British to the marrow ! "

A fact, doubtless — and all of a sudden it had begun to seem a very serious fact. So very serious, indeed, that the old trader did not notice the crisis in the chungke-yard, the increasing excitement in the crowds of spectators, the clamors presently when the game was declared a draw and the bets off, the stir of the departing groups. It was si lence at last that smote upon his senses

with the effect of interruption which the continuance of sound had not been able to compass. He drew himself up with a per plexed sigh, and looked drearily over the expanse of the river. Its long glittering reaches were vacant, a rare circumstance, for the Cherokees of that date were almost amphibious in habit, reveling in the many lovely streams of their mountain country; on the banks their towns were situated, and this fact doubtless contributed to the neat ness of their habitations and personal clean liness, to which the travelers of those times bear a surprised testimony. The light upon the water was aslant now from a westering sun, and glittering on the snowy breasts of a cluster of swans drifting, dreaming per haps, on the current. The scarlet boughs on the summit of Chilhowee were motion less against the azure zenith. Not even the vaguest tissue of mist now lingered about the majestic domes of the Great Smoky Moun tains, painted clearly and accurately in fine and minute detail in soft dense velvet blues against the hard polished mineral blue of the horizon. The atmosphere was so exqui sitely luminous and pellucid that it might

have seemed a fit medium to dispel uncer tainty in other than merely material sub jects of contemplation. Nevertheless he did not see his way clearly, and when he came within view of his trading-house he paused as abruptly as if he had found his path blocked by an obstacle.

There, seated on the step of the closed door which boasted the only lock and key in Tennessee Town, or for the matter of that in all the stretch of the Cherokee coun try west of the Great Smoky Range, was Otasite, the incongruity of his auburn curls and his Indian headdress seeming a trifle more pronounced than usual, since it had been for a time an unfamiliar sight. He was awaiting the coming of the trader, and was singing meanwhile in a loud and cheer ful voice, " Drink with me a cup of wine," a ditty which he had heard in his half-forgot ten childhood. The robust full tones gave no token of the draught made upon his en durance by the heavy exercise of the day, but he seemed a bit languid from the heat, and his doeskin shirt was thrown open at the throat, showing his broad white chest, and in its centre the barbarous blue discol-

orations of the " warrior's marks." These disfigurements, made by the puncturing of the flesh with gars' teeth and inserting in the wound paint and pitch, indelible testimonials to his deeds of courage and prowess, Otasite valued as he did naught else on earth, and he would have parted with his right hand as readily. The first had been bestowed upon him after he had gone, a mighty gun-man, against the Muscogees. The others he had won in the course of a long, furious, and stubborn contest of the tribe with the Chick-asaws, who, always impolitic, headlong, and brave, were now reduced by their own valor in their many wars from ten thousand fight ing men to a few hundred. He had attained the " warrior's crown " when he had shown their kindred Choctaws a mettle as fierce and a craft as keen as their own. And now he was looking at Abram Varney with kindly English eyes and an expression about the brow, heavily freckled, that almost smote the tears from the elder man. The trader knew from long experience what was com ing, but suddenly he had begun to regard it differently. Always upon the end of each journey from Charlestown he had been met

here within a day or two by Otasite on the same mission. The long years as they passed had wrought only external changes since, as a slender wistful boy of eleven years, heart-sick, homeless, forlorn, friendless, save for his Indian captors, likely, indeed, to forget all language but theirs, he had first come with his question, always in English, always with a faltering eyelash and a depre catory lowered voice, " Did you hear any thing in Charlestown of any people named < Queetlee ' ? "

This was the distorted version of his fa ther's name that Colannah had preserved. As to the child himself, his memory had perhaps been shaken by the events of that terrible night of massacre, which he only realized as a frightful awakening from sleep to smoke, flames, screams, the ear-splitting crack of rifle-shots at close quarters, the shock of a sudden hurt — and then, after an interval of unconsciousness, a transition to a new world of strange habitudes that grew speedily familiar, and of unexpected kind ness that became dear to a frank, affection ate heart. Perhaps in the isolations of the frontier life he had never heard his father

addressed by his surname by a stranger; he was called " Jan " by his wife, and her name was " Eelin," and this Otasite knew, and this was all he knew, save that he him self also had been called " Jan."

" They don't want you, my buck, or they would have been after you," the trader used to reply, being harder, perhaps when he was younger. Besides, he honestly thought the cadaverous brat, all legs, like a growing colt, and skinny arms, was better off here in the free woodland life which he himself considered no hardship, and affected long after necessity or interest had dictated his environment. The little lad was safe in the care of the powerful chief Colannah Gigagei of Tennessee Town, who had adopted him, and who was a man of great force and in fluence. Why should the child seek a home among his own people, unwelcome doubt less, to eat the meagre crust of charity, or serve as an overworked drudge somewhere on the precarious frontier ? The trader did not greatly deplore the lack of religious training, for in the remote settlements this was often still an unaccustomed luxury, al beit some thirty years had now gone by

since Sir Francis Nicholson, then the Gov ernor, declared that no colony could flourish •without a wider diffusion of the gospel and education, and forthwith ordered spiritual drill, so to speak, in the way of preaching and schooling. Although himself described as " a profane, passionate, headstrong man, bred a soldier," as if the last fact were an excuse for the former, he contributed largely to the furtherance of these pious objects, " spending liberally all his salary and per quisites of office," for which generous trait of character an early and strait-laced histo rian is obviously of the opinion that General Nicholson should have been suffered to swear in peace and, as it were, in the odor of sanctity.

More than once, when in Charlestown, Varney, notwithstanding his persuasions on the subject, had been minded to inquire concerning the " Queetlees," who he under stood from Colannah had come originally from Cumberland in England. With his mercantile cronies he had canvassed the ques tion whether the queer, evidently distorted name could have been " Peatley" or "Patey" or « Petrie," — for the Chero-

kees always substituted " Q " for " P," as the latter letter they could not pronounce, — and after this transient consideration the matter would drop.

As the child, running about the Indian town with his new-found playmates, grew robust and merry-hearted, and happiness, confidence, and strength brought their em bellishing influence to the expression. of his large dark gray eyes and straightened the nervous droop from his thin little shoulders, the trader noticed casually once or twice how comely the brat had become, and he experienced a fleeting, half-ridiculing pity for his mother — how the woman would have resented and resisted the persistent shearing and shaving of those silken, loosely twining red curls ! Then he thought of her no more. But when the child had come to man's es tate, when he was encased in a network of muscle like elastic steel wires, when stature and strength had made him alike formidable and splendid, when the development of his temperament illustrated virtues so stanch that they seemed the complement of his physical endowment and a part of his reso lute personality, the old trader thought of

the boy's father, and thought of him daily — how the sturdy Cumbrian yeoman would have rejoiced in so stalwart a son ! Thus, with this vague bond of sympathy with a man whom he had never seen, never known, so long ago, so cruelly dead, this intuitive divination of his paternal sentiment, Var-ney's fatherly attitude grew more definite daily and became accustomed, and he was jealous of the influence of Colannah, who in turn was jealous of his influence.

Now as Varney stood in the dusky trad ing-house among the kegs and bags and bales of goods, the high peak of the interior of the roof lost in the lofty shadows, he felt that he had been much in default in long-past years, and he experienced a very defi nite pang of conscience as Otasite swung abruptly around a stack of arms, a new rifle in his hand, the flint and pan of which he had been keenly examining.

He lifted his eyes suddenly with that long-lashed dreary look of his childhood.

" Did you hear of any Queetlees in Charles-town ? " he asked.

66 It is you who should seek your kindred, Jan Queetlee ! " Varney said impulsively, calling him by his unaccustomed English name. " It is you who should go to Charles-town to find the Queetlees ! "

Otasite's face showed suddenly the un wonted expression of fear. He recoiled ab ruptly, and Abram Varney was sensible of a deep depression. It was as he had thought. The wish for restoration to those of his name and his kindred which had animated the boy's earlier years had now dwindled to a mere abstract sentiment of loyalty as of clanship, but was devoid of expectation, of intention. All the members of his imme diate family had perished in the massacre, and he had been trained to regard this as the fortunes of war, cherishing no personal antagonism, as elsewhere among civilized people reconciliations are frequent between the victors and the friends of the slain in battle. Moreover, he was not brought close to it. The participators in the affray were of the distant Ayrate settlements of the tribe, southeast of the mountains, and not individualized. The Indians of Tennessee Town, which was then one of the most re mote of the Cherokee villages of the Ottare division, and this perhaps was the reason

it was selected as his home, were not con cerned in the foray, nor were any others o£ the Overhill towns. Thus he had grown up without the thirst for vengeance, which showed how little the methods of his Cher okee environment had influenced his heart. And truly the far-away Queetlees, if any such were cognizant of his existence, had troubled themselves nothing about it, and had infinitely less claim on his gratitude and filial affection than Colannah. They had left him to be as a waif, a slave. He had been reared as a son, nursed and tended, fed and fostered, bedecked in splendor, armed in costly and formidable wise, given com mand and station, carefully trained in all that the Indian knew.

" Colannah would never consent! " he said at last.

Abram Varney afterward wondered why he should then have had a vision — oh, so futile, so fleeting, so fantastic! — of the twenty, the forty, nay, the sixty years that this man, so munificently endowed by na ture, might pass here among the grotesque, uncouth barbarities of the savage Chero kee, while his heritage — his religion, the

religion into which he was born of Chris tian parents, his name and nation, his tongue and station, his opportunity — doubtless some fair, valid, valuable future — all lay there to the eastward but scant five hun dred miles away on the Carolina coast. He said as much, and the retort came succinctly, " You live here ! "

Otasite's English speech was as simple as a child's, but he thought as diplomatically as Colannah himself, whom he esteemed the greatest man in all the world, and he could argue in the strategic Cherokee method. Nevertheless, to give him full sway, that everything possible might be said in contra vention of the proposition, the old trader lapsed into the Indian speech, that was in deed from long usage like a mother tongue to them both. He stayed here, he said, from choice, it was true, but for the sake of the trade that gave him wealth, and with wealth he could return to the colonies at any time, and go whither he would in all the world. But Otasite was restricted; he had no goods for trade, no adequate capital to invest; he could only return to the colonies while young, to work, to make a way, to secure

betimes a place appropriate to his riper years. Even this could not be done without great difficulty,—witness how many settlers came empty-handed to barely exist on the frontier and wrest a reluctant living from the wilderness, — and it could not be done at all without friends. Now he, Abram Var-ney, was prepared to stand his friend; Otasite could take a place in the service of the company, in the main depot of the trade at Charlestown. His knowledge of

o

the details of the business of which Abram Varney's long absences had given him ex perience ; of the needs of the Cherokee na tion ; of the ever-continued efforts of the French traders, by means of the access to the Overhill towns afforded by the Cherokee and Tennessee rivers, despite the great dis tance from their settlements on the Mis sissippi, to insinuate their supplies at lower prices, in the teeth of the Cherokee treaty with the British monopolizing such traffic, and bring down profits — all would have a special and recognized value and be appreciated by his mercantile associates, who would further the young man's advance ment. Thence he could at his leisure make

inquiries concerning his father's family, and doubtless in the course of time be restored to his kindred.

Otasite listened throughout with the cour teous air of deliberation which his Indian training required him to accord to any dis course, without interruption, however un welcome or trivial it might be esteemed. Then, smiling slowly, he shook his head.

"You cannot be serious," he said. "It would break old Colannah's heart, who has been like a father to me."

Abram Varney too had the British bull dog tenacity. " What will you do, then," he asked slowly and significantly, "when Colannah takes up arms against the British government? Will you fight men of your own blood?"

He was reinforced in this argument by the habit of thought of the Indians — the absolute absence of tribal dissensions, of internecine strife, so marked among the Cherokees: here no man's hand was lifted against his brother.

Jan Queetlee palpably winced. Come what might, he could never fight for the Cherokees against the British — his father's

people, his mother's people—no more than he could fight for the British against his adopted tribe — the Cherokee — and he the "Man-killer!"

" They will fight each other/' said Var-ney weightily, " and the day is not far — the day is not far ! "

For in 1753 the cumulative discontents of the tribe were near the crisis, earnestly fostered by the French on the western boundaries, that vast domain then known as Louisiana, toward whose siren voice the Cherokees had ever lent a willing ear. The building by the British government, two or three years later, of those great defensive works, Fort Prince George and Fort Loudon, situated respectively at the eastern and western extremities of the Cherokee ter ritory, mounted with cannon and garri soned by British forces, served to hold them in check and quieted them for a time, but only for a time. Jan Queetlee, by rea son of his close association with the chiefs, knew far more than Varney dreamed of the bitterness roused in the hearts of the Indians by friction with the government, the aggressions of the individual colonist,

the infringements of their privileges in the treaty, and in opposition the influence of the ever seductive suavity of the French.

As with a sudden hurt, Jan Queetlee cried out with a poignant voice against the government and its patent unfaith, striking his clinched fist so heavily on the head of a keg of powder that the stout fibres of the wood burst beneath the passionate blow, and in a moment he was covered with the flying particles of the black dust. Kealizing the possibility of an explosion should a can dle or a pipe be lighted here, Varney did not wait for the return of one of the brawny packmen to remove the keg to a cave be neath the trading-house, which he utilized for storage as a cellar, but addressed himself to the job. Jan Queetlee silently assisted, his face darker, more lowering with the thought in his mind than with the smears of the powder.

Varney remembered this afterward, and that he himself, diverted by the accident from the trend of his argument, had launched out in a tirade against the government as they worked together, the young Briton's energy, industry, and persistence so at va-

riance with the aspect of his tufted topknot of feathers on his auburn curls, and the big blue warrior's marks on his broad white chest. For Varney too had his grievances against the powers that were; but his woes were personal. He vehemently condemned the reconciliation which the government had effected between the Muscogees and the Cherokees, for although there were more deerskins to be had for export when the Indian hunters were at pacific leisure, Var ney had considered the recent war between these tribes an admirable vent for gun powder and its profitable sale; and since the savages must always be killing, it was manifestly best for all concerned that they should kill each other. He could not suf ficiently deride the happy illustration which Governor Glen had given them (in his fatuity, Varney thought) of the values of peace and concord. In the presence of the two delegations the mediating Governor had taken an arrow and shown them with what ease it could be broken; then how impos sible he found it to break a quiverful of arrows, thus demonstrating the strength in union. Varney argued that the Indians

would readily perceive a further application of the principle and turn it to account, com bining* against the colonists. In the same spirit he animadverted upon a monopoly from which he was excluded in common with the traders in general, and which had been granted to a mercantile company seeking to establish posts among the Choctaws. The enterprise, although favored by the govern ment, obviously because, undertaken on a scale of phenomenal magnitude, it promised to dislodge the French and their long-estab lished trade among the Choctaws, and bring that powerful tribe to a British allegiance, had finally proved a failure; and with a bit ter joy in this fact he alternately contemned and pitied the government, because it could not wrest this valuable opportunity from the iron grasp of the " Mississippi Lou-isianians." He had, too, a censorious word for the French commercially — called them " peddlers," celebrated their deceitful wiles, underrated the quality of their cloths, and inconsistently berated them for their low prices, finding a logical parity in all these matters in the tenets of their religion, which they had so vainly and so zealously sought

to instill into the unreceptive hearts of the unimpressionable Choctaw. 4

With the plethora of interest involved in these subjects, Varney grew oblivious of the theme that had earlier occupied his mind. It recurred no more to his thoughts until several days had passed. He then chanced to be occupied with his new goods in his cavern. It was illumined only from above; there was a trap-door in the floor of the trading-house, and thence a pale tempered light drifted down, scarcely convenient, but sufficient for his purposes. Once he noticed that a shadow flickered across it. He experi enced a momentary surprise, for he had left no one in the building, and the outer door being locked, he imagined it could not be forced without noise enough to rouse him. Again the shadow flickered across the trap door ; then ensued a complete eclipse of the scant glimmer of light. There was a step upon the ladder which served as stair way — a man was descending.

Varney felt a sudden constriction about his throat. He realized an impending crisis; the door above had been closed; by the sound he knew that the ladder was now re-

moved and laid upon the ground. He had an idea — he could see naught — that the unknown invisible man had seated himself on the ladder on the ground, where he re mained motionless, silent, in anger, in grief, or some strange savage whim hardly possible for a civilized creature to divine.

The time that passed in this black nul lity — he never could compute it — mo ments, doubtless, but it seemed hours, tried to the utmost the nerve of the entrapped trader, albeit inured by twenty years' ex perience to the capricious temper of the Cherokee Indians. He felt he could better endure the suspense could he only see his antagonist, identify him, and thus guess his purpose, and shape his own course from his knowledge of character. But with some acquired savage instinct he, too, remained silent, null, passive; one might have thought him absent. Perhaps his quiescence, indeed, fostered some doubt of his presence here, for suddenly there sounded the rasping of flint on steel, the spunk was aglow, and then in the timorous flame of the kindling candle, taken from his own stores above, Varney recognized the face and figure of the stately

and imperious old chief Colannah. The next moment he remembered something far more pertinent. He called out in an agitated voice to the Indian to beware of the powder with which the place was largely stocked.

" I came for that/' said Colannah in Cher okee, with unaccustomed fingers snuffing the wick as he had seen Varney perform the process, for the Indians used torches and fires of split cane for purposes of illu mination.

" For God's sake, what have I done ? " cried the trader in an agony of terror, desir ous to bring his accusation to the point as early as might be and compass his release, thus forestalling the violent end of an ex plosion.

" What do the English always ? — you have robbed me ! " said Colannah, the light strong on his fierce indignant features, his garb of fringed buckskin, his many rich strings of the ivory-like roanoke about his neck, his gayly bedecked and feathered head, and in shadowy wise revealing the rough walls of the cave, the boxes and bales of goods, the reserve stock, as it were, the stands of arms, and the kegs and bags of powder.

As Varney,half crouching on the ground, noted the latter in the dusk, he cried out precipitately, " Bobbed you of what ? My God ! let us go upstairs. I '11 give it back, whatever it is, twice over, fourfold ! Don't swing the candle around that way, Colan-nah ! the powder will blow us and the whole trading-house into the Tennessee Biver."

Cola*hnah nodded acquiescence, the stately feathers on his head gleaming fitfully in the clare-obscure of the cavern. " That is why I came ! Then the British government could demand no satisfaction for the life of the British subject — an accident — the old chief of Tennessee Town killed with him. And I should be avenged."

"For what? My God!" Varney had not before called upon the Lord for twenty years. To hold a diplomatic conversation with an enraged wild Indian, flourishing a lighted candle in a powder magazine, is calculated to bring even the most self-sufficient and forgetful sinner to a sense of his dependence and helplessness. The lighted candle was a more subjugating weapon than a drawn sword. He had con templated springing upon the stanch old

warrior, although, despite the difference in age, he was no match for the Indian, in or der to seek to extinguish it. He reflected, however, that in the struggle a flaring spark might cause the ignition of scattered parti cles of the powder about the floor, and thus precipitate the explosion which he shuddered to imagine. " For what, Colannah ? " he asked again, in a soothing smooth cadence, " for what, my comrade, my benefactor for years, my best-beloved friend — avenged on me for what ? Let's go upstairs ! "

The flicker of the wavering candle showed a smile of contempt on the face of the an gry Indian for a moment, and admonished Varney that in view of the Cherokees' rel ish of the torture his manifestations of anx iety but prolonged his jeopardy. It brought, too, a fuller realization of the gravity of the situation in that the Indian should so valiantly risk himself. He evidently in tended to take the trader's life, but in such wise that no vengeance for his death should fall upon the Cherokee nation. Abram Varney summoned all his courage, which was not inconsiderable, and had been culti vated by the wild and uncertain conditions

of his life. Assured that he could do naught to hasten his release, he awaited the event in a sort of stoical patience, dreading, how ever, every motion, every sound, the least stir setting his expectant nerves aquiver. Silence, quiescence, brought the disclosure earlier than he had feared.

" When I took the boy Jan Queetlee — why do I call him thus, instead of by the name he has earned for himself, the noble Otasite of Tennessee Town?"—the old chief began as deliberately, as disregardfully of the surroundings as if seated under the boughs of one of the giant oaks on the safe slopes of Chilhowee yonder — " when I took him away from the braves who had overcome the South Carolina stationers, I owed him no duty. He was puny and ill and white and despised! You British say the Indian has no pity. A man's son or brother or father or mother has claims upon him. Otasite was naught to me, a mere eeankke !" (a captive). " I owed the child no duty. My love was voluntary. I gave it a free gift; no duty! And he was little, and drooping, and meagre, and ill all the time ! But he grew ; soon no such boy

in the Cherokee nation, soon hardly such a warrior in all the land — not even Otasite of Watauga, nor yet Otasite of Eupharsee; perhaps at his age Oconostota excelled " (Oconostota always was preeminently known as the " Great Warrior "). He paused to shake his head and meditate on difficult comparisons and instances of prowess. Af ter an interval which, long enough, seemed to the trembling trader illimitable, he re commenced abruptly : " Says the Goweno long time ago to me, ' Is not there a white youth among you ? ' I say, ' He is content; he has no white friends, it seems.' Says the Goweno to me, ' Ah, ah, we must look into this !' and says no more."

Colannah flung back his head and laughed so long and so loud that every echo of the sarcastic guttural tones, striking back from the stone walls of the cavern, smote Varney with as definite a shock as a blow.

" And now," the Cherokee resumed, with a changed aspect and a pathetic cadence, "I am an old man, and I lean upon Ota site. My sons are all dead — one in the wars with the Muscogee and two slain by the Chickasaw. And the last he said to me,

with his lingering latest breath, loath to go and leave me desolate, 'But you have an adopted son, you have the noble Otasite.' And now," his voice was firm again, "if I have him not, I go too, and you go. We go together."

" I will not advise him to quit the nation — never again! " cried Varney, suddenly enlightened, fervently repudiating his inter ference. " Since you disapprove, he shall not return to Carolina. He cannot go with out me — my help; he could not find a place — a home. Bold and fine as he is here, he would be strange there; he knows naught of the ways of the colonists. He would be poor, despised, while here he has been like the first, the best. His pride could never stoop to a life like a slave's; his pride would break his heart. Let me undo the mischief I have wrought; let me unsay the unthinking, foolish words I have spoken."

It was perhaps with the faith that the artful trader could best turn the young fellow's mind back to its wonted content, as his crafty arguments had already so potently aroused this wild, new dissatisfac tion, that Colannah at last consented to

liberate Varney for this essay, not without a cogent reminder that he would be held responsible for its failure. And indeed in recanting his former urgency, when he sought out Otasite, Varney exerted himself to the utmost.

" You are satisfied here. You know the life. Like me, you love it. If I, who can choose, prefer it, why not you ? "

But Otasite shook his head.

" When I talk to you of the colonies I speak as a man does of a dream," Varney continued. " It is something true and some thing false. I add here and I let slip there to make out the connection, and give the symmetry of truth to the picture. But did I ever tell you how they love money in the colonies, how they cheat and strive and slave their lives away to add to their store; how they reverence and worship the wealth of others till it seems that a rich man can do no wrong — if he is rich enough ? Did I ever tell you this? The poor, they are despised for being poor, and they are let to suffer. Here poverty is not permitted. If a man lose his dwelling by fire, the town builds him another house. You know this.

If a man fail in his winter hunt, the oth ers give of their abundance. Here one is rated by his personal worth. Here the deed is held to be fine, not the mere thing. Here you are valued as the great Otasite, and all men give you honor for your cour age. There you are Jan Queetlee, a penni less clod, and all men despise you and pass you by." 5

But again Otasite shook his head.

It was no spurious flare of ambition, in effectual, illusory; no discontented yearn ing for a different, a wider life that the trader's ill-advised words had roused. That sentiment of loyalty to the British govern ment, which had never sought to claim Jan Queetlee as a subject, seemed bred in his bone and born in his blood. Perhaps it was the stuff of which long afterward the Tories of the Eevolution were made. He could not lift his hand against this aloof, indifferent fetich. And yet take part against the Cherokees, whom he loved as they loved him ! For with his facilities for understand ing the trend of the politics of the day he could no longer blind himself to the ap proach of the war of the tribe with the

British government, which, indeed, came within the decade. The sons of Colannah, slain in the cruel wars with other Indians, had been to him like brothers, and in their loss he had felt his full and bitter share of the grief of a common household. Even yet he and Colannah were wont to sadly talk of them with that painful elimination of their names, a mark of Indian reverence to the dead, substituting the euphemism " the one who is gone," and linger for hours over the fire at night or on the shady river-bank in sunlit afternoons, rehearsing their deeds and recalling their traits, and repeating their sayings with that blending of affec tionate pride and sorrow that is the consola tion of bereavement when time has some what softened its pangs and made memory so dear. And Colannah had been like a father — it seemed to Jan Queetlee as if he had had no other father. He could not leave Colannah, old, desolate, and alone. Yet the war was surely coming apace, as they both knew, a war which already tore his heart in sunder, in which he could evade taking part against his own — his own of both factions — only by going at once and going far. He could decide no such weighty matter.

At last he determined he would leave it to fate, to chance, showing how truly a gambler his Indian training had made him. He would stake the crisis on a game at chungke; i£ he won, as he told Varney, he would go to Carolina, and take sides with neither faction; if he lost, he would cast his future with the Cherokee nation.

Varney, thoroughly uneasy, had come to feel a personal interest involved. If Otasite quitted the country, he felt his life would hardly be safe here, since the craft of Co-lannah had drawn from the unsuspecting young fellow the details of the plan of re moval to Charlestown which he had pro posed. And yet Varney himself was averse to any change, unless it was indeed neces sary. When put to the test he felt he would rather live in the Cherokee nation than any where else in all the world, and he valued his commerce with the tribe and his license from the government, under duly approved bond and security, to conduct that traffic in Tennessee Town and Tellico as naught else on earth. He manifested so earnest and gen uine a desire to repair the damage of his ill-starred suggestion that Colannah, showing

his age in his haste and his tremulousness and excitement, disclosed to him in a flutter of tri umphant glee that he had a spell to work which naught could withstand — a draught from Herbert's Spring to offer to Otasite. Thither some fifty miles he had dispatched a runner for a jar of the magic water, and after drinking of it Otasite could not quit for seven years the Cherokee nation even if he would.

It was in the council-house that the mys tic beverage was quaffed. There had been guests — head men from Great Tellico and Citico — during the afternoon, received in secret conclave, and now that their deliber ations were concluded and they were gone, Otasite, not admitted to the council, being one of those warriors who did the fighting of the battles devised by the " beloved men," strolled into the deserted, dome-like place. Its walls, plastered with red clay, were yet more ruddy for a cast of the westering sun. The building was large enough to accommo date several hundred people, and around the walls were cane seats, deftly constructed and artificially whitened, making, according to an old writer, " very genteel settees or

couches." Tired with the stress of mental depression and anxiety as physical effort could not tame him, and vaguely prescient of evil, Otasite had flung himself down on one of these, which was spread with dressed panther-skins, his hands clasped under his head, his scalp-lock of two auburn curls dangling over them.

Through the tall narrow doorway the au tumnal landscape was visible, blazing with all the fervors of summer; the mountains, however, were more softly blue, the sunlight of a richer glister; the river, now steel, now silver, now amber, reflected the atmosphere as a sensitive soul reflects the moods of those most dear; the forests, splendid with color, showed the lavish predominance of the rich reds characteristic of the Chilhowee woods; a dreamlike haze over all added a vague ideality that made the scene like some fond est memory or a glamourous forecast.

" Akoo-e-a ! " (summer yet!) said Colan-nah, his eyes too on the scene, as he sat on a buffalo-rug in the centre of the floor draw ing in the last sweet fragrant breaths from his long-stemmed pipe, curiously wrought of stone, for in the manufacture of these

pipes the Cherokees of that day were said to excel all other Indians. The young Briton experienced no mawkish pang to note that it was ornamented at one end by a dang ling scalp, greatly treasured, the interior of the skin painted red for its preservation. He had, in fact, a pipe of his own with a scalp much like it. Indeed, his trophy was a fine specimen, and it had been a feat to take it, for it had once covered a hot Chick-asaw head.

" Akoo-e-a! the day is warm !" remarked Colannah. He lifted his storied pipe, and with its long stem silently motioned to a young Indian woman, indicating a great jar of water. She quickly filled one of those quaint bowls, or cups, of the Cherokee man ufacture, and advanced with it to Otasite; but the proffer was in the nature of an in terruption of his troubled thoughts, and he irritably waved her away.

" I am displeased with you," said Colan nah sternly, lifting his dark, deeply sunken eyes to where the " Man-killer " lay at full length on the cane settee. " You set me aside. You have no thoughts for me — no words. Yet you can talk when you go to

the trading-house. You have words and to spare for the trader. You can drink with him. You can sing, f Drink with me a cup of wine." He lifted his raucous old voice in ludicrous travesty of the favorite catch, for sometimes the two Britons, so incongru ous in point of age, education, sentiment, and occupation, cemented their bond as compatriots by carousing together in a mild way.

But this ebullition of temper had naught of the ludicrous in Jan Queetlee's estima tion. He was pierced to the heart.

"Aketohta!" (Father!) he cried re proachfully. He had sprung to his feet, and stood looking down at the old chief, who would not look at him, but kept his eyes on the landscape without, now and then draw ing a long, lingering whiff from his pipe. " Aketohta ! /have no thought for you ! — who alone have taken thought for me / / have words for the trader and silence for you ! You say keen things, and you know they are not true! You know that I had rather drink water with you than wine with him. I am not thirsty; but since it is you who offer it" — His expression changed;

he broke into sudden pleasant laughter, and with a rollicking stave of the song, " Drink with me a cup of wine," he caught the bowl from the girl's hand and drained it at a draught.

" Seohsta-quo!" (Good!) cried Colannah, visibly refreshed, as if his own thirst were vi cariously slaked. But Otasite stood blankly staring, the bowl motionless in his hand. " It is well for wine to be old," he said wonderingly, " but not water."

For his palate was accustomed to the ex quisite sparkle and freshness of the moun tain fountains, and this had come from far.

The crafty Colannah stolidly repressed his delight, save for the glitter in his eyes fixed on the azure and crimson and silver landscape glimmering beyond the dusky portals of the terra-cotta walls. " Nawohti ! nawohti ! " (Rum!) he said, with an affectation of sever ity. " You drink too much of the trader's strong physic ! You have no love now for the sweet, clear water." And he shook his head with the uncompromising reproof of a mentor of present times as he growled disjointedly, " Nawohti ! nawohti! "

Otasite nothing questioned the genuine-ness of this demonstration, for the Cherokee rulers, in common with those of other tribes, had long waged a vigorous opposition to the importation of strong drink into their coun try ; indeed, as far back as 1704, when hold ing a solemn conference with Governor Daniel of North Carolina to form a general treaty of friendship, the chiefs of several tribes petitioned the government of the Lords Proprietors for a law, which was after ward enacted (and disregarded), forbidding any white man to sell or give rum to an Indian, and prescribing penalties for its in fringement. It was not the first time that Otasite had heard unfavorably of the influ ences of " nawohti," which, by the way, with the Cherokees signified physic, as well as spirituous liquor, a synonymous definition which more civilized people have sought to apply. He was content that he and the old chief were once more in affectionate ac cord, and he did not seek to interpret the flash of triumph in Colannah's face.

For seven years ! for seven years! the white " Man-killer" could not, if he would, quit the Cherokee country. Well might the old chief's eyes glisten ! The youth was

like a son to his lonely age, and Otasite's prowess the pride of his life. And like others elsewhere he had softened as age came on, and loved the domestic fireside and the companionship about the hearth, hearing without participating in the hilari ous talk of the young, and looking out at the world through the eyes of the new gen eration, undaunted, expectant, aglow with a spirit that had long ago smouldered in his own; for the fierce Indian at the last was but an old man.

Abram Varney, too, experienced a recur rence of ease. He had unwittingly imbibed much outlandish superstition in his resi dence among the Cherokees, and indeed other traders and settlers long believed in the enchaining fascination of Herbert's Spring, and drank or refrained as they would stay or go.

Otasite, however, was all unaware of the spell cast upon him when he came into the chungke-yard the next day, arrayed in his finest garb, the white dressed doeskin glit tering in the sun, his necklaces of beads, his belt of wolf fangs, his flying feet in their white moccasins — all catching the light with a differing effect of brilliancy.

Varney watched him; — with the two eagle feathers stiff and erect on his proud head, his two incongruous long auburn curls, that did duty as a " war-lock/' floating back ward in the breeze, he ran so deftly, so swiftly, with so assured and so graceful a gait that the mere observation of such sym metrical motion was a pleasure. The trader had scarcely a pulse of anxiety. Indeed, dis ingenuously profiting by the tip afforded by Herbert's Spring, he was heavily backing Wyejah as a winner !

A windy day it was; the clouds raced through the sky, and their shadows skim ming over the valleys and slopes challenged their speed. The Tennessee River was sing ing, singing ! The mountains were as clearly and definitely blue as the heavens. That revelation of ranges on the far horizon unaccustomed to the view, only vouchsafed by some necromancy of the clarified autum nal air, never before seemed so distinct, so alluring — new lands, new hopes, new life they suggested. Wyejah's scarlet attire, its fringes tasseled with the spurs of the wild turkey, rendered his lithe figure strongly marked against these illusory ethereal tints

as he sped abreast with Otasite along the level sandy stretch of the chungke-yard. And how well he played ! Varney realized this with a satisfaction as of having already won his wagers, many and large, for Otasite would leave the nation should he be victo rious, and having drunk unwittingly of Her bert's Spring, he could not quit the Chero kee country, although he himself was still unaware of having quaffed of those mystic waters. Therefore defeat was obviously his portion. "Whenever the trader thought anew of his secret knowledge of this fact he of fered odds on Wyejah, and glanced at him with approbation —at the young Indian warrior's face fiercely, eagerly smiling, his great flattened ears distended on their wire hoops, his dark eyes full of sombre brilliance. How well he played ! and how hard the skill of his opponent pressed him ! How accurate was the aim of the long lance of Otasite as he poised his weight on the supple tips of his white moccasins and hurled the missile through the air; how strong and firm his grasp that sent the circular, quartz chungke-stone, whirling along the sand; how tire lessly his long sinewy steps sped back and

forth in the swift dashes up and down the smooth spaces of the chungke-yard ; how faithfully he was doing his best, regardless of his own preference in the interests that he had adventured on the result! How like a Briton born it was, Abram Varney thought, for he alone knew of Otasite's resolution, and the significance of the game to him, that the boy could thus see fair play between the factions that warred within him for his future. He had staked the future on the event, — and suddenly it was the present!

A wild clamor of excitement, of applause, rose up from the throats of the crowd in the natural amphitheatre, clanging and clatter ing in long guttural cries, — all intensi fied by a relish of the unexpected, a joy in a new sensation, for Wyejah had never before been beaten, and Otasite was the victor at chungke.

Abram Varney felt his heart leap into his throat, then sink like lead ; Colannah, triumphant, knowing naught of the subtler significance of the contest, joyful, aglow with pride, rose up in his splendid feathered mantle, standing high on the slope, to sign to the boy his pleasure in the victory. The sunlight fell, glittering very white, on the young fellow's doeskin garb, his prickly belt of fangs, his bare chest with the blue warrior's marks, the curls of his auburn scalp-lock tossing in the wind. He had seemed hitherto stoical, unmoved by victory as he would have appeared in defeat; but Varney, eager to get at him, to combat his resolution, knew that he was stunned by the complications presented by this falling out of the event. He visibly faltered as his eye met the triumph and affection expressed in Colannah's quivering old face. He could not respond to its congratulation. He dropped on one knee suddenly, bending low, affecting to find something amiss with one of his moccasins.

Wyejah, too, could seem unmoved by vic tory, but indifference to defeat was more difficult to simulate. He had in the first moment of its realization felt the blood rush to his head; despite his strong nerve his hand trembled; the smile of placidity which it was a point of honor to preserve became a fixed grin. Several other young braves had come into the yard, and were idly toss ing the lance at the great chungke-pole —

as a billiardist of the civilized life of that day might pocket the balls with a purpose less cue after a match. Wyejah, too, had cast his lance aslant; then he idly hurled the chungke-stone with a muscular fling along the spaces of the white sand. His nerve was shaken, his aim amiss, his great strength de flected. The heavy discoidal quartz stone skimmed through the air above the stretch of sand, and striking with its beveled edge the kneeling figure on the temple, the future of the victor at chungke became in one moment the past.

The trader could only have likened the scene that ensued to the moment of an earthquake or some other stupendous con vulsion of nature. In the midst of the confusion, the wild cries, the swift run ning figures, the surging of the crowds into the chungke-yard that obliterated the wide glare of the sun on the white sand, he made good his escape. He knew enough of the trend of Cherokee thought to be pre scient of the fate of the scapegoat. Colan-nah in the first burst of grief he knew would blame himself that he should have tempted fate by the mystic draught from

Herbert's Spring to hold here that bright young form for seven years longer. How sadly true ! — for seven years Otasite would remain, and seven to that, and, alack, seven more, and forever ! Soon, however, the natu ral impulses of the Indian's temper, intensi fied by long cultivation, would be reasserted. He would cast about for revenge, remem bering the first suggestion of the departure of Otasite, and from whom it had ema nated. But for the English trader and his specious wiles, the old chief would argue, would Otasite have thought of forsaking his foster nation, his adopted father, for the selfish, indifferent British, the "Goweno" at Charlestown, who cared for him nothing ? The trader it was who had brought this calamity upon them, who had in effect, by the hand of another, administered the fatal draught. Seek for him ! — hale him forth ! — wreak upon him the just, unappeasable vengeance of the forever bereaved !

The old trader had evinced an instinct in flight and concealment that an animal might envy. No probable hiding-place he selected, such as might be known or di vined— a cave, the attic of his trading-

house, the cellar beneath — all obvious, all instantly explored. Instead, he slipped into a rift in the rocks along the river-bank. Myriads of such crevices there were in the tilted strata — unheeded, unremarked, too strait and restricted to suggest the idea of refuge, too infinitely numerous for search. There, unable in the narrow compass to turn, even to shift a numbing muscle of his lean old body, in all the constraint of a standing posture, he was held in the flex ure of the rock like some of its fossils, — as unsuspected as a ganoid of the days of eld that had once been imprisoned thus in the sediment of seas that had long ebbed hence, — or the fern vestiges in a later for mation finding a witness in the imprint in the stone of the symmetry of its fronds.

He listened to the hue and cry for him; then to the sudden tramp of hoofs as a pursuing party went out to overtake him, presumably on his way to Charlestown, maintaining a very high rate of speed, for the Cherokees of that period had some famously fine horses.

Straining his senses — all unnaturally alert — he distinguished, as the afternoon wore on, the details of the preparations for the barbarous sepulture of the young Briton. Now and then the cracking of rifle-shots betokened the shooting of his horses and cattle and all the living things among his possessions — a practice already in its decadence among the Cherokees, and later, influenced by the utilitarian methods of civilization, altogether abandoned. Swift steps here and there throughout the town intimated errands to gather all his choicest effects to be buried with him, for his future use. To this custom, it is said, and the great security of the fashioning of the sepulchres of the Cherokees, may be attributed the fact that little of their pottery, arms, beads, med als, the more indestructible of their personal possessions, can be found in this region where so lately they were a numerous peo ple ; for the effects of the dead, however valued, were never removed or the graves robbed, even by an Indian enemy. The Cherokees rarely permitted the presence of an alien at the ceremonies of the interment of one of the tribe; but Varney in times past had seen and heard enough to realize, with out any definite effort of the imagination,

how Otasite, arrayed in his most gorgeous apparel, his beautiful English face painted vermilion, would be placed in a sitting pos ture in front of his house, and there in the sunlit afternoon remain for a space, looking in, as it were, at the open door. Presently sounded the wild lamentations and melan choly cadences of the funeral song; the tones rose successively from a deep bass to a tenor, then to a shrill treble, falling again to a full bass chorus, with the progression of the mystic syllables, " Yah ! Yo-he-ioah ! Yah! Yo-he-wah! " (said to signify " Jeho vah "). This announced that the funeral procession, bearing the body, was going thrice around the house of the dead, where he had lived in familiar happiness these many years, and beneath which he would rest in solemn silence in his deep, deep grave, covered with heavy timbers and many layers of bark, and the stanch red clay, main taining a sitting posture, and facing the east, while the domestic life of homely cheer would go on over his unheeding head as he awaited the distant and universal resurrec tion of the body, in which the Cherokee re ligion inculcated a full and firm faith.

The sun went down, and through all the night sounded the plaints of grief. Late the moon rose, striking aslant on the melan choly Tennessee River, full of deep shad ows and vaguely pathetic pallid glimmers. A wind sprang up for a time, then suddenly sank to silence and stillness. A frost fell with a keen icy chill. Mists gathered, and the day did not break, — it seemed as if it might never dawn again; only a pallid visi bility came gradually upon clouds that had enshrouded all the world. The earth and the sky were alike indistinguishable; the mountains were as valleys, the valleys as plains. One might scarcely make shift to see a hand before the face. Through this white pall, this cloud of nullity, came ever the dolorous chant," Yo-he-ta-wah ! Yo-he-ta-weh ! Yo-he-ta-hah ! Yo-he-ta-heh ! " as in their grief and poignant bereavement the ignorant and barbarous Indians called upon the God who made them, and He who made them savages doubtless heard them.

Creeping out into the invisibility of the clouded day, Abram Varney had not great fear of detection. The mists that shielded him from view furthered still his flight, for his footsteps were hardly to be distin guished amidst the continual dripping of the moisture from the leaves of the dank autumnal woods. At night he knew the savages would be most on the alert. They would scarcely suspect his flight in the broad day. Moreover, their suspicions of his presence here were lulled; craftily enough he followed after the horsemen who fancied they were pursuing him — they would scarcely look for their quarry hard on their own heels. He experienced no sentiment but one of intense satisfaction when, as invisible as a spirit, he passed his own trading-house, and divined from the sounds within that the Indians were busy in sacking it, albeit a greater financial loss than seems probable at the present day; for the Indian trade was a very consider able commerce, as the accounts of those times will show. The English and French governments did not disdain to compete for its monopoly with various nations of In dians, for the sake of gaining control of the savages thereby, in view of supplies fur nished by the white traders vending these commodities and resident in the tribes.

Recollections of the items and values of his invoices, afflicting to Varney's commer cial spirit, threaded his consciousness only when again safe in Charlestown. He reached that haven at last by the exercise of great good judgment. He realized that another party would presently be sent out when no news of capture came from the earlier pur suers ; he divined that the second expedition would take the Chickasaw path, for being friendly to the British, that tribe would naturally be thought of as a refuge to an Englishman in trouble with the Cherokees; therefore Varney, lest he be overtaken on the way, avoided with a great struggle the temptation, mustered all his courage, and adopting an unprecedented expedient, turned off to the country of the Muscogees. These Indians, always more or less in imical to the colonists, bloodthirsty, cruel, crafty, and but recently involved in a furious war against the Cherokees, were glad to thwart Colannah in any cherished scheme of revenge, and received the fugitive kindly. Although but for this fact his temerity in venturing among them would have cost him his life, they ministered to his needs

with great hospitality, and forwarded him on his way to Charlestown, sending a strong guard with him as far as Long Cane settle ment, a little above Ninety-Six.

Wyejah also made his escape. Appalled by the calamity of the accidental blow, he " took sanctuary." In the supreme moment of excitement he flung himself into the Ten nessee Kiver, and while eagerly sought by the emissaries of Colannah in the woods, he swam to Chote, " beloved town," the city of refuge of the whole Cherokee nation, where the shedder of blood was exempt from vengeance. As years went by, how ever, either because of the death of Colan nah, or because time had so far softened the bereavement of the friends of Otasite that they were prevailed upon to accept the " satisfaction," the presents required even from an involuntary homicide, he was evi dently freed from the restricted limits of the " ever-sacred soil," for his name is re corded in the list of warriors who went to Charlestown in 1759 to confer with Gov ernor Lyttleton on the distracted state of the frontier, and being held as one of the hostages of that unlucky embassy, he per-

ished in the massacre of the Cherokees by the garrison of Fort Prince George, after the treacherous murder of the commandant, Captain Coytmore, by a ruse of the Indian king, Oconostota.

Abram Varney never ventured back among " the Nation/' as he called the Cher okees, as if they were the only nation on the earth. Now and again in their frequent conferences with the Governor at Charles-town, rendered necessary by their ever-recur rent friction with the British government, he sought out members of the delegation for some news of his old friends, his old haunts. Not one of them would take his hand; not one would hear his voice; they looked be yond him, through him, as if he were the impalpable atmosphere, as if he did not exist.

It was a little thing,—the displeasure of such men — mere savages, — but it cut him to the heart. So long they had been his friends, his associates, as the chief furni ture of the world !

He busied himself with the affairs of his firm at Charlestown, but for a time he was much changed, much cast down, for he had

a sense of responsibility, and his conscience was involved, and although he had sought to do good he had only wrought harm, and irreparable harm. He grew old very fast, racked as he was by rheumatism, a continual reminder of the stern experiences of his flight. He had other reminders in his un quiet thoughts, but he grew garrulous at a much later date. Years intervened before he was wont to sit in front of the ware house, with his stick between his knees, his hands clasped on the round knob at its top, his chin on his hands, and cheerily chirp of his days in " the Nation." The softening touch of time brought inevitably its gla mours and its peace; his bleared old eyes, fixed on the glittering expanse of the har bor, beheld with pleasure, instead of the sea, the billowy reaches of that mighty main of mist-crested mountains known as the Great Smoky Eange, and through all his talk, and continually through his mind, flitted the bright animated presence of the victor at chungke.

THE CAPTIVE OF THE ADA-WEHI

THE CAPTIVE OF THE ADA-WEHI

ATTUSAH was obviously an impostor. Many, however, had full faith in his supernatural power, and often he seemed to believe in his own spectral account of himself.

" Tsida-wei-yu! " (I am a great ada-wehi! 6) the young warrior would cry with his joyous grandiloquent gesture, waving his many braceleted right arm at full length as he held himself proudly erect. " Akee-o-hoosa! Akee-o-hoosa! " (I am dead). Then triumphantly, " And behold I am still here."

Attusah had gone unscathed through that bloody campaign of 1761 in which the Cher-okees suffered such incredible rigors. After their total defeat at Etchoee the Indians could offer no further resistance to the troops of Colonel Grant, who triumphantly bore the authority of the British king from one end of the Cherokee country to the other, for there was no more powder to be had hi the

tribe. The French, from whom they had hoped a supply, failed them at their utmost need, and now those massive crags of the Great Smoky Mountains, overhanging the Tennessee River, no longer echoed the " whoo-whoop ! " of the braves, the wild cry of the Highlanders, " Claymore ! Clay more ! " the nerve-thrilling report of the vol leys of musketry from the Royal Scots, the hissing of the hand grenades flung bursting into the jungles of the laurel. Instead, all the clifty defiles of the ranges were filled with the roar of flames and the crackling of burning timbers as town after town was given to the firebrand, and the homeless, helpless Cherokees frantically fleeing to the densest coverts of the wilderness, — that powerful truculent tribe ! — sought for shel ter like those " feeble folk the conies " in the hollows of the rocks.

Thus it was that Digatiski, the Hawk, of Eupharsee Town, long the terror of the southern provinces, must needs sit idle, for lorn, frenzied with rage and grief, in a re mote and lofty cavity of a great cliff, and looking out over range and valley and river of this wild and beautiful country, see fire

and sword work their mission of destruction upon it. By day a cloud of smoke afar off bespoke the presence of the soldiery. At night a tremulous red light would spring up amidst the darkness of the valley, and ex panding into a great yellow flare summon mountains and sky into an infinitely sad and weird revelation of the landscape, as the great storehouses of corn were burned to the ground, leaving the hapless owners to starvation.

His pride grudged his very eyes the sight of this humiliation, for despite the oft-re peated assertion of the improvidence of the Indian character, these public granaries, whence by the primitive Cherokee govern ment food was dispensed gratis to all the needy, were always full, and their destruction meant national annihilation or subjugation. After one furtive glance at the purple ob scurities of the benighted world he would bow his head, and with a smothered groan ask of the ada-wehi, " Where is it now, At-tusah?"

The young warrior, half reclining at the portal of the niche, would lift himself on one elbow, — the glow of the little camp-fire

within the recess on his feather-crested head, his wildly painted face, the twenty strings of roanoke passed tight like a high collar around his neck, thence hanging a cascade of beads over his chest, the devious ara besques of tattooing on his bare, muscular arms, the embroideries of his buckskin rai ment and gaudy quiver, — and searching with his gay young eyes through the stricken country reply, " Cowetchee," " Si-nica," "Tamotlee," whichever town might chance to be in flames.

Doubtless Attusah realized equally the significance of the crisis. But a certain joy ous irresponsibility characterized him, and indeed he had never seemed quite the same since he died. He had been much too reck less, however, even previous to that event. Impetuous, hasty, tumultuously hating the British colonists, he had participated several years earlier in a massacre of an outlying station, when the Cherokees were at peace, without warrant of tribal authority, and with so little caution as to be recognized. For this breach of the treaty his execution was demanded by the Royal Governor of South Carolina, and reluctantly conceded

by the Cherokees to avert a war for the chastisement of the tribe. Powder must have been exceedingly scarce !

Attusah was allowed to choose his method of departure to the happy hunting-grounds, and thus was duly stabbed to death. He was left weltering in his blood to be buried by his kindred. The half king, Atta-Kulla-Kulla, satisfied of his death, himself re ported the execution to the Carolina au thorities, and as in his long and complicated diplomatic relations with the colonial gov ernment this Cherokee chief had never broken faith, he was implicitly believed.

Whether the extraordinary vitality and vigor of the young warrior were reasserted after life had been pronounced wholly ex tinct, and thus his relations were induced to defer the obsequies, or that he was enabled to exert supernatural powers and in the spirit reappear in his former semblance of flesh, — both theories being freely ad vanced, — certain it is that after a time he returned to his old haunts as gay, as reckless, as impetuous as ever. He bore no token of his strange experience save sundry healed-over scars of deep gashes in his

breast, which he seemed at times to seek to shield from observation ; and this he might have accomplished but for his solicitude that a very smart shirt, much embroidered and bedizened with roanoke, should not suffer by exposure to water; wherefore he took it off when it rained, and in swimming, and on the war-path. He manifested, too, a less puerile anxiety to escape the notice of Atta-Kulla-Kulla and other head men, who were supposed to be well affected at that time to the British government. This he was the better enabled to do as his habitat, Kanoo-tare, was the most remote of the Cherokee towns, his name, Attusah, signifying the " Northward Warrior."

After the capitulation of Fort Loudon and the massacre of the garrison the pre vious year, and the organized resistance the Cherokees had made in the field of battle against Colonel Montgomerie, then com manding the expeditionary forces, he had felt that the tribe's openly inimical rela tions with the British government warranted him in coming boldly forth from his retire ment and competing for the honors of the present campaign of 1761. His friends

sought to dissuade him. The government had had, as assurance of his death, the word of Atta-Kulla-Kulla, who might yet insist that the pledge be made good. That chief, they urged, had a delicate conscience, which is often an engine of disastrous efficiency when exerted on the affairs of other people. Attusah was advised that he had best stay dead. Although he finally agreed with this, he could not stay still, and thus as he ap peared in various skirmishes it became gradually bruited abroad among the Chero-kees that Attusah, the Northward Warrior, was a great ada-wehi, a being of magical power, or a ghost as it might be said, of special spectral distinctions. Thus he lived as gayly yet as before the dismal day of his execution, always carefully, however, avoiding the notice of Atta-Kulla-Kulla, whose word had been solemnly accepted by the British government as the pledge of his death.

It is impossible to understand how a man like Digatiski of Eupharsee could believe this, — so sage, despite his ignorance, so crafty, so diplomatic and acute in subter fuge, yet he was sodden in superstition.

" Can you see Colonel Grant, the Bar barous ?" 7 he asked suddenly, lifting his head and gazing steadily at the young In dian's face, which was outlined against the pallid neutral tint of the sky. The dark top most boughs of a balsam fir were just on a level with the clear high-featured profile; a single star glittering beyond and above his feathered crest looked as if it were an orna ment of the headdress; the red glow of the smouldering fire within, which had been carefully masked in ashes as the darkness came on, that its sparkle might not betray their presence here to any wandering band of troopers, still sufficed to show the impos tor's painted red cheek. He was armed with a tomahawk and a pistol, without powder as useless as a toy, and a bow borne in default of aught better lay on the floor beside him, while a gayly ornamented quiver full of poi soned arrows swung over his shoulder.

o

" Ha-tsida-wei-yu ! " he proclaimed. " I am a great ada-wehi! I see him! Of a surety I see him ! "

Attusah gazed at the sombre night with an expression as definitely perceptive as if the figure in his thoughts were actually be fore his eyes.

" And he is not dead ? " cried Digatiski, in despair.

Some such wild rumor, as of hope gone mad, had pervaded the groups of Cherokee fugitives.

" He would be if I could get close enough with a bare pinch of powder that might charge my gun !" declared Attusah discon solately. Then himself again, " But I will tell you this ! He is waiting for my poi soned arrow! And when he dies he will come back no more. He is not like me."

He paused to throw out his hand with his splendid pompous gesture. "Akee-o-hoo-sa ! Tsida-wei-yu ! " (I am dead ! I am a great ada-wehi!)

Digatiski groaned. It mattered not to him whether Colonel Grant came back or abode in his proper place when dead. The grievous dispensation lay in the fact that he was here now, in the midst of the wreck he was so zealously wreaking.

There were three women in the niche. One with her head muffled in her mantle of fringed deerskin sat against the wall, silently weeping, bemoaning her dead slain in the recent battle, or the national calami-

ties, or perhaps the mere personal afflictions of fatigue and fear and hunger and sus pense. Another crouched by the fire and gazed dolorously upon it with dreary tear-filled eyes, and swollen, reddened eyelids. The sorrowful aspect of a third was oddly incongruous with her gay attire, a garb of scarlet cloth trimmed with silver tinsel tas sels, a fabric introduced among the Chero-kees by an English trader of the name of Jeffreys, and which met with great favor. Her anklets, garters, and bracelets of sil ver "bell-buttons" tinkled merrily as she moved, for she had postponed her tears in the effort to concoct some supper from the various scraps left from the day's scanty food. The prefatory scraping of the coals to gether caused a sudden babbling of pleasure to issue from the wall, where, suspended on a projection of rock, was one of the curious upright cradles of the people, from which a pappoose, stiff and perpendicular, gazed down at the culinary preparations, evidently in the habit of participating to a limited ex tent in the result, having attained some ten months of age.

The mother glanced up, and despite the

tear stains about her eyes, dimpled and laughed in response. Griefs may come and pleasures go, nations rise and fall, the world wag on as it will, but this old joy of mother and child, each in the other, is ever new and yet ever the same.

Resuming her occupation, the woman hes itated for a moment as she was about to lay the meat on the coals, the half of a wood duck, fortunately killed by an arrow, for larger game was not attainable, the wild beasts of the country being in flight as never heretofore. The conflagration of the towns of a whole district, the turmoils of the heady victorious troops, hitherto held together, but now sent through the region in separate detachments, each within reach of support, however, had stripped the tribe of this last means of subsistence. Years and years afterward the grim dismantled fragments of these buildings were still to be seen, the charred walls and rafters mere skeletons against the sky, standing, melan choly memorials of war, on the hillsides and in the valleys, along the watercourses " transparent as glass," of that lovely coun try where these pleasant homes had been.

The Indian woman doubted if the bit of fat could be spared ; then poising it in her hand under the watchful eyes of all, she flung it into the fire, the essential burnt-offering according to their old religious custom.

Digatiski, bowing his head still lower, once more groaned aloud. He would not have stayed her hand, — but to hunger even for the offering to the fire ! The woman whose head was muffled had only to re peat her sobs anew; she could not sorrow more ! But the pappoose in its primitive cradle on the wall babbled out its simple pleasure, and now and again the tearful little mother must needs lift smiling eyes.

The great ada-wehi looked out at the night. On the whole he was glad he was dead !

He took no bite, nor did Digatiski. The Indian men were accustomed to long fasts in war and in hunting, and they left the trivial bits to the women. The muffled figure of grief held out her hand blindly and munched the share given her in the folds of her veil. Then, for tears are of no nutritive value, she held out her hand again. Feeling it still empty, she lifted the veil from a swollen tear-stained face to gaze aghast at the others. They silently returned the gaze, aghast themselves, and then all three wo men fell to sobbing once more. But the pap-poose was crowing convivially over a bone.

Hunger does not dispose to slumber, nor does war with the sight of a dozen towns aflame. They slept, but in fitful starts, and the first gray siftings of light through the desolate darkness found them all gazing drearily at it, for what might a new day signify to them but new dangers, fresh sor rows, and quickened fears.

A flush was presently in the east, albeit dusk lingered westward. The wonderful crystalline white lustre of the morning star palpitated in the amber sky, seeming the very essence of light, then gradually van ished in a roseate haze. The black moun tains grew purple, changing to a dark rich green. The deep, cool valleys were dewy in the midst of a shadowy gray vapor. The farthest ranges showed blue under a silver film, and suddenly here were the rays of the sun shooting over, all the world, aiming high and far for the western hills.

And abruptly said the ada-wehi, as he still lay at length on the floor of the niche, —

« Skee ! " (Listen !)

Naught but the breeze of morning, delicately freighted with the breath of bal sams, the dew, the fragrance of the awak ening of the wild flowers, the indescribable matutinal freshness, the incense of a new day in June.

« Skee ! "

Only the sound of the rippling Tennes see, so silver clear, beating and beating against the vibrant rocks as its currents swirl round the bend at the base of the cliff.

« Skee ! "

The sudden fall of a fragment of rock from the face of the crag to the ground far below! — the interval of time between the scraping dislodgment and the impact with the clay beneath implies a proportional in terval of distance.

The conviction is the same in the mind of each. A living creature is climbing the ascent! A bear, it may be. A great bird, an eagle, or one of the hideous mountain vultures, very busy of late, alighting in

quest of food —which it might find in plenty elsewhere, in the track of the invaders.

Attusah does not rely, however, on a facile hypothesis with a triumphant enemy at hand, and a dozen towns charring to ashes in sight.

As noiseless as a shadow, as swift, Attu sah is on his feet. At the back of the great niche, so high that none could con ceive that it might afford an exit, a fissure lets in a vague dreary blur of light from spaces beyond. Leaping high into the air, the lithe young warrior fixes his fingers on the ledge, crumbling at first, but holding firm under a closer grasp. The elder man, understanding the ruse as if by instinct, lays hold of the knees of the other, held out stiff and straight below. Then by a mighty effort Attusah lifts the double weight into the fissure, the elder Indian aiding the manosuvre by walking up the wall, as it were, with his feet successively braced against it.

Outside, now and again bits of rock con tinued to fall, seeming to herald a cautious approach, for after each sound a consider able interval of silence would ensue. So

long continued was this silence at last that the three women, now alone, began to deem the alarm of an intrusion vain and fantas tic. The elder of them motioned to one of the others to look out and terminate the painful suspense.

The young squaw, brilliant in her scarlet dress and silver tassels, the pappoose piously quiet in his perpendicular cradle on her back, slipped with gingerly caution to the verge of the precipice and looked down.

Nothing she saw, and in turn she was in visible from without. She wheeled around briskly to reassure the others, and at that moment a young soldier of the battalion of Scotch Highlanders stepped from the hori zontal ledge alongside, which he had then gained, and into the niche, bringing up short against the pappoose, stiff and erect in its cradle.

" Hegh, sirs! " he cried in jocular sur prise, happy to find naught more formidable, perhaps, although a brave man, for he had volunteered to examine the source of the smoke from this precarious perch, — which had attracted the attention of the ensign commanding a little detachment, — despite

the fact that a Cherokee in his den and brought to bay was likely to prove a dan gerous beast.

The Highlander had a piece of bread in his hand, from which he had been recklessly munching as he had stood for a moment's breathing spell on the horizontal ledge be side the niche before venturing to enter, for the command had broken camp with scant allowance of time for breakfast. With a genial laugh he thrust a morsel into the pappoose's open mouth and put the rest in its little fingers.

Perhaps it was because of his relief to find no bigger Cherokee man stowed away here in ambush ; perhaps because he was himself hearty and well-fed and disposed to be gracious; perhaps because he had a whole-souled gentle nature hardly conso nant with the cruel arts of war which he practiced, — at all events he was thoughtful enough of others to mark the ravenous look which the women cast upon the food in the child's hand.

" Gude guide us ! " he exclaimed. " This is fearfu' wark ! The hellicat hempies are half starved! "

For if Colonel Grant compassionated the plight of the savages, as he has recorded, and shrank from the ruin wrought in the discharge of his duty of destroying their capacities for resistance and the mainte nance of existence other than as peaceful dependents of the British colonies, the rank and file of his command, weighted with no such responsibilities, may well have indulged now and then a qualm of pity.

The British soldier had been ordered to halloo for help should he encounter armed resistance, but otherwise to rest a bit at the top of the precipice before making the effort to descend, lest he become dizzy from fatigue and the long strain upon his facul ties, and fall; the ensign added a pointed reminder that he had no means of trans portation for " fules with brucken craigs." The opportunity was propitious. The High lander utilized the interval to open his haversack and dispense such portion of its contents as he could spare. While thus en gaged he was guilty of an oversight inex cusable in a soldier : the better to handle and divide the food, he leaned his loaded gun against the wall.

A vague shadow flickered across the niche.

The young Highlander was a fine man physically, although there was no great beauty in his long, thin, frank, freckled face, with its dare-devil expression and bantering blue eyes. But he was tall, heavily muscled, clean-limbed, of an admirable symmetry, and the smartest of smart soldiers. His kilt and plaid swung and fluttered with martial grace in his free, alert, military gait as he stepped about the restricted space of the cavity, be stowing his bounty on all three women. His " bonnet cocked f u sprash " revealed certain intimations in his countenance of gentle nur ture, no great pretensions truly, but betoken ing a higher grade of man than is usually found in the rank and file of an army. This fact resulted from the peculiar situation of the Scotch insurgents toward government after the " Forty-Five," and the consequent breaking up of the resources of many well-to-do middle-class families as well as the leaders of great clans.

The Highlander hesitated after the first round of distribution, for there would be no means of revictualing that haversack until

the next issuance of rations, and he was him self a " very valiant trencher-man." Never theless their dire distress and necessity so urged his generosity that he began his rounds anew.

Once more a shadow. Whence should a shadow fall ? It nickered through the niche.

o

The three women stood as mute as statues. The pappoose in its cradle on its mother's back, its face turned ignominiously toward the wall, and perhaps aware that something of interest in the commissariat department was going forward, had begun to whimper in a very civilized manner, and doubtless it was this trivial noise that deterred the young Scotchman from hearing sounds of more moment, calculated to rouse his suspicions. He had already added to the portions of the elder women and was bestowing his dona tions upon the young mother, when suddenly the shadow materialized and whisked past him.

It fell like a thunderbolt from above.

Bewildered, agitated, before he could turn, his gun was seized and presented at his breast by a warrior who seemed to have fallen from the sky. The soldier, nevertheless, instantly

laid his hand on the great basket-hilt of his claymore. Before he could draw the blade, the warrior and the three women flung them selves upon him, their arms so closely wound about him that his own arms were effectually pinioned to his sides. With a violent effort he shook himself free from their grasp for one moment; yet as the blade came glitter ing forth from the scabbard, a sharp blow scientifically administered upon the wrist by the ada-wehi almost broke the bone and sent the weapon flying from his hand and clat tering to the floor of the niche. The wo men had taken advantage of the opportu nity afforded by the struggle between the two men to substitute the coils of a heavy hempen rope for the clasp of their arms, and Attusah had only to give a final twist to the knots of their skilled contriving, when the captive was disarmed and bound.

He had instantly bethought himself of his comrades and an appeal for rescue, and sent forth a wild, hoarse yell, which, had it been heard, must have apprised them of his plight. But as he had not at once given the signal of danger agreed upon, they had naturally supposed the coast clear, and while

he rested presumably at the top of the pre cipice they gave their attention to other de tails of their mission, firing several houses at a little distance down the river. There fore they would have heard naught, even if Attusah had not precluded further efforts of his captive to communicate with his com rades by swiftly fashioning a gag out of the Highlander's bonnet and gloves.

Perhaps never was a brave man more dis mayed and daunted. Not death alone, but fire and torture menaced him. The shining liquid delight in the eyes of the women re minded him of the strange fact that they were ever the most forward in these cruel pleasures, for the ingenuity of which the Cherokees were famous among all the tribes. Yet the realization of his peril did not so diminish his scope of feeling as to prevent him from inwardly upbraiding his ill-starred generosity as the folly of a hopeless fool, more especially as the elder woman — she of the many tears — held up the substantial gift of provisions, jeering at him with a look in her face that did not need to be supple mented by the scoffing of language.

" The auld randy besom ! " the soldier

commented within himself. " But eh, I didna gie it to be thankit, — nae sic a fule as that comes to, neither ! "

Hoping against hope, he thought that the length of his absence would inevitably alarm the ensign for his scout's safety, when it should attract attention, and induce the officer to send a party for his relief and for further investigation of the precipice, whence the smoke intimated an ambush of the enemy. This expectation had no sooner suggested its solace and the exercise of pa tience in the certainty of ultimate rescue, than the Highlander began to mark the preparations among the Indians for a swift departure. But how? The precipice was a sheer descent for eighty feet, the rugged-ness of its face barely affording foothold for a bird or a mountaineer; and at its base hovered the ensign's party within striking distance. A resisting captive could not be withdrawn by this perilous path. The sol dier looked in doubt and suspense about the restricted limits of the cavity in the great crag. The mystery was soon solved.

The position of all had changed in the struggle, and from where Kenneth Mac-

Vintie now stood he noted a scant suggestion of light flickering down from a black fissure in the roof of the cavity, and instantly real ized that it must give an exit upon the moun tain slope beyond. The agility with which Attusah of Kanootare sprang up and leaped into it was admirable to behold, but MacVin-tie did not believe that, although knotted up as he was in his own plaid passed under his arms and around his waist for the pur pose, he could be lifted by the ends of the fabric through that aperture by the strength of any one man. Naturally he himself would make no effort to facilitate the enterprise. On the contrary, such inertness as the sheer exercise of will could compass was added to his dead weight. Nevertheless he rose slowly, slowly through the air. As he was finally dragged through the rift in the rocks, his first feeling was one of gratification to per ceive that no one man could so handle him. The feat had required the utmost exer tions of two athletic Indians pulling strenu ously at the ends of the plaid passed over a projection of rock, thus acting pulley-wise, and the good Glasgow weave was shedding its frayed fragments through all the place by reason of the strain it had sustained.

The next moment more serious consider ations claimed his thoughts. He saw that two men, fully armed, for Digatiski had secured ammunition for his own gun from the cartouch-box of the soldier, could force his withdrawal, bound as he was, farther and farther from the ensign and his party, whose attention had been temporarily di verted from the scout's delay in returning by signs of the enemy ambushed in another direction.

MacVintie still struggled, albeit he knew that it was vain to resist, more especially when another Cherokee joined the party and dedicated himself solely to the enter prise of pushing and haling the captive over the rugged way, — often at as fair a speed as if his good will had been enlisted in the endeavor. Now and again, however, the Highlander contrived to throw himself prone upon the ground, thus effectually hampering their progress and requiring the utmost exertions of all three to lift his great frame. The patience of the Indians seemed illimitable ; again and again they performed this feat, only to renew it at the distance of a few hundred yards.

At length the fact was divined by Mac-Vintie. More than the ordinary fear of capture animated Attusah of Kanootare. Colonel Grant's treatment of his prisoners was humane as the laws of war require. Moreover, his authority, heavily reinforced by threats of pains and penalties, had sufficed, except in a few instances, to restrain the Chickasaw allies of the British from wreak ing their vengeance on the captive Chero-kees in the usual tribal method of fire and torture. The inference was obvious. Attu sah of Kanootare was particularly obnox ious to the British government, the civil as well as the military authorities, and flee ing from death himself, he intended at all hazards to prevent the escape of his prisoner, who would give the alarm, and inaugurate pursuit from the party of the ensign.

In this connection a new development attracted the attention of MacVintie. As they advanced deeper and deeper into the Cherokee country and the signs and sights of war grew remote, — no sounds of volleys nor even distant dropping shots clanging from the echoes, no wreaths of smoke float ing among the hills, no flare of flames

flinging crude red and yellow streaks across the luminous velvet azure of distant moun tains with their silver haze, viewed through vistas of craggy chasms near at hand, — he observed a lessening of cordiality in the manner of the other two Indians toward the Northward Warrior, and a frequency on his part to protest that he was a great ada-wehi, and was dead although he appeared alive. The truth soon dawned upon the shrewd Scotchman, albeit he understood only so much Cherokee as he had chanced to catch up in his previous campaign in this region with Montgomerie and the present expedi tion. Attusah was for some reason obnox ious to his own people as well as to the Brit ish, and was in effect a fugitive from both factions. Indeed, the other two Indians pre sently manifested a disposition to avoid him. After much wrangling and obvious discon tent and smouldering suspicion, one lagged systematically, and, the pace being speedy, contrived to fairly quit the party. Digatiski accompanied them two more days, then, openly avowing his intent, fell away from the line of march. It was instantly diverted toward the Little Tennessee River, on the

western side of the Great Smoky Moun tains; and as Attusah realized that without his connivance his captive's escape had be come impossible, MacVintie found himself unbound, ungagged, and the society of the ada-wehi as pleasant as that of a savage ghost can well be.

There was now no effort to escape. Mac-Vintie's obvious policy was to await with what patience he might the appearance of the British vanguard, who in the sheer vaunt of victory would march from one end of the unresisting territory to the other, that all might witness and bow before the tri umph of the royal authority. As yet remote from the advance of the troops, he dared not quit his captor in these sequestered regions lest he fall into the power of more inimical Cherokees, maddened by disaster, overwhelmed in ruin, furious, and thirst ing for revenge for the slaughter of their nearest and dearest, and the ashes of their homes.

Attusah made known his reason for his own uncharacteristic leniency to a soldier of this ruthless army, as they sat together by the shady river-side. He went through the

dumb show of repeatedly offering to his captive guest the fish they had caught, pressing additional portions upon him, laughing significantly and joyously through out his mimicry. Then suddenly grave, he seized the Highlander's left arm, giving it an earnest grasp about the wrist, the elbow, then close to the shoulder to intimate that he spared him for his gift to the needy and helpless.

But Kenneth MacVintie, remembering his ill-starred generosity, flushed to the eye brows, so little it became his record as a soldier, he thought, that he should be cap tured and stand in danger of his life by reason of the unmilitary performance of feeding a babbling pappoose.

Attusah, however, could but love him for it; he loved the soldier for his kind heart, he said. For great as he himself was, the Northward Warrior, he had known how bit ter it was to lack kindness.

" It is not happy to be an ada-wehi!" he confessed, "for those who believe fear those who do not! "

And tearing open the throat of his bead-embroidered shirt to reveal the frightful

208 THE CAPTIVE OF THE ADA-WEHI

gashes of the wounds in his breast, he told the story of his legal death, with tears in his gay eyes, and a tremor of grief in the proud intonations of his voice, that thus had been requited a feat, the just guerdon of which should have been the warrior's crown, — in the bestowal of which, but for a cowardly fear of the English, all the tribe would have concurred.

" Akee-o-hoosa! " (I am dead!) he said, pointing at the scars. And the Highlander felt that death had obviously been in every stroke, and hardly wondered that they who had seen the blows dealt should now ac count the appearance of the man a spectral manifestation, his unquiet ghost.

Then, Attusah's mood changing suddenly, " Tsida-wei-yu !" (I am a great ada-wehi!) he boasted airily.

That he was truly possessed of magical powers seemed to MacVintie least to be questioned when he angled, catching the great catfish, after the manner of the In dians, with the open palm of his hand. In these fresh June mornings he would dive down in some deep shady pool under the dark ledges of rock where the catfish are

THE CAPTIVE OF THE ADA-WEHI 209

wont to lurk, his right arm wrapped to the fingers with a scarlet cloth. Tempted by the seeming bait, the catfish would take the finger-tips deep in its gullet, the strong hand would instantly clinch on its head, and Attusah would rise with his struggling gleaming prey, to be broiled on the coals for breakfast.

But for these finny trophies they too might have suffered for food, in the scarcity of game and the lack of powder; but thus well fed, the two enemies, like comrades, would loiter beside their camp-fire on the banks, awaiting as it were the course of events. The dark green crystalline lustre of the shady reaches of the river, where the gigantic trees hung over the current, contrasted with the silver glister of the rip ples far out, shimmering in the full glare of the sun. The breeze, exquisitely fra grant, would blow fresh and free from the dense forests. The mockingbird, a feath ered miracle to the Highlander, would sway on a twig above them and sing jubilantly the whole day through and deep into the night. The distant mountains would show softly blue on the horizon till the sun was

210 THE CAPTIVE OF THE ADA-WEHI

going down, when they would assume a translucent jewel-like lustre, amethystine and splendid. And at night all the stars were in the dark sky, for the moon was new.

So idle they were they must needs talk and talk. But this was an exercise requir ing some skill and patience on the part of each, for the Scotchman could only by the closest attention gather the meaning of the Cherokee language as it was spoken, and the magic of the ada-wehi compassed but scanty English. Attusah was further ham pered by the necessity of pausing now and then to spit out the words of the tongue he abhorred as if of an evil taste. Never theless it was by means of this imperfect linguistic communication that Kenneth Mac-Vintie, keenly alive to aught of significance in this strange new world, surrounded with unknown unmeasured dangers, was enabled to note how the thoughts of his companion ran upon the half king Atta-Kulla-Kulla. Yet whenever a question was asked or curi osity suggested, the wary Attusah diverted the topic. This fact focused the observation of the shrewd, pertinacious Scotchman. At

first he deemed the special interest lay in a jealousy of artistic handicraft.

Atta-Kulla-Kulla's name implied the su perlative of a skillful carver in wood, Attu-sah told him one day.

" An' isna he a skilly man ? " MacVintie asked.

" Look at that! " cried the braggart, holding aloft his own work. He was carv ing a pipe from the soft stone of the region, which so lends itself to the purpose, hard ening when heated. " Tsida-wei-yu ! "

There was a long pause while the mock ingbird sang with an exuberant magic which might baffle the emulation of any ada-wehi of them all. MacVintie had almost forgot ten the episode when Attusah said suddenly that the colonists translated the name of Atta-Kulla-Kulla as the " Little Carpen ter."

" Hegh ! they hae a ship named for his honor ! " exclaimed the Highlander. " I hae seen the Little Carpenter in the harbor in Charlestoun, swingin' an' bobbin' at her cables, just out frae the mither country ! Her captain's name wull be Maitland."

This evidence of the importance of the

Cherokee magnate in the opinion of the British colonists did not please the ada-wehi. He spat upon the ship with ostentatious contempt as it were, and then went on si lently with his carving.

The mockingbird paused to listen to a note from the hermit thrush in the dense rhododendron, still splendidly abloom on the mountain slope. The Scotchman's eyes nar rowed to distinguish if the white flake of light in the deep green water across a little bay were the reflection of the flower known as the Chilhowee lily, or the ethereal blos som itself.

Attusah's mind seemed yet with the sea going craft. He himself knew the name of another ship, he said presently; and the Highlander fancied that he ill liked to be outdone in knowledge of the outer world.

But it was immediately developed that in this ship Atta-Kulla-Kulla had sailed to England many years before to visit King George II. in London. 8 Attusah could not at once anglicize the name " Chochoola," but after so long a time MacVintie was ena bled to identify the Fox, then a noted British man-of-war.

In these leisurely beguilements the days passed, until one morning Attusah's fears and presentiments were realized in their seizure by a party of Cherokees, who swooped down upon their hermitage and bore them off by force to the council-house of the town of Citico, where Atta-Kulla-Kulla and a number of other head men had assembled to discuss the critical affairs of the tribe, and decide on its future policy.

So critical indeed was the situation that it seemed to MacVintie that they might well dispense with notice of two factors so inconsiderable in the scale of national im portance as the ada-wehi and his captive. But one was a British prisoner, calculated to expiate in a degree with his life the woe and ruin his comrades had wrought. The more essential was this course since the triumph of putting him to the torture and death would gratify and reanimate many whose zeal was flagging under an accumu lation of anguish and helpless defeat, and stimulate them to renewed exertions. For before the Cherokees would sue for peace they waited long in the hope that the French would yet be enabled to convey to them a

sufficient supply of powder to renew and prosecute the war.

As to the arrest of the other, Attusah of Kanootare, this was necessary in the event that submission to the British government became inevitable. For since he claimed to be a ghost, surely never was spectre so reck less. He had indeed appeared to so many favored individuals that the English might fairly have cause to doubt his execution in satisfaction of his crimes against the gov ernment ; and the breach of faith on the part of the Cherokee rulers in this conspicu ous instance might well preclude the grant ing of any reasonable terms of peace now, and subject the whole nation to added hard ship.

This was the argument advanced by Atta-Kulla-Kulla as he stood and addressed his colleagues, who sat on buffalo-skins in a circle on the floor of the council-house of Citico, — the usual dome-shaped edifice, daubed within and without with the rich red clay of the country, and situated on a high artificial mound in the centre of the town.

The council-fire alone gave light, flashing

upon the slender figure and animated face of this chief, who, although of slighter physique and lower stature than his com peers, wielded by reason of his more intel lectual qualities so potent an influence among them.

The oratorical gifts of Atta-Kulla-Kulla had signally impressed Europeans of cul ture and experience. 9 Imagine, then, the effect on the raw young Highland soldier, hearing the flow of language, watching the appropriate and forceful gestures, noting the responsive sentiment in the fire-lit coun tenances of the circle of feather-crested Indians, yet comprehending little save that it was a masterpiece of cogent reasoning, richly eloquent, and that every word was as a fagot to the flames and a pang to the torture.

Attusah of Kanootare, the Northward Warrior, rose to reply in defense of him self and his captive, and Atta-Kulla-Kulla listened as courteously as the rest, although the speech of the ada-wehi depended, like the oratory of many young men, chiefly on a magical assurance. He had an ally, how ever, in the dominant superstition of the

Ckerokees. Numbers of the warriors now ascribed their recent disasters to the neglect of various omens, or the omission of certain propitiatory observances of their ancient re ligion, or the perpetration of deeds known to be adversely regarded by the ruling spirits of war.

Moreover, they were all aware that this man had been killed, left for dead, reported as dead to the British government, which accepted the satisfaction thus offered for his crimes, — the deeds themselves, however, accounted by him and the rest of the tribe praiseworthy and the achievements of war.

And here he was protesting that he was dead and a ghost. " Akee-o-hoosa ! Akee-o-hoosa! Tsida-wei-yu I " he cried contin ually.

Indeed, this seemed to be the only reason able method of accounting for the renewed presence in the world of a man known to be dead. This was his status, he argued. He was a dead man, and this was his cap tive. The Cherokee nation could not pre tend to follow with its control the actions of a dead man. They themselves had pro nounced him dead. He had no place in the

war. He had been forbidden, on account of his official death, to compete for the honors of the campaign. Apart from his former status as a Cherokee, merely as a supernatural being, a spirit, an ada-wehi, he had captured this British soldier, who was therefore the property of a dead man. And the Cherokee law of all things and before all things forbade interference with the effects of the dead.

Despite the curling contempt on the lip of Atta-Kulla-Kulla the council did not im mediately acquiesce in his view, and thus for a time flattered the hope of the ada-wehi that they were resting in suspension on the details of this choice argument. There was an illogical inversion of values in the experience of the tribe, and while they could not now accept the worthless fig ments of long ago, it was not vouchsafed to them to enjoy the substantial merits of the new order of things. Reason, powder, diplomacy, had brought the Cherokee na tion to a point of humiliation to which superstition, savagery, and the simplicities of the tomahawk had never descended in " the good old times." Reason was never so

befuddled of aspect, civilization never so undesired as now. In their own expanded outlook at life, however, they could not af ford to ignore the views of Atta-Kulla-Kulla, the advocate of all the newer methods, in so important a matter as the release of a British prisoner of war on the strange pre text that his captor was a ghost of a pe culiar spectral power, an ada-wehi, although this course would have been more agreeable to the "old beloved" theories of their hal cyon days of eld, when the Cherokee name was a terror and a threat.

Therefore, averse as they were to subscribe to the modern methods which had wrought
o
them such woe and humiliation and defeat, the dominant superstition of the race now fell far short of the fantasy of liberating a British prisoner at this crisis under the influence of any spectral manifestation whatsoever. The council was obviously steeled against this proposition, as MacVin-tie shortly perceived, and equally deter mined that the ada-wehi must needs exert phenomenal and magical powers indeed to avoid yet making good the nation's pledge of his death to the British government, and

becoming a ghost in serious earnest. Mac-Vintie's heart sank within him as he noted the hardening of the lines of their grave harsh faces and the affirmative nodding of the feather-crested heads, conferring to gether, as the decision was reached.

It accorded, however, with their ancient custom to postpone over a night the execu tion of any sentence of special weight, and therefore the council adjourned to the next day, the two prisoners being left in the de serted building, each securely bound with a rope to a pillar of the series which upheld the roof of the strange circular edifice. This colonnade stood about four feet from the wall, and the interval between was oc cupied by a divan, fashioned of dexterously woven cane, extending around the room; and as the prisoners could seat themselves here, or lie at full length, they were sub jected to no greater hardship than was con sistent with their safe custody.

A sentinel with his musket on his shoul-
• der stood at the door, and the sun was
going down. Kenneth MacVintie could see

through the open portal the red glow in
the waters of the Tennessee River. Now and

then a flake of a glittering white density glided through it, which his eyes, accus tomed to long distances, discriminated as a swan. Thunder-heads, however, were gath ering above the eastern slopes and the mountains were a lowering slate-toned pur ple, save when a sudden flash of lightning roused them to a vivid show of green.

The dull red hue of the interior of the council-house darkened gradually; the em bers of the council-fire faded into the gray ash, and the night came sullen and threat ening before its time.

The young Highlander sought to bend his mind to the realization that his days on earth were well-nigh ended, and that it be hooved him to think on the morrow else where. He had an old-fashioned religious faith presumed to be fitted for any emer gency, but in seeking to recall its dogmas and find such consolation in its theories as might sustain a martyr at the stake, he was continually distracted with the momentous present.

The two prisoners could no longer see each other, and the little gestures and sig nificant glances which had supplemented

their few words, and made up for the lack of better conversational facilities were im practicable in the darkness.

The silent obscurity was strangely lonely. MacVintie began to doubt if the other still lived.

" Attusah ! " he said at length.

" Tsida-wei-yu! " (I am a great ada-wehi) murmured the ghost mechanically.

He was quite spent, exhausted by the effort to logically exist as a ghost in a world which had repudiated him as a live man.

MacVintie, who found it hard enough to reconcile himself to die once, felt a poign ant sympathy for him, who must needs die again. But the Highlander could not think. He could not even pray. He desisted from the fitful effort after a time. He had a de pressing realization that a good soldier relies upon the proficiency acquired by the daily drill to serve in an emergency, not a spe cial effort at smartness for an occasion. The battle or the review would show the quality of the stuff that was in him.

Despite the stunned despair which pos sessed his mental faculties, his physical senses were keenly acute. He marked un-

consciously the details of the rising of the wind bringing the storm hitherward. A searching flash of lightning showed the fig ure of the sentinel, half crouching before the blast, at his post in the open portal. The rain was presently falling heavily, and ever and anon a great suffusion of yellow glare in its midst revealed the myriads of slanting lines as it came. He inhaled the freshened fragrance it brought from the forests. He noted the repeated crash of the thunder, the far-away rote of the echoes, the rhythmic beat of the torrents on the ground, and their tumultuous swift dash down the slope of the dome-shaped roof, and suddenly among these turmoils, — he could hardly believe his ears, — a mild little whim per of protest.

The sentinel heard it too. MacVintie saw his dark figure in the doorway as he turned his head to listen. A woman's voice sounded immediately, bidding a child beware how he cried, lest she call the great white owl, the Oo-koo-ne-kah, to catch him !

The flare of the lightning revealed a pappoose the next moment, upright in his perpendicular cradle, as it swung on his

mother's back, in the drenching downpour of the rain, for the woman had advanced to the sentinel and was talking loudly and eagerly.

Kenneth silently recognized the small creature who had moved him to a trivial charity which had resulted in so strangely disproportionate a disaster. Doubtless, how ever, the squaws would never have been able to return to their accustomed place but for the food which he had given them, sustain ing them on the journey home.

It would imply some mission of impor tance surely, he thought, to induce the wo man to expose the child to a tempest like this; and indeed the pappoose, buffeted by the wind, the rain full in his face, lifted up his voice again in a protest so loud and ve hement that his mother was enabled to see the great white owl, whose business it is to remove troublesome little Cherokees from the sphere of worry of their elders, already winging his way hither. One might won der if the Oo-koo-ne-kah would do worse for him than his maternal guardian, but pelted by the pitiless rain he promptly sank his Heatings to a mere babble of a whimper.

Thereby Kenneth was better enabled to hear what the woman was saying to the sentinel.

An important mission indeed, as Mac-V in tie presently gathered, for she must needs lift her voice stridently to be heard above the din of the elements. Some pow der, only a little it was true, had been sent by the French to the town, and a share had been left at the house of the sentinel that night in the general distribution. But there was no one at home. All his family were across the mountains, whither, according to the custom of the Cherokees, they had gone to find and bring back the body of his brother, who had been killed in the fight at Etchoee. And the leak in the roof ! She, his nearest neighbor, had just bethought herself of the leak in the roof ! Would not the powder, the precious powder, be ruined? Had he not best go to see at once about it ?

He hesitated, letting the butt of his gun sink to the ground. She seized the weapon promptly. She would stand guard here till he returned, she promised. The prisoners were bound. They could not move. It would require but an instant's absence, — and the powder was so scarce, so precious!

The next moment the sentinel was gone ! The darkness descended, doubly intense, after a succession of electric flashes; the rain fell with renewed force. MacVintie suddenly heard the babbling whimper quite close beside him, somewhat subdued by a fierce maternal admonition to listen to the terrible voice of the Oo-koo-ne-kah, coming to catch a Cherokee cry-baby !

A stroke of a knife here and there, and the two prisoners were freed from their bonds. The Highland soldier did not know whether Attusah looked back while in flight, but his last glimpse of the Cherokee town of Citico showed the broad glare of light ning upon the groups of conical roofs in the slanting lines of rain ; the woman on the high mound at the portal of the coun cil-house, with the pappoose on her back and the gun in her hand; the sentinel once more climbing the ascent to his post. And the last words he heard were chronicling the adverse sentiments entertained toward bad children by the Oo-koo-ne-kah, the mysterious great white owl.

The escape was not discovered till the next day, and was universally attributed to

the magic of the ada-wehi. Even the senti nel himself doubted naught, having left a trusty deputy in his stead, for the devotion of the Cherokee women to the tribal cause was proverbial, and gratitude, even for a res cue from starvation, is not usually an urgent motive power.

Kenneth Mac Vintie was seen again in the Cherokee country only in his place as a marker in the march of his regiment, and as he was evidently exceedingly desirous to permit no one to incur penalties for his lib eration, his officers spared him questions con cerning his escape, save in a general way.

When the ada-wehi next reappeared in a remote town of the district and was sedu lously interrogated as to how his freedom had been achieved, he threw out his right hand at arm's length in his old, boastful, airy gesture.

" Cheesto kaiere ! " (An old rabbit!) he exclaimed. " A little old rabbit ran down the slope. I turned the soldier into a rabbit, and he ran away. And I turned myself into a fish, and I swam away. Ha ! Tsida-wei-yu ! " (I am a great ada-wehi!)

THE FATE OF THE CHEEBA-TAGHE
THE FATE OF THE CHEERA-TAGHE

ALONG the old " trading-path " that was wont to wind from the Cherokee country among the innumerable spurs and gorges of the Great Smoky Mountains, and through the dense primeval forests full five hundred miles to the city of Charlestown, was visible for many years, on the banks of the Little Tennessee, an "old waste town,"as the aban doned place was called in the idiom of the Indians. An early date it might seem, in 1744, in this new land, for the spectacle of the ruins of a race still in possession, still unsubdued. Nearly twenty years later, after the repeated aggressive expeditions which the British government sent against the Cherokees, such vestiges became more numer ous. This " waste town, " however, neither fire nor sword had desolated, and the grim deeds of British powder and lead were still of the future. The enemy came in more sub tle sort.

230 THE FATE OF THE CHEERA-TAGHE

Only one of the white pack-men employed to drive a score of well-laden horses semi-annually from Charlestown to a trading-sta tion farther along on the Great Tennessee — then called the Cherokee River — and back again used to glower fearfully at the u waste town "as he passed. He had ample leisure for speculation, for the experienced animals of the pack-train required scant heed, so regularly they swung along in single file, and the wild whoops of their drivers were for the sake of personal encouragement and the simple joy which very young men find in their own clamor. It grew specially bois terous always when they neared the site of Nilaque Great, the deserted place, as if to give warning to any vague spiritual essences, unmeet for mortal vision, that might be lurk ing about the " waste town," and bid them avaunt, for the place was reputed haunted.

The rest of the Carolina pack-men, troop ing noisily past, averted their eyes from the darkened doors of the empty houses; the weed-grown spaces of the "beloved square/' where once the ceremonies of state, the re ligious rites, the public games and dances were held; the council-house on its high

THE FATE OF THE CHEERA-TAGHE 231

mound, whence had been wont to issue the bland vapors of the pipe of peace or the far more significant smoke emitted from the cheera, the " sacred fire/' which only the cheera-taghe, the fire-prophets, 10 were per mitted to kindle, and which was done with pomp and ceremony in the new year, when every spark of the last year's fire had been suffered to die out.

Cuthbert Barnett, however, always looked to see what he might, — perhaps because he was a trifle bolder than the other stalwart pack-men, all riding armed to the teeth to guard the goods of the train from robbery as well as their own lives from treachery, for although the

Cherokees professed friend ship it was but half-hearted, as they loved the French always better than the English; perhaps because he had a touch of imagi nation that coerced his furtive glance; per haps because he doubted more, or believed less, of the traditions of the day. And he saw — silence ! the sunset in vacant spaces, with long, slanting, melancholy rays among the scattered houses of the hamlet; an empty doorway, here and there; a fall ing rotting roof; futile traces of vanished

homes. Once a deer and fawn were graz ing in the weed-grown fields that used to stand so thick with corn that they laughed and sung; once — it was close upon win ter— he heard a bear humming and hum ming his content (the hunters called the sound " singing ") from the den where the animal had bestowed himself among the fallen logs of a dwelling-house, half cov ered with great drifts of dead leaves; often an owl would cry out in alarm from some dark nook as the pack-train clattered past; and once a wolf with a stealthy and sinister tread was patrolling the " beloved square." These were but the natural incidents of the time and the ruins of the old Cherokee town. Little did Cuddy Barnett imagine, as he gazed on the deserted and desolate place, that he was yet to behold the smoke of the " sacred fire" flaring up into the blue sky from the portal of the temple, as the cheera-taghe would issue bearing the flame aloft, newly kindled in the opening year, and calling upon many assembled people to light therefrom their hearths, rekindling good resolutions and religious fervor for the fu ture, and letting the faults of the unavail-

ing past die out with the old year's fire; that he was to mark the clash of arms in the " beloved square/' once more populous with the alert figures of warriors in mar tial array, making ready for the war-path ; that he was to hear the joyful religious songs of greeting to the dawn, and the sonorous trumpeting of the conch-shells, as the vanished Indians of the " old waste town " would troop down at daybreak into the water of that bright stream where long ago they had been wont to plunge in their mystic religious ablutions. All this, how ever, the pack-men might see and hear, to believe the tradition of the day, in camping but a single night near the old "waste town."

And so anxious were these gay itinerant companies to see and hear nothing of such ghostly sort that whatever the stress of the weather, the mischances of the journey, the condition of the pack-animals, this vicinity was always distinguished by the longest day's travel of the whole route, and the camp was pitched at the extreme limit of the endurance of man and horse to compass distance from Nilaque Great. For believe

what one might, the fact remained indisput able, that a decade earlier, when the place was inhabited, strange sounds were rife about the locality, the " sacred fire " was unkin-dled on the great " Sanctified Day," the two cheera-taghe of the town mysteriously disappeared, and their fate had remained a dark riddle.

One of these men, Oo-koo-koo, was well known in Charlestown. Both were of influ ence in the tribe, but often he had been specially chosen as one of the delegations of warriors and "beloved men" sent to wait in diplomatic conference on the Gov ernor of South Carolina, to complain of in justice in the dealings of the licensed tra ders or the encroachments of the frontier settlers, or to crave the extension of some privilege of the treaty which the Cherokee tribe had lately made with the British gov ernment.

Two white men, who had become con spicuous in a short stay in the town of Nilaque

Great, disappeared simultaneously, and the suspicion of foul dealing on their part against the cheera-taghe, which the Cherokee nation seemed disposed to enter-

tain, threatened at one time the peace that was so precious to the "infant settlements/' as the small, remote, stockaded stations of the Carolina frontiersmen were tenderly called.

Therefore the Governor of South Caro lina, now a royal province, — the event oc curred during the incumbency of Robert Johnson, who having acted in that capacity for the Lords Proprietors, well understood the menace of the situation, — busied him self with extreme diligence to discover the subsequent movements of the two white men, whose names were Terence O'Kim-mon and Adrien L'Epine, in order to ascer tain the fate of the cheera-taghe, and if evilly entreated, to bring the perpetrators of the deed to justice.

With a long, unguarded, open frontier such as his province presented to the incur sions of the warlike and fierce Cherokees, who, despite their depopulating wars with other tribes, could still bring to the field six thousand braves from their sixty-four towns, the inhabitants of which were esti mated at twenty thousand souls, he was by no means disposed to delay or to indulge

doubts or to foster compatriot commisera tion in meting out the penalty of the male factors. The united militia of South Caro lina and Georgia at this time numbered but thirty - five hundred rank and file, these colonies being so destitute of white men for the common defense that a memorial addressed to his majesty King George II. a little earlier than this event, bearing date April 9, 1734, pathetically states that " money itself cannot here raise a sufficient body of them." The search for the sus pects, however, although long, exhaustive, and of such diligence as to convince the

o

Indians of its sincerity of purpose, resulted fruitlessly. The government presently took occasion to made some valuable presents to the tribe, not as indemnity, for it could re cognize no responsibility in the strange dis aster, but for the sake of seeming to comply with the form of offering satisfaction for the loss, which otherwise the Indians would retaliate with massacre.

Nilaque Great with this cloud upon it grew dreary. The strange disappearance of its cheera-taghe was canvassed again and again, reaching no surmise of the truth.

Speculations, futile as they were continu ous, began to be reinforced with reminis cences of the date of the event, and certain episodes became strangely significant now, although hardly remarked at the time; people remembered unexplained and curious noises that had sounded like muffled thun der in the deep midnight, and again, scarcely noted, in the broad daylight. The " sacred fire " remained unkindled, and sundry mis fortunes were attributed to this unprece dented neglect; an expert warrior, young and notably deft-handed, awkwardly shot himself with his own gun; the crops, cut short by a late and long-continued drought, were so meagre as to be hardly worth the harvesting; the days appointed for the an nual feasts and thanksgiving were like days of mourning; discontents waxed and grew strong. Superstitious terrors became rife, and at length it was known at Charles-town that the Cherokees of Nilaque Great had settled a new place farther down upon the river, for at the old town the vanished cheera-taghe were abroad in the spirit, per vading the " beloved square " at night with cries of " A-kee-o-hoo-sa ! A-kee-o-hoo-sa! "

(I am dead ! I am dead !) clamoring for their graves and the honors of sepulture due to them and denied. And this was a grief to the head men of the town, for of all tribes the Cherokees loved and revered their dead. Thus when other cheera-taghe kindled for the municipality the " sacred fire " for a new year it was distributed to hearths far away, and Nilaque Great, deserted and depopu lated, had become a " waste town."

A fair place it had been in its prime, and so it had seemed one afternoon in June, 1734, when for the first time the two white strangers had entered it. Mountains more splendid than those which rose about it on every hand it would be difficult to imagine. The dense, rich woods reach in undiminished vigor along the slopes covering them at a height of six thousand feet, till the "tree line" interposes ; thence the great bare domes lift their stately proportions among the clouds. Along these lofty perspectives the varying distance affords the vision a vast array of gradations of color, — green in a thousand shades, and bronze, and purple, and blue, — blue growing ever fainter and more remote till it is but an illusion of

azure, and one may believe that the summits seen through a gap to the northeast are sheer necromancy of the facile horizon.

In the deep verdant cove below, groups of the giant trees common to the region towered above the stanchly constructed cabins that formed the homes of the Indians, for the Cherokees, detesting labor and ex perts in procrastination, builded well and wisely that they might not be forced to rebuild, and many of the distinctive fea tures of the stout frontier architecture were borrowed by the pioneers from ab original example. Out beyond the shad ows were broad stretches of fields with the lush June in the wide and shining blade and the flaunting tassel. The voices of wo men and young girls came cheerily from the breezy midst as they tilled the ground, where flourished in their proper divisions the three varieties of maize known to In dian culture, " the six weeks' corn, the hom iny corn, and the bread corn." A shoal of canoes skimmed down the river, each with its darting shadow upon that lucent current and seeming as native, as indigenous to the place as the minnows in a crystal brown

pool there by the waterside — each too with its swift javelin-like motion and a darting shadow. Sundry open doors here and there showed glimpses of passing figures within, but the arrival of the strangers was un noticed till some children playing beside the river caught sight of the unaccustomed faces. With a shrill cry of discovery, they sped across the square, agitated half by fright and half by the gusto of novelty. In another moment there were two score armed men in the square.

" Now hould yer tongue still, an' I '11 do the talkin'," said one of the white adven turers to the other, speaking peremptorily, but with a suave and delusive smile. "If yez were n't Frinch ye 'd be a beautiful Englishman ; but I hev got the advantage of ye in that, an' faix I '11 kape it."

He was evidently of a breeding inferior to that of his companion, but he had so sturdy and swinging a gait, so stalwart and goodly a build, so engaging a manner, and so florid a smile, that the very sight of him was disarming, despite the patent crafty de ceit in his face. It seemed as if it could not be very deep or guileful, it was so

frankly expressed. It was suggestive of the roguish machinations of a child. He had twinkling brown eyes, and reddish hair, plaited in a club and tied with a thong of leather. His features were blunt, but his red, well-shaped lips parted in a ready, reassuring smile, and showed' teeth as even and white as the early corn. Both men were arrayed in the buckskin shirt and leggings gen erally worn by the frontiersmen, but the face of the other had a certain incongruity with his friend's, and was more difficult to decipher. It looked good, — not kind, but true. It had severe pragmatic lines about the mouth, and the lips were thin and some what fixedly set. His eyes were dark, seri ous, and very intent, as if he could argue and protest very earnestly on matters of no weight. He would in a question of theory go very far if set on the wrong line, and just as far on the right. The direction was the matter of great moment, and this seemed now in the hands of the haphazard but scheming Irishman.

" If it plaze yer honor, " said O'Kimmon in English, taking off his coonskin cap with a lavish flourish as a tall and stately Indian

hastily garbed in fine raiment of the aborigi nal type, a conspicuous article of which was a long feather-wrought mantle, both brilliant and delicate of effect, detached himself from the group and came forward, " I can't spake yer illigant language, — me eddication bein' that backward, — but I kin spake me own so eloquent that it would make a gate-post prick up the ears of understanding. We Ve come to visit yez, sor."

The smile which the Hibernian bent upon the savage was of a honeyed sweetness, but the heart of his companion sank as he sud denly noted the keen, intuitive power of comprehension expressed in the face of the old Indian. Here was craft too, but of a different quality, masked, potent, impossible to divine, to measure, to thwart. The sage Oo-koo-koo stood motionless, his eyes nar rowing, his long,flat, cruel mouth compressed as with a keen scrutiny he marked all the characteristics of the strangers, — first of one, then deliberately of the other. A war captain (his flighty name was Watatuga, the Dragon-fly, although he looked with his high nose and eagle glance more like a bird of prey), assuming precedence of the others,

pressed up beside the prophet, and the chal lenge of his eyes and the contempt that di lated his nostrils might have seemed more formidable of intent than the lacerating gaze of the cheera-taghe, except that to an Irish man there is always a subtle joy even in the abstract idea of fight. The rest of the braves, with their alert, high-featured cast of countenance, inimical, threatening, clus tered about, intent, doubtful, listening.

Adrien L'fipine had his secret doubts as to the efficacy of the bold, blunt, humorous impudence which Terence O'Kimmon fan cied such masterful policy, — taking now special joy in the fact that its meaning was partially veiled because of the presumable limitations of the Indian's comprehension of the English language. The more delicate nurture that L'Epine obviously had known revolted at times from this unkempt brus-querie, although he had a strong pulse of sympathy with the wild, lawless disregard of conventional standards which characterized much of the frontier life. He feared, too, that O'Kimmon underrated the extent of the Cherokee's comprehension of the lan guage of which, however, the Indians gener-

ally spoke only a few disconnected phrases. So practiced were the savages in all the arts of pantomime, in the interpretation of facial expression and the intonation of the voice, that L'Epine had known in his varied wan derings of instances of tribes in conference, each ignorant of the other's language, who nevertheless reached a definite and intricate mutual understanding without the services of an interpreter. L'Epine felt entrapped, regretful, and wished to recede. He winced palpably as O'Kimmon's rich Irish voice, full of words, struck once more upon the air.

" Me godson, the Governor o' South Car olina," Terence O'Kimmon resumed, lying quite recklessly, "sint his humble respects, — an' he's that swate upon yez that he licks his fingers ter even sphake yer name ! (Pity I furgits ut, bein' I never knew ut!)"

Although possessing an assurance that he could get the better of the devil," could he but identify him," as O'Kimmon frequently said, he felt for one moment as if he were now in the presence. Despite his nerve the silence terrified him. He was beginning to cringe before the steady glare of those search ing eyes. It was even as a refreshment of

spirit to note a sudden bovine snort of rage from the lightsome Dragon-fly, as if he could ill bridle his inimical excitement.

The adventurers had not anticipated a reception of this sort, for the hospitality of the Indians was proverbial. Credentials surely were not necessary in the social cir cles of the Cherokees, and two men to six thousand offered no foundation for fear. O'Kimmon had such confidence in his own propitiating wiles and crafty policy that he did not realize how his genial deceit was emblazoned upon his face, how blatant it was in his voice. But for its challenging duplicity there would hardly have arisen a suggestion of suspicion. Many men on vari ous errands easily found their way into the Indian tribes when at peace with the Brit ish, and suffered no injury. Nevertheless as the wise Oo-koo-koo looked at O'Kimmon thus steadily, with so discerning a gaze, the Irishman felt each red hair of his scalp rise obtrusively into notice, as if to suggest the instant taking of it. He instinctively put on his coonskin cap again to hold his scalp down, as he said afterward.

" Why come ? " Oo-koo-koo demanded sternly.

" Tell the truth, for God's sake ! " L'Epine adjured O'Kimmon in a low voice.

" I 'm not used to it! 'T would give me me death o' cold ! " quavered the Irishman, in sad sincerity, at a grievous loss.

" Asgaya uneka (White man), hut no Ingliss," said the astute Indian, touching the breast of each with the bowl of his pipe, still in his hand and still alight as it was when the interruption of their advent had occurred.

" No, by the powers, — not English ! " exclaimed the Irishman impulsively, seeing he was already discovered. " I 'm me own glorious nation ! — the pride o' the worruld, — I was born in the Emerald Isle, the gem o' the say! I 'm an Oirishman from the tip o' me scalp — in the name o' pity why should I mintion the contrivance " (dropping his voice to an appalled muffled tone) — may the saints purtect ut! But surely, Mister Injun, I 've no part nor lot with the bloody bastes o' English ers either over the say or in the provinces. If I were the brother-in-law o' the Governor o' South Carolina I 'd hev a divorce from the murtherin' Englisher before he could cry, ' Quarter !'

Oo-koo-koo, the wise Owl, made no direct answer.

" Asgaya uneka (White man), but no Ingliss," he only said, now indicating L'fipine.

" Frinch in the mornin', plaze yer wor ship, an' only a bit o' English late in the afternoon o' the day," cried O'Kimmon, of ficiously, himself once more.

" French father, English mother, " ex plained L'Epine, feeling that the Indian was hardly a safe subject for the pleasantries of conundrums.

" But his mother was but a wee bit of a woman, " urged O'Kimmon ; " the most of him is Frinch, — look at the size of him ! "

For O'Kimmon was now bidding as high against the English aegis as earlier he had been disposed to claim its protection, when he had protested his familiarity with the Royal Governor of South Carolina. In an instant he was once more gay, impudent, confident of carrying everything before him. He divined that some recent friction had supervened in the ever-clashing interests subsisting between the Cherokee nation and the British government, and was relying

on the recurrent inclination of this tribe to fraternize with the French. Their influence from their increasing western settlements was exerted antagonistically to the British colo nists, by whom it was dreaded in anticipation of the war against a French and Cherokee alliance which came later. Oo-koo-koo, com placent in his own sagacity in having detected a difference in the speech of the new-comers from the English which he had been accus tomed to hear in Charlestown, and animated by a wish to believe, hearkened with the more credulity to an expansive fiction de tailed by the specious Irishman as to their mission here.

They were awaiting the coming of cer tain pettiaugres from New Orleans, — a long journey by way of the Mississippi, the Ohio, the Cherokee, and the Tennessee rivers, — with a cargo of French goods cheaper than the English. They designed to establish a trading-post at some con venient point, out of reach of the grasp ing British, and thus to compete with the monopoly of the Cherokee commerce which the English government sought to foster. And then, to furnish a leaven of truth to

this mass of lies, he detailed, with such a relish as only an Irishman can feel in a happy incongruity, that the French, having no market in old France for deerskins, the chief commodity of barter that the Indians possessed, disposed of them to ships of the British colonies, from New York and else where, lured thus to New Orleans, in ex change for English cloths and other British manufactures, which the French then sur reptitiously furnished to the Indians of the British alliance, underselling them on every hand.

" The intellects of the Frinch are so handsome ! " cried O'Kimmon, the tears of delighted laughter in his eyes. "Faix, that is what makes 'em so close kin to the Oirish!"

Albeit the Cherokee treaty with the Brit ish forbade the Indians to trade with white men of any other nationality than the Eng lish, these professed aliens were promised protection and concealment from the Brit ish government, and the pretext of their mission served to countenance their linger ing stay.

Soon their presence seemed a matter of

course. The Indians had recurred to their methods of suave hospitality. The two strangers encountered only friendly looks and words, while affecting to gratify curi osity by peering into all the unaccustomed habitudes, — the preparation of food, the manufacture of deerskin garments, the care of the sick, the modeling of bowls and jars of clay, in which the Cherokees were notably expert as well as in the weaving of feather-wrought fabrics and baskets, the athletic games, the horse-races, the continual dances and pantomimic plays, — and were presently domiciled as it were in the tribe. Of so little note did they soon become that when they gradually ceased these manifestations of interest, as if familiarity had sated their curiosity, it seemed to occasion no com ment. They were obviously free to rove, to stay, to live their lives as they would with out interference or surveillance.

Nevertheless, they still maintained the utmost caution. Sometimes, idleness being no phenomenon, they would lie half the day in the shade on the river-bank. The Tennessee was shrunken now in the heated season, and great gravelly slopes were ex-

posed. The two loiterers were apparently motionless at first, but as their confidence increased and the chances of being ob served lessened, L'Epine, always dreading discovery, began to casually pass the gravel and sand through his fingers as he lay; sometimes he idly trifled with the blade of a hoe in a shallow pool left by the receding waters, while the jolly Irishman, now grave and solicitous, watched him breathlessly. Then Lupine would shake his head, and the mercurial O'Kimmon groaned his deep despondency.

Once the Frenchman's head was not shaken. A flush sprang up among the pragmatic lines of L'Epine's face; his dark eyes glittered; his hand shook; for as he held out the hoe, on its blade were vaguely glimmering particles among the sand.

Later the two adventurers cherished a small nugget of red, red gold!

This find chanced below a bluff in a sort of grotto of rock, which the water filled when the river was high, and left quite dry and exposed as it receded in the droughts of summer.

Whether the two strangers were too

much and too long out of sight; whether attention was attracted by certain perfo rated dippers or pans which they now brought into assiduous use, but which they sought to conceal; whether they had been all the time furtively watched, with a sus picion never abated, one can hardly say. They had observed every precaution of secrecy that the most zealous heed could suggest. Only one worked with the pan while the other lay motionless and idle, and vigilantly watched and listened for any stealthy sign of approach. They fully real ized the jealousy of the Indians concern ing the mineral wealth of their territory, lest its discovery bring hordes of the crav ing white people to dispossess them. This prophetic terror was later fulfilled in the Ayrate division of the tribe, but to the northward, along the Tennessee River, they sedulously guarded this knowledge. Tra ditions there are to the present day in the Great Smoky Mountains concerning mines of silver and lead, and of localities rich in auriferous gravel which are approximately ascertained, but which the Cherokees knew accurately and worked as far as they listed;

—they carried their secret with them to the grave or the far west.

The exploration of L'Epine and O'Kim-mon of necessity was conducted chiefly by day, but one night the prospectors could not be still, the moon on the sand was so bright!

The time which they had fixed for a silent, secret departure was drawing near. Their bags were almost filled, but they lingered for a little more, and covetously a little more still. And this night, this memorable night, the moon on the sand was as bright as day !

The light slanted across the Tennessee River and shimmered in the ripples. One could see, if one would, the stately lines of dark summits along a far horizon. A mock ingbird was singing from out the boscage of the laurel near at hand, and the night wind was astir. And suddenly the two gold-washers in the depths of the grotto became conscious that they were not alone.

There, sitting like stone figures one on each side of the narrow portal, were the two cheera-taghe of the town, silent, motionless, watching with eyes how long alert, listening with ears how discerningly attentive, it is im possible to divine.

The gold-washers sprang to their feet, each instinctively grasping for his weapon, but alack, neither was armed ! The pan had come to seem the most potent of accoutre ments, with which, in good sooth, one might take the world by storm, and the rifle and knife were forgotten, in their absorption. Doubtless the Cherokees interpreted aright the gesture, so significant, so obvious to their methods of life. Both the cheera-taghe were armed with pistol as well as tomahawk and scalping-knife.

Perhaps because of this they felt secure, at leisure, acquiescently allowing the event to develop as it needs must, — or perhaps realizing the significance of the discovery to the young strangers, their palpitant eager ness to gauge its result, their dread of re prisal, of forced renunciation of their booty, the Indians permitted themselves a relish of the torture of an enemy on a more aesthetic scheme than their wont.

The two cheera-taghe, the shadow of their feather-crested heads in the moonlight on the sand of the grotto almost as distinct as the reality, spoke suddenly to each other, and the discomfited gold-seekers, who had

learned to comprehend to a certain extent the language, perceived with dismay the sar casm that lengthened their suspense. For it was thus that the rulers among the Chero-kees rebuked their own young people, not upbraiding them with their misdeeds, but with gentle satire complimenting them for that in which they had notably failed.

" A reward for hospitality we find in these young men," said one, whose voice was hoarse and croaking and guttural and who was called Kanoona (the Bull-frog).

" Strangers to us, yet they requite us, for we treated them as our own," said Oo-koo-koo.

" They treat us as their own ! " the croak ing, satiric, half-smothered laughter of this response intimated an aside. Then Kanoona in full voice went on, " Open and frank as the day, they keep no secrets from us! "

" They are honest! They rob us not of the yellow stone which the Carolina people think, so precious!" rejoined Oo-koo-koo, while O'Kimmon and L'Epine looked from one to the other as the cheera-taghe sus tained this fugue of satiric accusation.

" Not they," croaked the responsive voice,

"for behold, we have long time fed and lodged them and given them of our best. We have believed them and trusted them. We have befriended them and loved them."

" And they have befriended and loved us! " said Oo-koo-koo.

Then silence. The river sang, but only a murmurous rune ; the mute moonlight lay still on the mountains; the wind had sunk, and the motionless leaves glistened as the dew fell; a nighthawk swept past the portal of the grotto with the noiseless wing of its kind.

" Had they desired to explore our land they would have asked our consent," the croaking voice of Kanoona resumed the an-tiphonal reproach. " They would not have brought upon us the hordes of British colo nists, who would fain drive us from our habitations for their greed of the yellow stone."

" Oh, no ! never would they make so base a recompense ! — to bring upon us the de struction of our men and women and chil dren, the wresting from us of our land, the casting of us forth from our homes, — be cause the poor, unsuspecting Indians gave

them food and shelter and a haven of rest while waiting for the pettiaugres that are coming up from New Orleans."

" The pettiaugres from New Orleans!" Kanoona repeated with a burst of raucous laughter. "Hala! Hala!"

But Oo-koo-koo preserved his gravity. " They would not lie ! Surely the white men would not lie ! "

Then turning to O'Kimmon he asked point-blank, " Chee-a-koh-ga f " (Do you lie?)

The direct address was a relief to O'Kim-mon. He had often wondered to see the stanch young braves reduced almost to tears by this seemingly gentle discipline; he felt its poignancy when the keen blade of satire was turned against himself.

" I did lie !" he admitted, as unreservedly as if he were at confession. " But Oo-koo-koo, we will pay for what we 've got. This is all of ut! An' f aix, yez have thrated us well, — an' begorra, we would have axed yer consint if we had dhramed we could have got ut! " he concluded ingenuously.

The two Indians gazed at him with a sur prise so evident that a chill ran through his every nerve.

258 THE FATE OF THE CHEERA-TAGHE

" We will never reveal the secret, — the place of the gold/' declared L'Epine. Then perceiving in his turn something uncompre-hended in their expression he reinforced his promise with argument. " We will want to come back — alone — to get more of it — all for ourselves. We will not be willing to share our discovery with others."

The cheera-taghe still silently gazed at the two young men; then turned toward each other with that patent astonishment yet on their faces. At last they burst forth into sarcastic laughter.

L'Epine and O'Kimmon, albeit half bewildered, exchanged appalled glances. There was no need of speech. Each under stood at last.

Return! There was no chance of depar ture. They were to pay the penalty of the dangerous knowledge they had acquired. Already some vague report, some suspicion of the hidden gold of the locality had been bruited abroad,— thus the Indians must rea son,— or these white men would not have come so far to seek it. Should they be per mitted to depart, their sudden wealth would proclaim its source, even though as they had promised they should keep silence.

THE FATE OF THE CHEERA-TAGHE 259

This was equally true should they even tually escape. Therefore — hideous realiza tion ! — the actual possession by the Indians of their own country depended upon the keeping of the secret inviolate. Dead men tell no tales!

O'Kimmon, with a swelling heart, be thought himself of his status as a British subject and the possible vengeance of the province. It would come, if at all, too late. For the Cherokees believed the two to be without the pale of the English protection. One had repudiated the government, de claring himself an Irishman, a nationality then unknown to the Cherokees. The other was French, — no reprisal for his sake was possible to a tribe under British allegiance. Death it must be ! — doubtless with all the pomp and circumstance of the torture, for from the standpoint of the Indians they had requited hospitality with robbery. Death was inevitable, — unless they could now es cape. Had they but one weapon between them they might yet make good their flight.

An Irishman rarely stops to count the odds. With the thought O'Kimmon, heavy, muscular, yet alert, threw himself upon

260 THE FATE OF THE CHEERA-TAGHE

Oo-koo-koo, and in an instant he had almost wrenched the knife from the Indian's belt.

The other Cherokee cried warningly, "Akee-rooka! Akee-rooka!" (I will shoot!) Then drew his pistol and fired.

The next moment, perhaps for many mo ments thereafter, none of them knew very definitely what had happened. There was a cloud of dust, a terrific detonation, a sudden absolute darkness, as in some revul sion of nature, a stifling sensation. They were penned within the grotto by a great fragment of the beetling cliff. Doubtless it had been previously fractured by the action of continuous freezes, and the concussion of the pistol shot in the restricted space of the cave below had brought it down.

The days went on. The men were missed after a time, but a considerable interval had elapsed. The two strangers had of late kept themselves much apart, owing to their ab sorption and their covert methods of seeking for gold. It was an ill-ordered, roaming, sylvan life they led at best. The cheera-taghe, although " beloved men " and priests of their strange and savage religion, were but wild Indians, and their temporary absence

created no surprise. In fact, until sought with anxiety when the drought had become excessive and threatened the later crops, and the services of the cheera-taghe were necessary to invoke and with wild barbaric ceremonials bring down the lightning and thunder to clear the atmosphere and the rain to refresh the soil, it was not ascertained that the prophets had definitely disappearedo

Then it was that excitement supervened, search, anxiety, grief, fear. There began to be vague rumors of untoward sounds, re membered rather than noticed at the time. Faint explosions had been heard in the night as if under the ground, and again in broad daylight as if in the air. None could imagine that the doomed men had sought to attract the attention of the town by firing off their pistols, thus utilizing their scanty ammunition. The strain grew intense ; superstitious fancies supplemented the real mystery ; the place was finally abandoned, and thus Nilaque Great became a " waste town."

It was ten years, perhaps, after this blight had fallen upon it, that one day as the pack-train came down the valley of the

Little Tennessee, on its autumnal return trip to Charlestown, the snow began to sift down. An unseasonable storm it was, for the winter had hardly set in. A north wind sprang up; the snow was soon heavily driving; within an hour the woods, still in the red leafage of autumn, were covered with snow and encased in ice. Only by a strenuous effort would the train be able to pass the old " waste town " before the early dusk, — a mile or two at most; but it was hoped that this might suffice to keep the ghosts out of the bounds of visibility. The roaring bacchanalian glees with which the pack-men set the melancholy sheeted woods aquiver might well send the ghosts out of earshot, presuming them endowed with vo lition.

Suddenly Cuddy Barnett discovered that one of the pack-horses of his own especial charge was missing, — a good bay with a load of fine dressed deerskins to take to Charlestown, then the great mart of all this far region. A recollection of a sharp curve in the trading-path, running dangerously near a bluff bank, came abruptly into his mind. Drifts had lodged in its jagged crev-

ices, and it might well have chanced that here the animal had lost his footing and slipped out of the steadily trotting file along the river bank unnoticed in the blinding snow.

This theory seemed eminently plausible to his comrades, but when they learned that he was of the opinion that the disaster had happened at the old " waste town," as he had there first missed the animal in the file, not one would go back with him to search the locality, — not for the horse, not for the peltry, not even to avert the displeasure of their employer in Charles town. Barnett besought their aid for a time, urging the project of rescue as they all sat around the roaring camp-fire under the sheltering branches of a cluster of fir trees that, acting as wind-break, served to fend off in some degree the fury of the storm. The ruddy flare illumined far shadowy aisles of the snowy wilderness, all agloom with the early dusk. Despite the falling flakes, they could still see the picketed pack-horses, now freed from their burdens, huddling together and holding down their heads to the icy blast as they munched their forage. The supper of

the young 1 pack-men was broiling on the coals ; their faces were florid with the keen wind, their coonskin caps all crested with snow; and the fringes of their buckskin raiment had tinkling pendants of icicles; but although they had found good cheer in a chortling jug, uncorked as the first pre liminary of encamping, they had not yet imbibed sufficient fictitious courage to set at naught their fears of the old "waste town."

Barnett at last acquiesced in the relin-quishment of his desire of rescue. Some losses must needs occur in a great trade, and considering the stress of the weather, the long distances traversed, the dangers of the lonely wildernesses in the territory of savages, the incident would doubtless be leniently overlooked. And then he be thought himself of the horse, — a good horse, stout, swift, kindly disposed; a hard fate the animal had encountered, — aban doned here to starve in these bleak winter woods. Perhaps he might be lying there at the foot of the cliffs with a broken leg, suf fering the immeasurable agonies of a dumb beast, for the lack of a merciful pistol-ball

to put him at peace. Barnett could not re sist the mute appeal of his fancy.

Presently he was trudging alone along the icy path. The flare of the red fire grew dim behind him; the last flicker faded. The woods were all unillumined, ghastly white, with a hovering gray shadow. The song of the bivouac fainted in the distance and failed; the echo grew doubtful and dull; and now in absolute silence that somehow set his nerves aquiver he was com ing in with the dreary dusk and the driving snow to the old " waste town/' Nilaque Great.

More silent even than the wilderness it seemed with the muffling drifts heavy on the roofs, blocking the dark open doors of the tenantless dwellings, lying in fluffy masses on the boughs of* the trees that had once made the desert spaces so pleasantly umbrageous in those sweet summers so long ago. The great circular council - house, shaped like a dome, was whitely aglimmer against the gray twilight and the wintry background of the woods and mountains, — only the vaguest suggestions of heights seen through the ceaseless whirl of the

crystalline flakes. No wolf now, although remembering the casual glimpse he had had he was prepared with rifle and pistol, and held his knife in his hand ; no bear; no sign of living creature until, as he skirted the jagged bluff of the river where he fancied the horse might have lost his footing, he heard a sudden whinny of welcome, the sound keen and eerie and intrusive in the strange breathless solemnity of the silent place.

Gazing cautiously over the verge of the precipice, he saw the animal despite the gath ering shadows. The horse was quite safe, having doubtless slipped down in the soft densities of a great drift dislodged from the crevice by his own weight. His pack was still on his back, now piled twice as high with snow. He lifted his arched neck as he sprang about with undiminished activity, vainly seeking to ascend the almost sheer precipice.

Daylight, however, was essential for his rescue. The effort now on these icy steeps might cost either man or beast a broken limb, if no more. With an instinct of self-protection the animal had chosen the lee of a great buttress of the cliff, and could stand there safely all night though the tempera ture should fall still lower. The young pack man called out a word or two of encourage ment, listening fearfully as the sound struck back in the silence from the icy bank of the river, the craggy hillsides, and the reso nant walls of the deserted houses in the old " waste town." Himself suddenly stricken to silence, he realized as he turned that the night had at last closed in. It lay dark and desolate in the limitless woods', where a vague sense of motion gave token that the snow was stih 1 viewlessly falling in the dense ob scurities.

But in the "waste town" itself a pallid visibility lingered in the open spaces where the trees were few, and gloomily showed the empty cabins, the deserted council-house, the vacant "beloved square." Somehow, turn as he would, this dim scene in the midst of the dense darkness of the stormy night was before his eyes. Again and again he plunged into the woods seeking to fol low the well-known trail of the trading-path to the camp and rejoin his companions, but invariably he would emerge from the wilder-

ness after a toilsome tramp, entering the old "waste town" at a different angle.

He perceived at length that he could not keep the direction, that he was wandering in a circle after the manner of those lost in forests. His clothing, freezing upon his body, was calculated for warmer weather ; the buckskin shirt and leggings, the garb of the frontiersmen, copied from the at tire of the Indians, were of a thin and pli able texture, owing to the peculiar skill of the savages in dressing peltry. An early historian describes such costume in a curi ously sophisticated phrase as the " summer visiting dress of the Indians." The south ern tribes were intensely averse to cold, for in winter they wore furs and garments made of buffalo hides, the shaggy side in ward ; this raiment was sewed with the sinews of deer and a kind of wild hemp for thread, and with needles dexterously fash ioned of fishbone.

Barnett had now no thought of the ghosts of the old " waste town." His first care was to save his life this cruel night; without fire, without food, without shelter, it might be that he had indeed come to the end.

He was induced by this reflection to climb the mound to the old council-house. For here the walls, plastered both within and without with the strong adhesive red clay of the region, admitted no wind, while in the cabins which had been dwellings the drifts lay deep beneath the rifts in the di lapidated roofs and the crevices in the wall, and the flying flakes sifted in as the keen gusts surged through. He had had the forethought to gather as he went bits of wood, now a loose clapboard or piece of bark from low-hanging eaves, now a frag ment of half-rotten puncheon from a door step, and as he groped into the dense darkness of the council-house with his steel and flint he set them alight on the hearth in the centre of the floor.

When he was once more warm and free of the fear of death, other fears took hold upon him. In the first glimmers of the fire he could see through the tall narrow door-less portal only the dark night outside and a flickering glimpse against its blackness of the quivering crystals of the snow, — these but vaguely, for the blue smoke eddying through the great room veiled the opposite

side, there being no chimney or window, and he sat in the interior behind the fire.

He gazed furtively over his shoulder ever and anon, as the flames flared up, revealing the deeply red walls of the dome-like place with here and there a buffalo skin sus pended against them, the inside of the hide showing, painted in curious hieroglyphics, brilliant with color, and instinct with an untranslated meaning; a number of conch shells lay about, with jars and vases of clay, and those quaintly fashioned earthen drums, the heads of tightly stretched deer skin,— all paraphernalia of the savage wor ship which the cheera-taghe had conducted, now abandoned as bewitched.

Sitting here comfortably in the place of those men of the " divine fire," Cuthbert Barnett, his rifle by his side, his knife in his belt, his coon skin cap pushed back from his face, once more florid, warm, tingling from the keen wind of the day and the change to this heated air, and with per chance a drowsy eyelid, began to marvel anew as to the fate of the cheera-taghe. Hardly a drowsy eyelid, he consciously had, however, for he had resolved that he would

not sleep. His situation here alone was too dangerous ; he feared wolves, — the fire that would otherwise affright them might un-tended sink too low. He feared also some wandering Indian. Should he be discovered here by means of the unaccustomed light he might be wantonly murdered as he slept, or in revenge for the sacrilege of his intrusion

o o

among these things that the savages had esteemed sacred.

Therefore, when he suddenly saw the cheera-taghe he saw them quite plainly. Tall, stately, splendidly arrayed in their barbaric garb, draped with their iridescent feather-wrought mantles, their heads dressed with white plumes, a staff of cane adorned with white feathers in the right hand, a green bough in the left, preceded by those curiously sonorous earthen drums, of which the drone blended with the notes of the religious song, Yo-he-wah-yah ! Yo-he-wah-yah ! they thrice led the glittering proces sion of the " holy dance " around and around the " beloved square."

A blank interval ensued. And then again he saw them, nearer now, more distinct; they were entering the temple; they were

close at hand; triumphant of mien, assured, so full of life!—he could laugh to think that he had had a dream, or had heard somehow, that they were dead or lost or vaguely gone. For here, without seeming in the least to notice his presence, they kindled anew with friction of bits of poplar or white oak the fire for the new year, the cheera, the " sacred flame," to bear it outside to distribute it to the assembled people of Nilaque Great. Without was summer; the trees were full of green leaves; canoes were glancing along the shimmering river; the " beloved square " was crowded with braves, — he saw their feathered crests wave and glisten ; the wind was blowing fresh and cool; the sun shone. And suddenly it was shining in his face, as it came up over the Great Smoky Moun tains, sending its first long slanting wintry beams through the narrow portal to the hearth where he had lain asleep before the ashes of the once " sacred fire," covered with the fresh ashes of last night's vigil, for they too were dead. He staggered to his feet and went out into the glistening dawn of this snowy sunlit day, hardly able to recon cile its aspect with the summer-tide scene

he had just quitted. Now and again he paused, half-bewildered, as if unfamiliar with the pathetic miseries of the old " waste town " — the scene in his mind savored far more of reality.

The necessity of caring for the pack-horse, perhaps better than aught else, served to restore his faculties. He found it easy now to climb down the jagged face of the bluffs of the river bank, whence the snow had vanished, for in the changeable south ern climate a sudden thaw had begun in the earlier hours and now the warm sun was setting all the trees and eaves adrip. As he stood below the cliff on the sandy slope whence the snow had slipped down into the river, the volume of which the storm of last night would much increase after the long drought of the summer, he carefully exam ined the horse to ascertain what injuries he might have sustained ; a few abrasions on the right flank seemed to be all, until the animal moved, a bit stiffly with the near fore leg. This attracted Barnett's attention to a gash on the knee received doubtless when the horse first fell on the ground, — a queer gash, long, jagged, unaccountable,

as if it had been made by a dull blade. Glancing down to search the gravel, the pack-man discerned, half-imbedded in the sand, the edge of a fragment of a knife, a scalping-knife, broken half in two; and there, lying not three yards away, was a handle attached to a belt heavily wrought with roanoke, — only a bit of the belt, — and the other half of the knife.

The pack-man's hand trembled and his florid cheek went pale, for these lay just under the sharp edge of a huge fragment of rock that had evidently fallen from the cliff above, breaking the blade and holding the belt fast.

How long he stood and stared he did not know. For a time he heard without realiz ing the significance of the sounds the whoops and shouts of his comrades, wildly racing back through the old " waste town" in search of him; but although in the strenu ous duty of his rescue they would venture to pass it in broad daylight, no ardor of per suasion could induce them to linger there to investigate the locality of his find, or to aid in moving the rock and exploring the grotto that had evidently proved a sepulchre.

On the contrary, they deemed the discov ery might be resented by the Indians as in trusive, and, keeping the secret, they made haste to get out of the country with even more speed than their wont. Cuthbert Bar-nett, however, carried his information to the authorities in Charlestown, who, promptly acting upon it, solved the mystery of the fate of the cheera-taghe.

Since peace with the Cherokees was be coming more and more precarious, some satisfaction was experienced by the Royal Governor of South Carolina, James Glen, at that time, in being able to urge upon the attention of the head-men of the tribe the fact that, although the two white strangers had obviously been captured in the act of robbing Cherokee soil of its gold, they had as evidently been unarmed, and the Irish man, a British subject, had been shot down by one of the cheera-taghe, for there was the bullet still imbedded firmly in the sternum of his broad chest. Thus a political crisis, which the event had threatened, was averted.

Despite the evil chance that had befallen the gold-seekers, now widely bruited abroad, stealthy efforts were ever and anon made

by the hardy frontier prospectors of those days, already busy in the richer deposits of the Ay rate division of the Cherokee coun try, to pan also the sands of the banks of the Tennessee; but the yield here was never again worth the work, and the interest in the possibility of securing " pay gravel" in this region died out, until the later excite ments of the discovery of the precious metal in a neighboring locality, Coca Creek, dur ing the last century.

The old " waste town " long remained a ruin, and at last fell away to a mere mem ory.

THE BEWITCHED BALL-STICKS
THE BEWITCHED BALL-STICKS

AT no time in the history of mankind, ex cept during that brief Paradisiac courtship in the Garden of Eden, has the heart of a lover been altogether unvexed by the pre sence, or even the sheer suspicion, of that baleful being commonly denominated " an other." Here, however, it would seem that the field must needs be almost as clear. The aspect of the world was as if yet young; the swan, long ago driven from the rivers, still snowily drifted down the silver Ten nessee ; the deer, the bear, the buffalo, the wolf in countless hordes roamed at will throughout the dense primeval wildernesses; the line of Cherokee towns along the banks represented almost the only human habita tions for many hundred miles, but to Tus-ka-sah the country seemed to groan under a surplus of population, for there yet dwelt right merrily at loco Town the youthful Amoyah, the gayest of all gay birds, and a

280 THE BEWITCHED BALL-STICKS

painful sense of the superfluous pressed upon the brain at the very sight of him.

This trait of frivolity was to Tus-ka-sah the more revolting, since he himself was of a serious cast of mind and possessed of fac ulties, rare in an Indian, which are called " fine business capacity." He was esteemed at an English trading-house down on the Eupharsee River as the best " second man " in any of the towns ; this phrase " second man " expressing the united functions of al derman, chief of police, chairman of boards of public improvements, and the various executive committees of civilization. His were municipal duties, — the apportionment of community labor, the supervision of the building of houses and the planting of crops, the distribution of public bounty, the trans action of any business of loco Town with vis itors whom individual interest might bring thither. So well did he acquit himself when these errands involved questions of com mercial policy that the English traders were wont to declare that Tus-ka-sah, the Terra pin, had " horse sense " — which certainly was remarkable in a terrapin !

His clear-headed qualities, however, val-

THE BEWITCHED BALL-STICKS 281

ued commercially, seemed hardly calculated to adorn the fireside. In sensible cumbrous silence and disastrous eclipse he could only contemplate with dismayed aversion the pal pable effect of Amoyah's gay sallies of wit, his fantastic lies, his vainglorious boastings, and his wonderful stories, which seemed always to enchant his audience, the house hold of the damsel to whom in civilized par lance they were both paying their addresses. These audiences were usually large, and far too lenient in the estimation of Tus-ka-sah. First there was present, of course, Amoyah himself, seeming a whole flock instead of one Pigeon. Then must be counted Alt-sasti, who although a widow was very young, and as slight, as lissome, as graceful as the "wreath" which her name signified. She was clad now in her winter dress of otter skins, all deftly sewn together so that the fur might lie one way, the better to enable the fabric to shed the rain ; the petticoat was longer than the summer attire of doe skin, for although the tinkle of the metal " bell buttons " of her many garters might be heard as she moved, only the anklets were visible above her richly beaded moccasins.

282 THE BEWITCHED BALL-STICKS

She seldom moved, however; sitting beside the fire on a buffalo rug, she monotonously strung rainbow-hued beads for hours at a time. Her glossy, straight black hair was threaded with a strand of opaque white beads passing through the coils, dressed high, and copiously anointed with bear's oil, and on her forehead she wore a single pendant wrought of the conch-shell, ivory-white and highly polished. She maintained a busy silence, but the others of the group — her father, sometimes her mother and grandmother and the younger sisters and brothers — preserved no such semblance of gravity, and indulged in appreciative chuckles responsive to Amoyah's jests, idly watching him with twinkling eyes as long as he would talk.

It would be difficult to say how long this might be, for there were no windows to the winter houses of the Cherokees; in point of architecture these structures resembled the great dome-shaped council-house, plastered within and without with red clay ; the floor was some three feet lower than the surface of the ground out side, and the exit fashioned with a narrow winding passage before reaching the outlet of the door. The sun might rise or set; the night might come or go; no token how the hour waxed or waned could penetrate this seclusion. The replenishing of the fire on the chimneyless hearth in the centre of the floor afforded the only comment on the passage of time. Its glow gave to view the red walls; the curious designs of the painted interior of the buffalo hides stretched upon them, by way of decoration ; the cane di vans or couches that were contrived to run all around the circular apartment, and on which were spread skins of bear and pan ther and wolves, covering even the heads of the slumbering members of the household, for the Cherokees slept away much of the tedious winter weather.

The fire would show, too, how gayly bedight and feather-crested was Amoyah, wearing a choice garb of furs; — often, so great was his vanity, his face was elaborately painted as if for some splendid festive oc casion, a dance or the ball-play, instead of merely to impress with his magnificence this simple domestic circle. Tus-ka-sah dated the events that followed from one night when

this facial decoration of his rival was even more fantastic than usual. Like a fish was one side of the young Cherokee's profile; the other in glaring daubs of white and black and red craftily represented the head of a woodpecker. The effect in front was the face of a nondescript monster, that only a gleeful laughing eye, and now and then a flash of narrow white teeth, identified as the jovial Amoyah, the Pigeon of loco.

The snow lay on the ground without, he said as he shook a wreath of it from a fold of his fur and it fell hissing among the coals. The shadows were long, he told them, for the moon was up and the world was 'dimly white and duskily blue. The wind was abroad, and indeed they could hear the swirl of its invisible wings as it swooped past; the boughs of the trees clashed together and ice was in the Tennessee River. The winter had come, he declared.

Not yet, Tus-ka-sah pragmatically averred. There would be fine weather yet.

For the snowfall so early in the season was phenomenal and the red leaves were still clinging to the trees.

Had they been together among men

Amoyah would not have cared enough for the subject to justify contention, but in the presence of women he would suffer no con tradiction. He must needs be paramount, — the infinitely admired! He shook his head.

The winter had surely come, he insisted. Why, he argued, the bears knew, — they always knew ! And already each had walked the round with his shadow.

For in the approach of winter, in the light of the first mystic, icicled moon, the night when it reaches its full, a grotesque pageant is afoot in that remote town of the bears, immemorially fabled to be hidden in the dense coverts of the Great Smoky Moun tains, — the procession of the bears, each walking with his shadow, seven times around the illuminated spaces of the " beloved square."

The bears knew undoubtedly, the " sec ond man," the man of facts and method and management, soberly admitted. But how did Amoyah know that already they had trod den those significant circles, each with his shadow ? He smiled triumphant in his in controvertible logic.

And now Amoyah's face was wonderful

to view, whether as a fish on one side or a woodpecker on the other, with that most human expression of surprise and indigna tion and aversion as distinctly limned upon it as if in pigments, for he loved the " sec ond man's " facts no more than the " second man " loved his fancies. How did he know, forsooth ? Because, Amoyah hardily de clared, he himself had witnessed the march, — he had been permitted to behold that weird and grotesque progress!

He took note of the blank silence that en sued upon this startling asseveration. Then emboldened to add circumstance to sheer statement he protested, " I attended the ceremony by invitation. I had a place in the line of march — I walked beside the Great Bear as his shadow ! "

For, according to tradition, each bear, burly, upright in the moonlight, follows the others in Indian file, but at the side of each walks his shadow, and that shadow is not the semblance of a bear, but of a Chero kee Indian !

Now, as everybody has heard, the bears were once a band of Cherokee Indians, but wearying of the rigors and artificialities of

tribal civilization they took to the woods, became bears, and have since dwelt in se clusion.

The thoughts, however, persistently reach out for the significance of the fact that in the tradition of this immemorial progress each creature is accompanied by the shadow, not of the thing that he is, but of the higher entity that he was designed to be.

Whether this inference is merely the me chanical deduction of a lesson, or a subtlety of moralizing, with a definite intention, on the part of the Cherokees, always past-mas ters in the intricacies of symbolism, it is difficult to determine, but the bears are cer tainly not alone in this illustration of retro gression, and memory may furnish many an image of a lost ideal to haunt the paths of beings of a higher plane.

The picture was before the eyes of all the fireside group, — the looming domes of the Great Smoky Mountains, where the clouds, white and opaline, hung in the intervals be neath the ultimate heights; the silences of the night were felt in the dense dark lonely forest that encompassed the open spaces of that mysterious city, with the conical

thatched roofs of its winter houses and the sandy stretch of the " beloved square; " — and there was the line of bears, clumsy, heavy-footed, lumbering, ungainly, and be side each the feather-crested similitude of what he had been, alert, powerful, gifted with human ingenuity, the craft of weapons, mental endowment, and an immortal soul, — so they went in the wintry moonlight!

There was naught in this detail of the annual procession of the bears, always tak ing place before the period of their hiber nation, that surprised or angered Tus-ka-sah ; but that they should break from their ancient law, their established habit of ex-clusiveness, single out Amoyah (of all the people in the world), summon him to attend their tribal celebration, and participate in their parade, as the shadow of Eeon-a, the Great Bear, — this passed the bounds of the possibilities. This fantasy had not the shreds of verisimilitude!

Yet even while he argued within him self Tus-ka-sah noted the old warrior's gaze fix spellbound upon Amoyah, the hands of Altsasti petrify, the bead in one, the mo tionless thread in the other. The eyes of

the more remote of the group, who were seated on rugs around the fire, glistened wide and startled, in the shadow, as Amoyah proceeded to relate how it had chanced.

A frosty morning he said it was, and he was out in the mountain a-hunting. He re peated the song which he had been singing, and the wind as it swirled about the house must have caught his voice and carried it far. It was a song chronicling the deeds of the Great Bear, and had a meaningless re frain, " Eeon-a, Ha-hoo-jah ! Eeon-a, Ha-hoo-jah!" But when he reached the advent upon the scene of the secondary hero, the Great Bear himself, very polite, speaking excellent Cherokee (" since we are alone," he said), very recognizant of the merits of Amoyah,— the fame of which indeed was represented to have resounded through the remotest seclusions of the ursine realm, — fiction though it all obviously was, the man of facts could no longer endure this magni fication of his rival.

" The great Eeon-a said all that to you ? " he sneered. " The fire-water at the trading-house makes your heart very strong and your tongue crooked. This sounds to me like

the language of a simple seequa, not the Great Bear — a mere bit of an opossum! "

Amoyah paused with a sudden gasp; He was not without an aggressive temper, albeit, persuaded of his own perfection, he feared no rival, and least of all Tus-ka-sah.

" You, Tus-ka-sah," he retorted angrily, " have evidently strongly shaken hands with the discourse of the opossum, speaking its language like the animal itself, and also the wolfish English. You have too many tongues, and, more than all, the deceitful, forked tongue of the snake, which is not agreeable to the old beloved speech. For myself, the Great Bear made me welcome in the only language that does not make my heart weigh heavy, — the elegant Cherokee language."

The spellbound listeners had broken out with irritated protests against the interrup tion, and Tus-ka-sah said no more.

As the blasts went sonorously over the house and the flames swirled anew into the murky atmosphere of the interior, a weird, half-smothered voice suddenly invaded the restored quiet of the hearthstone: "Eeon-a, Ha-hoo-jah ! Eeon-a, Ha-hoo-jah ! "

Like an echo the barbaric chant vibrated through the room. One of the sleepers, a half - grown youth, had semi - consciously caught the familiar refrain and sang it in that strange uncanny voice of slumber. The tones gave fitting effect to the gro tesque details of the supernatural adventure, and as Tus-ka-sah rose and surlily took his way toward the door his departure did not attract even casual notice from the listeners, hanging enthralled upon the words of the Great Eeon-a, so veraciously repeated for their behoof. Their eyes showed intent even in the murky gloom and glistened lus trous in the alternate fitful flare ; the red walls seemed to recede and advance as the flames rose and fell; the sleeping boy on the broad bed-place stirred uneasily, fling ing now and again a restless arm from out the panther skins in which he was enveloped, and ever and anon his cry, " Eeon-a, Ha-hoo-jah! Eeon-a, ffa-hoo-jah!" punctuated the impressive dramatic tones of the racon teur.

The next instant Tus-ka-sah was in the utter darkness of the narrow tortuous little passage, but after threading this he came

out of the doorway into the keen chill air of a snowy world, the scintillations of frosty stars, the languid, glamourous radiance of the yellow moon, low in the sky, and his accustomed mental atmosphere of the plain est of plain prose. His thoughts were with the group he had just left, and he marveled if no influence could be brought to reduce the prestige with which the immaterial chief of the bears, the fabled Eeon-a, had contrived to invest the illusory Amoyah.

Tus-ka-sah's expectations concerning the weather were promptly justified. A contin ual dripping from the roofs and trees per vaded the early hours of the morning, and soon the snow was all gone here in the valley; even the domes of the mountains so early whitened with drifts showed now a bare, dark, sketch-like outline against the horizon and above-the garnet tint of the massed sere boughs of the forests of the slopes. A warm sun shone. Not a summer bird was yet lingering, but here and there a crisp red leaf winged the blue sky as gallantly as any crested cardinal of them all. The town of loco was now astir, and Tus-ka-sah noted how the softening of the

air had brought out the inhabitants from their winter houses. Children played about the doorways; boys in canoes shot down the shimmering reaches of the river; warriors congregated in the council-house and the half-open buildings surrounding the " be loved square," and in its sunny sandy spaces sundry old men were placidly engaged in the game of " roll the bullet."

It was at this group that Tus-ka-sah looked with an intent gaze and a sort of

o

indignant question in his manner, and pre sently an elderly Cherokee, one of the cheera-taghe of the town, detached himself from it and came toward him. Despite this show of alacrity Cheesto distinctly winced as he contemplated the sullen and averse mien of his client or parishioner, for the relation in which Tus-ka-sah stood to ward him partook of the characteristics of both. The professional wiseacre, however, made shift to recover himself.

" I will tell you what you have come to tell me," the prophet said quickly. " The spell on Amoyah does not work."

Tus-ka-sah assented surlily, gazing mean while at the face of the conjurer. It was a

face in which the eyes were set so close together as to suggest a squint, although they were not crossed. He had an uncer tain and dilatory tread, the trait of one who hesitates, and decides in doubt, and forthwith repents ; being in his prophetic character an appraiser of the probable, and the sport of the possible. He wore many beads in strings around his neck, and big earrings of silver, heavy and costly. His fur garments reached long and robe-like almost to his feet, the shaggy side of the pelt out ward, the weather being damp, for when it was dry and cold it was customary to wear the fur turned inward.

The wise man had been recently unfor tunate in his sorcery. The corn crop had been cut short by reason of a lack of rain which he had promised should fall in June. He had justified the drought, in the opinion of most of the Indians, by feigning illness and taking to his bed; for by these it was be lieved that if he had been able to be up and about his ordinary vocations the preposter ous conduct of the weather must needs have been restrained. The fields about loco had suffered especially, and Tus-ka-sah, as the

chief business man of that town, had mani fested half veiled suspicions that the art of the conjurer was incompetent; this ren dered Cheesto particularly solicitous to suc ceed when his magic had been invoked to reduce the attractions of Amoyah in the eyes of Altsasti and turn her heart toward Tus-ka-sah. For among the Indians the lives of the weather-prophets were not safe from the aggrieved agriculturists, and there are authentic cases in which the cheera-taghe suffered death by tribal law as false con jurers. Cheesto fixed an anxious gaze upon his interlocutor as Tus-ka-sah rehearsed, by way of illustrating how worthless were the charms wrought, the unsubstantial fiction that had so beguiled the 'fancy of Altsasti, and posed Amoyah in the splendid guise of the representative of the great Eeon-a in the shadow-march of the bears.

The fate of the over-wise is ever the sor rowful dispensation. The fool may be merry and irresponsible. Cheesto was at his wit's end. With that unlucky drought in June to confront him, and dealing with the sharp business man of loco, who exacted his due in the exchange of the Fates as rigorously

as if in a merely mundane market, the jeop ardy of the magician was great and his dis credit almost assured.

Old Cheesto set his jaw firmly. Somehow, somewhere, something must be wrought that would place Amoyah at a disadvantage and bring ridicule upon him. No great matter, it might be said, to compass the change of a fickle woman's mind, to disconcert a giddy young man. But how? Cheesto was aweary of his own incantations and his inef fectual spells. He would fain lend Fate a muscular hand.

This thought was uppermost in his mind for several days, even when he went with the other cheera-taghe of loco to share in the conjurations and incantations of the pre liminary ceremonials of the Ball-Play, with out which success would never be antici pated, for a great match between the towns of loco and Niowee was impending.

This game was usually played in the mid summer or fall, but it would seem that the unseasonable cold weather was well suited for such violent exercise and the severe physical training which preceded it, and al though Amoyah noticed ice in the river as

he dashed in for the ceremonial plunge which accompanies the incantations, he re membered the fact for a different reason than discomfort.

The eighty ball-players of loco stood in a row near the bank, submerged to the knees. They had gone in with a tumultuous rush, and with their faces painted, their heads crested with feathers, clad fantastically and gorgeously but scantily, they were hold ing their ball-sticks high in the air with an eager grasp,—all except Amoyah. Although still in his place in the line, he was looking over his shoulder with an amazed and startled gaze.

For there upon the bank, as if struck from his hand in the confusion and turmoil of first entering the water, lay his ball-sticks. He seemed about to return for them, as the implement of the game must be dipped also in the water at the appropriate moment of the incantation. But old Cheesto, the Rabbit, motioned him to forbear lest by this unprecedented quitting of the line during the ceremonial the efficacy of the spell be annulled; he himself stooped down and picked up the ball-sticks. Then, notwith-

standing his age and his fierce rheumatism, notwithstanding his long and cumbrous robe of buffalo skin, the skirt of which he seemed to clutch with difficulty, he plunged into the icy water, waded out to the young man, handed him the ball-sticks, and regained the bank just as the other cheera-taghe standing at the margin of the river began the incan tations supposed to influence the success of the competition.

This Indian game, which has left its name on one of the watercourses of Tennessee, Ball-Play Creek, required a level space of some five or six hundred yards in length but no other preparation of the ground. At one end, in the direction of Niowee, two tall poles were fixed firmly in the earth about three yards apart, and slanting out ward. At the end toward loco a similar goal was prepared. Every time the ball should be thrown over either goal the play would count one for the proximate town, and the game was of twelve or twenty points according to compact, the catcher of the twentieth ball being entitled to especial honor. It was of course the object of each side to throw the ball over the goal toward their own town, and to prevent it from going in the direction of the town of the opposing faction.

All the morning crowds of Cherokees of all ages and both sexes had been gather ing from the neighboring towns, and were congregated in the wide spaces about the course at Ioco. These fields had earlier been planted in corn, but the harvest had stripped the plain, and now the trampling of hundreds of feet erased all vestiges of the growth except for the yellow-gray tint of the stubble, spreading out on every side to the brown of the dense fallen leaves on the slopes where the forests began to climb the mountain sides. Here and there fires were kindled where some spectator felt the keen chill of the approaching winter, and more than one meal was in progress, — perhaps such groups had come from far. Pack-horses were in evidence laden with rich garments of fur, various peltry, blankets, valuable gear of every sort to be staked on the result of the game, and soon the men were betting heavily. All the various tones of the gamut were on the air, — the deep bass guttural laugh of the braves; the shrill

callow yelping of boys; the absent-minded bawl of spoiled pappooses interested in the stir, but with an ever-recurrent recollection of the business of vocally disciplining their patient mothers ; the keen treble chatter of women, — all were suddenly resolved into a strong dominant chord of sound as a tre mendous shout arose upon the appearance of the ball-players of Ioco. Fresh from the river, they made a glittering show with the tossing feathers of their crested heads, their faces painted curiously and fantastically in white, the bright tints of their gaudy though scanty raiment, their bare arms and legs sup pled with unguents and shining in the sun. This note of welcome had hardly died away and the echo of the encompassing moun tains grown silent, whesi an agitated murmur of excitement went sibilantly through the throng.

A cloud of dust was approaching in the distance, heralding a band of men. A new sound invoked the echoes. The breath was held to hear it. The throb of a drum — faint — far. And here thunderously beat ing, hard at hand, overpowering all lesser sounds, the drums of Ioco responded. To

the vibrations of these sonorous earthen cylinders, the sticks plied with a will on the heads of wet deerskins tightly stretched, the ball-players of Niowee advanced. In a diagonal direction and at a sturdy trot they came for a space, — a sudden halt ensued, and eighty pairs of muscular feet smote tumultuously on the ground. Then once more forward diagonally, at that swinging jaunty pace, and the stamping pause as be fore. The sound seemed to shake the ground, the impact of the feet with the earth was heard despite the turmoil of the drums ; the stamping vibrations were felt in the midst of the stir of the crowds, and now in the nearer approach the individual faces could be distinguished, wildly painted ; the ath letic figures, gaudily clad and barbarically decorated; the ball-sticks, held aloft in a sort of rhythmic vibration as if quivering for a chance at the ball; and fourscore wild young voices howled defiance at Ioco Town, whose youth in return howled its municipal pride, failing only with failing breath.

They were all in the course at last. The judges, elderly warriors and absolutely im partial, chosen from towns which had no

interest at stake in the match, were seated on a little knoll, commanding a view of the ground, but at a sufficient distance to be in no danger from a maladroit handling of the ball. This was made of deerskin, stuffed hard with hair, and sewn up with deer sinews. The ball-sticks, of which each player owned his pair, were also partly made of deerskin, the two scoops or ladles being fash ioned of a network of thongs on a wooden hoop, each furnished with a handle of hick ory three feet long, worked together with a thong of deerskin to catch the ball between the rackets, — it being of course prohibited to catch the ball in the hand.

The drums beat furiously; the word was given; the ball was flung high in the air in the middle of the course, and the next in stant one hundred and sixty young athletes rushed together with a mighty shock the force of which seemed to shake the ground. Some fell and were trampled in the crush; others madly clutched one another, friend or foe, with the ill-aimed ball-sticks, inflict ing a snapping hurt like a bite, — a wound by no means to be despised. One, an ex pert, sent the ball with an artful twirl •

through the air toward the loco goal, and in the midst of a shout that rent the sky the whole rout of players went frantically flying after it, whirling with an incredible swiftness and agility when it was caught midway, and hurled back toward Niowee with a force as if it had been flung from a catapult. Here and there individual play ers in the frenzied chase made wonderful records of leaps in their efforts to catch the ball, springing into the air with a surpris ing strength and elasticity, and a lightness as of creatures absolutely without weight.

A good match they were playing; for more than half an hour neither side was permitted by the other to score a single point. The ball seemed for a time as if it were awing forever, and would fall to the ground no more. The casualties were many; almost always after one of those sudden rushes together of both factions that had a tremendous momentum as of galloping squadrons, the ground would show as the moving masses receded half a dozen figures prone upon the course ; one with a^broken arm perhaps ; another badly snapped by the inartistically plied ball-sticks of friend or

foe and crawling off with a bloody pate ; sometimes another lying quite still, evidently stunned and to be hastily dragged off the course by spectators, before another stam pede of the ball-players crush the life out of the unconscious and prostrate wight. Nev ertheless only the normal interest, which however was very great, appertained to the match until at a crisis a strange thing hap pened, inexplicable then, and perhaps never fully understood.

The ball was flying toward the Niowee goal and the whole field was in full run after it. The blow that had impelled it had been something tremendous. A shout of triumph was already welling up from the throat of all Niowee, for to prevent the scoring of a point in its favor it would seem that there must be a thing afoot whose fleetness could exceed the speed of a thing awing.

Amoyah, the deftest runner of all the Tennessee River country, was foremost in the crown of swift athletes; presently he was detached by degrees from it; now he was definitely in advance; and soon, spurt ing tremendously, he had so neared the

Niowee goal that the ball just above must needs pass over it if a spring might not enable him to capture it at the last mo ment. As agile as a deer, and as light as a bird, he leaped into the air, both arms upstretched, holding the rackets aloft and ready. He was a far-famed player, and even now the loco spectators were shouting, Amoyah needs must win !

A mysterious silence fell suddenly. They all saw what had happened. There could be no mistake. The rackets parted at the propitious moment to receive the ball. The netting closed about it. And then, as if it had met with no impediment whatever, the ball passed through the stanch web of thongs and over the poles, and falling to the ground counted one for Niowee.

The spectators from that town in their astonishment forgot to shout. The onrush-ing crowd of players, bearing down upon Amoyah, having intended to force him to drop the ball, which he had seemed predes tined to catch, or to throw it so ill as to deliver it into the power of Niowee still to secure the point, could not arrest their own momentum, and went over the startled

306 THE BEWITCHED BALL-STICKS

and dumfounded player in a swift dash, leaving him prone upon the ground. He was on his feet in an instant, his physical faculties rallying promptly, but so bewil dered and doubtful that he had but one definite mental process, the resolve to regain for loco the point he had so mysteriously lost. Twice afterward his fine playing fo cused the attention of the crowd. Twice their plaudits of his skill rang through the vibrating air. Then the ball, hardly checked by the web of his racket, passed through the ball-sticks, and all realized their be witchment.

Amoyah heard the gossip afloat concern ing the matter before he had well quitted the course. The Great Bear had torn the net of the ball-sticks with his claw, one brave was telling another as he passed, be cause Amoyah had unveraciously boasted that he had walked by invitation in the pro cession of the bears during their annual march with their shadows at their hidden mysterious town in the Great Smoky Moun tains.

Amoyah paused, tired, excited, panting, and critically examined the web. Surely

THE BEWITCHED BALL-STICKS 307

enough the interlacing thongs had parted in twain in two straight lines, invisible save on close inspection, as deftly and as evenly severed as if cut with a keen knife.

It was late in the day. The sun was now on a westering slant. The parties of spec tators were breaking up, some to journey homeward, others going into the town with friends. The place that the crowd had occu pied had that peculiarly dreary aspect char acteristic of a deserted pleasure ground. Trampled heavily it was, and the charred remnant of a fire showed black here and there; broken bits of food were scattered in places where feasting had been ; a great gourd that had held some gallons of water lay shattered on the ground at his feet; a group at a distance were doubtfully retra cing their steps, searching for something they had lost; at the farthest limits a wolf like a dog, or a dog like a wolf, was gnaw ing at a bone, and snarling as he gnawed. It was all frowzy, jaded, forlorn.

Somehow suddenly he had a sense of freshness, an illumination, as it were a vision, of the early morning light striking through a network of bare trees upon the

308 THE BEWITCHED BALL-STICKS

shimmering reaches of a river. And there on the bank lay his ball-sticks, — quite good and sound then, he would have staked his life. And now a picture was before him, — being a man of fancy, he thought in pictures, — a picture of old Cheesto the Rabbit holding the ball-sticks half hidden in the folds of his great fur robe and wad ing out into the ice-cold water to restore them. And old Cheesto, he reflected, was one of the cheera-taghe of loco, and could work a spell quite as well as the Great Bear, who had gone to bed for the winter two weeks ago, and had not heard of ball-sticks within the memory of man, — perhaps not since he was a Cherokee himself, and play ing with the rest on the course at Tennessee Town.

In fact, old Cheesto, in common with many men not Cherokees, cared little for the public weal when it interfered with pri vate interest. But he had not realized how much he had jeopardized the success of loco Town in cutting the netting of the ball-sticks. He had imagined the incompleteness of the racket would merely show Amoyah as incompetent, render his play futile and ineffective, and discredit him with both friend and foe. Never, however, had the play of any one man been so important and conspicuous as his to-day when the be witched ball-sticks became the salient fea ture and the living tradition of the match between loco and Niowee. For despite these points, thus lost by supernatural agency to Niowee, the bewitchment of the ball-sticks only served to illustrate the superior skill of the loco team, and to embellish their victory.

Amoyah had nothing but his imagination to support his theory, but it seemed singu larly credible to Altsasti, to whom he re hearsed it, finding her seated on the ground before the door of her winter house in great dreariness of spirit, that he should in play ing so well have won nothing and merely jeopardized the game.

"I am afraid of that Great Bear/' she declared, eying the ball-sticks askance as he came up.

Then revealing his theory of the spell that old Cheesto had wrought upon him in Tus-ka-sah's interest, Amoyah proposed a counter-spell which would defeat Tus-ka-sah.

" But Cheesto can still send you trouble if you have a wife," she argued.

" Ah, no," the specious Amoyah replied. " Everybody knows that a man's wife makes him all the trouble that he needs."

To save him from these woes devised by others Altsasti undertook to give him all the trouble he needed. But he seemed quite cheerful in the prospect, and as she cooked the supper within doors he sat at the en trance, much at home, singing, " Eeon-a y Ha-hoo-jah f Eeon-a, Ha-hoo-jah ! "

Tus-ka-sah upbraided the magician with the result of this victory, by which he was defeated. And the wise man threw up eyes and hands at his ingratitude.

" I set the Great Bear after Amoyah for you! I made the Eeon-a acquainted with his boastful lies, and he bewitched Amoyah's ball-sticks that his fine play might come to nothing."

Very little to the purpose, the disaffected man of facts reflected, remembering the im pression produced by his rival's display of skill. Somehow Amoyah seemed beyond the reach of logic. " Why did you not instead bewitch the woman ? " Tus-ka-sah asked.

But this wiliest of the cheera-taghe shook his head.

"If she had been a mere woman/' he said. " But a widow is a witch herself."

" Eeon-a, Ha-hoo-jah ! Eeon-a, Ha-hoo-jah ! " sang Amoyah at the door of the winter house.

Eeon-a, the Great Bear, made no sign and slept in peace at his town house in the mountains.

And since then, as always before, under the first icy moon of the winter the com pany of bears with their feather-crested shadows take up their mysterious march seven times around the " beloved square " of their ancient secluded town in the Great Smoky Mountains, which it is said may be seen to this day — by all who can find it!

THE VISIT OF THE TURBULENT GRANDFATHER

THE VISIT OF THE TURBU LENT GRANDFATHER

IT was long remembered in the Cherokee nation. Their grandfather came to the Overhill towns on the banks of the Ten nessee River in a most imperious frame of mind.

" Give me a belt! " he cried in irrelevant response to every gracious overture of hos pitality. For although presents were heaped upon him, the official belt of the Cherokee nation was not among them, and he cast them all aside as mere baubles.

Even the clever subterfuges of that mas ter of statecraft, the half-king, Atta-Kulla-Kulla, might not avail. " N'tschutti ! " (Dear friend) he said once in eager propi tiation ; " Gooch Hi lehelecheu ? " (Does your father yet live ?) He spoke in a gentle voice and slowly, the Delaware language being unaccustomed to his lips. " Tell the great sakimau I well remember him ! " And he laid a string of beads on the arm of the

quivering Lenape, for their grandfather was of that nationality.

But what flout of Fate was this? Not the coveted string of wampum, the official token, its significance not to be argued away, or overlooked, or mistaken — but instead a necklace of pearls, the fine fresh water gems of the region, so often men tioned by the elder writers and since held to be mythical or exaggeration of the pol ish of mere shell beads till the recent dis coveries have placed once more the yield of the Unio margaritiferus of the rivers of Tennessee on metropolitan markets.

A personal gift — of the rarest, it is true — but a mere trifle in the estimation of Tscholens, in comparison with that national recognition which he craved and which a tribe of warriors awaited.

The irate grandfather flung the glossy trinket from him down among the ashes of the fire, which glowed in the centre of the floor of the great council-house of the town of Citico, one of the dome-shaped buildings, plastered as usual within and without with richly tinted red clay. The flicker from the coals revealed the rows of posts that like

a colonnade upheld the roof; the cane-wrought divan encircling the apartment between these columns and the window-less walls; the astonished faces and feather-crested heads of the conclave of Chero kee chiefs from half a dozen towns as they clustered around the fire and stared at Tscholens.

The grave emotion in his face dignified its expression despite its savagery. Paradox ically the grandfather was young, slender, and, rated by any other standard than that of the Cherokees, an unusually tall people, would have been considered of fine height. His muscular arms were bare except for his heavy silver bracelets; a tuft of feathers quivered high on his head; his leggings were of deerskin, embroidered with parti colored quills of the porcupine, and his shirt was of fine sable fur. His voice was sono rously insistent.

"N'petcdogalgun! " (I am sent as a mes senger) he declared urgently. " Give me a belt."

He turned his flaming eyes directly upon Atta-Kulla-Kulla, himself in the prime of life now, in 1745, who it seemed must act

definitely under this coercion. He must either refuse to testify to the truth, which he knew, or involve his people, the Chero-kees, in a quarrel which did not concern them, of which a century was tired, between the Lenni Lenape and the Mengwe.

So long ago it had begun ! The Mengwe, hard pressed by other nations and long at war with the Lenape, besought peace of this foe, and that they would use their in fluence with the others. Usually women, prompted always by the losing side, pro tested against the further effusion of blood and went with intercessions from one fac tion to the other. This, in view of the number and devious interests of the war ring forces, was then impracticable, and therefore the Mengwe besought the Lenape to act as mediator for the occasion. Only so noted a race of warriors could afford this magnanimity, the Mengwe argued. It might impair the prestige of a less high-couraged and powerful tribe. And with these spe cious wiles the cat was duly belled.

But alas for the Lenape! Magnanimity is the most dangerous of all the virtues — to its possessor ! Presently the Mengwe

claimed to have conquered the Lenape in battle, and cited the well-known fact that they had inaugurated peace proposals. As the Mengwe confederation grew more pow erful they assumed all the arrogance of a protectorate. They sold the lands of their dependents. They resented all action of the Lenape on their own account. If the Lenape went to war on some quarrel of their mak ing, they had the Mengwe to reckon with as well as the enemy. As the years rolled by in scores, this fiction gradually assumed all the binding force of fact, till now it was felt that only by the avowal of the truth by some powerful tribe, both ancient and contemporary, such as the Cherokee, — who, although allied neither linguistically nor consanguineously, by some abstruse figment of Indian etiquette affected an affiliation to the Lenape and called them "grand father," — could their rightful independ ence be recognized, reestablished, and main tained. Therefore, " Give me a belt! " cried Tscholens pertinaciously, offering in ex change the official belt of the Delawares, or, as they were called, Lenni Lenape. Nothing less would content him. He

hardened himself as flint against all suave beguilements tending to effect a diversion of interest. He would not see the horse race. He would not " roll the bullet." He would not witness the game of chungke, expressly played in honor of his visit. He even refused to join in the dance, although young and nimble. But it chanced that the three circles were awhirl on the sandy spaces contiguous to the " beloved square " when the first break in the cohesion of his pertinacity occurred. The red sunset was widely aflare; the dizzy rout of the shad ows of the dancers, all gregarious and in tricately involved in the three circles, kept the moving figures company. These suc cessive circles, one within another, followed each a different direction in their revolu tions to the music of the primitive flute, fashioned of the bone of a deer (the tibia), and the stertorous sonorities of the earthen drums; and as the fantastically attired fig ures whirled around and around, their dull gray shadows whisked to and fro on the golden brown sand, all in the red sunset glow.

Tscholens, quitting the council-house,

glanced but indifferently at them and then away at the lengthening perspective of the azure mountains of the Great Smoky range. The harbingers of the twilight were ad vancing in a soft blue haze over the purple and garnet tinted slopes near at hand, their forests all leafless now, although the au tumn had lingered long, and the burnished golden days of the Indian summer were loath to go. Lights were springing up here and there in the town as the glow of the hearths of the dwellings, where supper was cooking, flickered out to meet on the thresh old the rays of the departing sun, which seemed to pause there for a farewell glance in at the open door. In the centre of the " beloved square" the fire which always burned here was slowly smouldering. It flung a red reflection on the front of the building devoted to the conferences of the aged councilors, painted a peaceful white and facing the setting sun. At this mo ment was emerging from it a figure which Tscholens had not before seen.

A man so old he was that even the In dian's back was bent. His face was of weird effect, for amid its many wrinkles

were streaks of parti-colored paint such as he had worn more than three quarters of a century earlier, when his fleet foot and the old war-trace were familiar. In common with all the Cherokees, his head was polled and bare save for a tuft, always spared to afford a'grasp for any hand bold enough and strong enough to take the scalp; but this lock, although still dense and full, was of a snowy whiteness, contrasting sharply with the red paint and belying the warlike aspect of the red-feathered crest that trembled and shivered with the infirmities of his step. A heavy robe of fur reached almost to his feet, and a mantle, curiously wrought of the iri descent feathers of the neck and breast of the wild turkey, bespoke his consequence and added to the singularity of his aspect; for Indians seldom attained such age in those wild days, the warriors being usually cut off in their prime. It is to be doubted if Tscholens had ever seen so old a man, for this was Tsiskwa of Citico, reputed then to be one hundred and ten years of age.

The step of the young grandfather, saun tering along, came to an abrupt halt. He stood staring, exclaiming to the Cherokee

warrior Savanukah, "Pennau wullihl Au-ween won gintsch pat ? " (Look yonder ! Who is that who has just come ?)

It was an eagle-like majesty which looked forth from the eyes of Tsiskwa of Citico, as he seated himself on the long cane-wrought divan, just within the entrance of the cabin on the eastern side of the " beloved square." Time can work but little change in such a spirit. An eagle, however old, is always an eagle.

The sage lifted one august claw and majestically waved it at the young Dela ware illau (war-captain) standing before him, while Savanukah turned away to join the dancers. " Lenni Lenape ? — I remem ber— I remember very well when you came from the West! "

Tscholens was not stricken with astonish ment, although that migration is held by investigators of pre-Columbian myths 11 to have occurred before the ninth century ! It was formerly a general trait among the Indians to use the first person singular in speaking of the tribe, and to avoid, even in its name, the plural termination. Tsiskwa went on with the tone of reminiscence rather

than legendary lore, and with an air of bated rancor, as of one whose corroding grievance still works at the heart, to describe how the Lenni Lenape crossed the Mississippi and fell upon the widespread settlements of the Alligewi (or Tallegwi) Indians — considered identical with the Cherokee (Tsullakee) — and warred with them many years in folly, in futility, in hopeless defeat.

He lifted his eyes and gazed at the sun. A curve of pride steadied his old lips. His face was as resolute, as victorious, in looking backward as ever it had been in vaunting forecast. His was the temperament that al ways saw in prophecy or retrospect what he would wish to see. And that sun, now go ing down, had lighted him all his life along a path of conscious triumph.

And then, he continued, the Lenni Len ape, after years of futile war, combined with the Mengwe, 12 and before their united force the Cherokee retired into the impreg nable stronghold of their mountains, their beautiful country, the pride of the world!

He waved his hand toward the landscape — lying out there in the lustre of its ex quisite coloring, in the clarified air and the

enhancing sunset; in the ideality of the contour of its majestic lofty mountains; in the splendor of its silver rivers, its phenome nally lush forests, its rich soil — pitying the rest of the world who must needs dwell else where.

" And here/' he went on, " the European found me two centuries ago."

He proceeded to narrate the advent of De Soto and his followers into the country of the Cherokees, embellishing his account with unrecorded particulars of their stay, especially in their digging for gold and sil ver, in which enterprise he himself seemed to have actively participated — only some two centuries previous!

Tscholens, listening, looked about ab sently at the " beloved square," which was vacant, with its open piazza-like building on each of the four sides. Two or three men were talking in the " war cabin," painted a vivid red. On the western side of the square the roof of the " holy cabin " showed dark against a lustrous reach of the shimmering river; despite the shadows within the broad entrance, the " sacred white seat" and the red clay transverse wall that partitioned off

the sanctum sanctorum were plainly visible, but all was empty, deserted — the cheera-taghe had departed for the night.

As Tsiskwa paused to cough, the Dela ware, suddenly taking heart of grace, ob served that it had always been the boast of the Lenni Lenape that they were the first tribe to welcome the European, the Dutch, to the land that they now called New York.

Whereupon Tsiskwa retorted in a tem pest of racking coughs that, whoever wel comed the Europeans here or there, it was no credit that the Lenape should be so for ward to appropriate it! The white people were not the friends of the red man. They wanted the whole country. FinaUy they would have it.

" Mattapewiwak nik schwannakwak!" (The white people are a deceiving lot!) said Tscholens, seeking some common ground on which they could meet with a mutual sen timent.

And at once Tsiskwa was all animation and as aggressive as at twenty. Well, in deed, might the Lenape say that! They were forever an easy prey — not only of the astute Europeans, but of the simple Indian

as well. For a hundred years they had been the dupe of the Mengwe ! As the mind of Tsiskwa dwelt on the various subtleties of the diplomatic attitude of the Mengwe to ward the Lenape, its craft so appealed to him that his lips curved with relish; a smile irradiated his blurred eyes and intensified his wrinkles; his cough, shaking the folds of his outer fur garments above his wasted chest, mingled with his gay chuckle of mer riment, as young as a boy's, while he cried, " Iroquois ! Iroquois ! " — the characteristic exclamation of the Mengwe confederation, whence they take their modern and popular name, and signifying, " I have spoken! I have spoken!"

At the familiar and detested sound the Lenape suddenly smote his breast with his braceleted arms, and a strong cry involun tarily broke from him — so poignant, so bitter, so shrill, that it sounded high above the bleating flute, the guttural drone of the drum, the vibratory throb of the dancing feet, and brought the pastime to a sudden close. In another moment the "beloved square " was filled with crowds of the Chero-kees and their huddling shadows, all a med-

ley in the last red suffusions of the sinking sun. To the tumult of eager, anxious, polite questions, Tscholens faltered to Savanukah, who had hastily returned : —

" N'schauwihilla ! N'dagotschi ! Lo-wanneunk undchen! " (I am fainting! I am cold! The wind comes from the north !)

He looked ill enough, but Savanukah's sharp eyes scanned suspiciously the aged countenance of Tsiskwa of Citico. Tsiskwa was, however, the image of venerable and respected innocence. His aged lips mumbled one upon the other silently. He hardly seemed to take note of the tumult. When the afflicted " grandfather " was being led away from the scene, Savanukah loitered to ask, with well-couched phrase and the show of deep reverence, what had been the tenor of the discourse, and it was with a galvanic jerk that the old man appeared to gather his faculties together.

"Of what did he talk?" Tsiskwa fixed august eyes upon Savanukah as he repeated the query. " Am / to remember of what young men talk ? — the mad young men ? — mad, mad — all quite mad ! "

For not to Savanukah, surely, would he

confess; and although because of this reti cence that discerning party believed that Tsiskwa had wittingly wounded their emo tional " grandfather " in his tenderest pride till he roared like a bull, Savanukah after ward had cause to repudiate this opinion in a conviction which was less to the credit of the acumen of Tsiskwa than a full con fession of his breach of etiquette in torment ing his young " grandfather " might have been. At the time Savanukah felt a certain malicious pride in the old man's keenness and poise and capacity, and he said apart to the inquisitive bystanders that, as might have been expected, the big bird, Tsiskwa-yah, had pounced upon the little bird, Tscholen-tit — for the name of each signifies a bird in their respective languages, and the suffixes imply great and small. And mightily pleased was Savanukah with his own wit.

That night came a sudden change. A keen frost was falling soon after the sun went down, for the wind was laid, and such a chill glittering white moon came gliding out of the mists about the dark Great Smoky domes that it seemed the winter incarnate. All adown the desert aisles of the leafless

woods the light lay with a flocculent glister like snow, so enhanced was its whiteness in the rare air and the blackness of the forest shadows — spare, clearly drawn, all filar and fine like the intricacies of a delicate line en graving. Something that the daylight might have shown, blue and blurred, was about the mountains ; it followed the progress of that wintry moon westward. Presently, drawn up from across the ranges, it proved to be a purple cloud, and despite the broad section of the heavens still clear and the glittering whorls of the constellations, that cloud held snow.

As the loitering southern winter had been long in abeyance, many of the Cherokees of Citico Town were still in their airy summer residences, but in one of the conical " win ter houses," stove-like, air-tight, windowless, plastered within and without with the im pervious red clay of the region, after the fashion of the great rotunda, Tscholens, in view of his sudden seizure and complaint of the gentle breeze of the south as freighted with the chill of the north, was consigned to rest. Half a dozen Cherokee braves were detailed to accompany him, nominally as a

guard ; but, there being no menace, this was in recognition of his importance and distinc tion, his escort of Delaware Indians having been billeted about in the town. There was no chimney, and although the fire which burned in the centre of the clay floor ex haled but little smoke, it hung in the air for the lack of the means of escape, and seemed to add to the warmth which the fuel sent forth. Now and again the superfluity of ashes encroached on the live coals. Where upon one or another of the occupants of the restricted apartment, silent and recumbent upon the cane divan, which served now as bed and extended all around the room be tween the walls and the row of posts that upheld the roof, would reach out a long stick, furnished for the purpose to each sleeper, and touch off the incumbering ash from the glow of the embers. As the night wore deeper into the dark hours these inter vals of waking were rarer.

Tscholens, muffled in bed draperies of otter furs and feathered mantles, his cane-wrought couch softened with panther and wolf skins, heard the wind going its rounds, and he realized that the direction of the

currents of the air had veered and it came straight from the north. With the mere suggestion his heart sank. How should he return whence it came? — baffled, denied, empty-handed! — from these specious Cher-okees, who yet called the Lenape "grand father."

The young war-captain had divined since he had been among them that the Chero-kees were making ready for war against the British government; they would attack the South Carolina colonists, and for this rea son, if for no other, they would do nothing to anger the Mengwe, the Iroquois, whom, however, they had often fought: for they loved war — they loved war !

Gradually the room grew less warm. A sudden stir sounded under the divan, and a dog presently crept out to the fire, stretch ing lengthily and yawning widely as he went. He bestowed himself in an upright posture by the coals and looked down with drowsy gravity at the glow. His pendant ears, his long, pointed muzzle, his upright, rotund body, and his pose of solemn pon dering made a queer shadow on the wall. He was no Cherokee, so to speak, but was the

property of a French officer, and, following his master here from Fort Toulouse, aux Alibamons, had been left in the care of a Cherokee friend to await his owner's return from a mission to Fort Chartres and other French settlements " in the Illinois." The dog spoke any language, it might seem ; for when one of the braves, half-awakened by his loud, unmannerly yawn, called out a reproof to him in Cherokee, he wagged his tail among the cold ashes till he stirred up a cloud of gritty particles; then he made his way across the room to the speaker, wheezing and sniffing, and bantering for a romp, till he was caught by the muzzle and, squeaking and shriUing, thrust under the divan anew.

Once more silence, save for the patrol of the wind again on its rounds. Once more the flare of the fire, dying gradually down to a smouldering red glow, akin to the smothered red tone of the terra-cotta waU. Once more the hot, angry eyes of the young war-captain, staring hopelessly, sleeplessly into the red gloom and the dull mischance of the future, sequel of the past.

Suddenly a thought struck him. It seemed

at first to take his breath away. He gasped at the mere suggestion of its temerity. Then it set his blood beating furiously in his veins. After a space, in which he sought to calm himself, to still his nerves, to tame his quivering muscles, he rose slowly to a sit ting posture, then stepped deftly, lightly to the floor. Standing motionless, he glanced keenly about in the dull red gloom. All si lence — no stir save the regular rise and fall of the breathing of the slumbering Indians. Nevertheless, with his keen perceptions all alert and tense, he felt an eye upon him. He looked back warily over his shoulder through the lucid red gloom, like a palpable medium, as one looks through a veil or tinted glass.

It was the eye of the dog ! The animal lay under the couch, his muzzle flat on the clay floor. A serious yet doubtful vigilance was in his aspect. Tscholens was already at the exit, which was a narrow winding pas sage serving as a wind-break, and with a sudden turn leading to the outer world. He heard the abrupt patter of the dog's feet on the clay floor, and a drowsy voice calling to the animal in Cherokee, admonishing him to

be still. Tscholens waited without, and, as the dog issued and with half-aroused sus picions sniffed dubiously around him, he stooped down and patted the creature's head. It was well, after all, that he should follow ; the noise of the dog's exit and return would serve to cover his own absence.

He sought craftily to make friends with the dog. " Mon chou ! Mon cochon !" he said, aping the endearments addressed to dog or horse which he had heard from the French officers at Fort Chartres, where he had recently been. Then suddenly in agita tion : " Tais toi ! Sois sage ! "

For the animal was indeed no Cherokee. At the sound of his native tongue, as it were, he demonstrated how little he cared to be in his skin, for his joyous bounces almost took him out of that integument. Luckily his gambols were noiseless, — for the ground was covered with snow.

Tscholens stood for a moment motion less, his brain still afire with the imminent emprise, but his hot heart turning cold, and failing; for the snow — oh, treacherous cloud! — the snow would betray his steps and the trail disclose the mystery.

" Oh, Lowannachen ! " (Oh, north wind!) he moaned, holding up both hands out stretched to the north. " Oh, wischiksil! Witschemil! " (Oh, be thou vigilant! Help me!)

Then suddenly lowering his head, he sped like the wind itself through the town, along the river bant and into the sacred precincts of the " beloved square." Ah ! here he had stood this evening with what different hope and heart. Here in front of the eastern cabin he had sat beside the wily Tsiskwa of Citico, who might hardly make feeble shift to sway a reed, and yet with sharp sarcasms had stabbed him again and again to the very heart.

"Pihmtonheu ! Oh, pihmtonheu ! " (He has the crooked mouth! Oh, he has the crooked mouth !) Tscholens muttered be tween his set teeth as he crossed the open space and paused before the western " holy cabin."

But for his rage, perhaps, but for his smarting wounds, Tscholens might have la bored with some deterrent sense of sacri lege. But no ! With one elastic bound he leaped upon the " holy white seat," whence

he surmounted the tier of places still behind and higher; then he lightly swung himself down into the intervening space in front of the inner partition formed by a red clay wall.

A momentary pause — a monition of cau tion. He looked back over his shoulder at the pallid world without, visible across the barrier of seats through the broad entrance of the loggia-like place. With the reflec tion from the drifts on the ground and the tempered radiance of the moon behind the tissues of cloud, the scene seemed more wan, more illumined with ghastly light, because of the density of the gloom wherein he stood. The conical-shaped winter tenements had each a thatch of snow; the great cir cular council-house, with its whitened dome, glimmered as stately as some marble rotunda on its high mound, distinct against the blur ring blue shadow of the night and the gray clouds and the bare boughs of the encom passing forest. No living creature was to be seen, save the dog that had followed him, and that had paused to investigate some real or fancied find beneath the snow, — a bone, perhaps, flung out from the feastings of

overnight; perhaps some little animal, young or hurt, whelmed in the drift. Now the dog thrust down a tense, inquiring muzzle, sniff ing tentatively, cautiously, and again he plied alternately his forefeet and his hind-feet, digging out the snow from the quarry; then once more, with a motionless body and a straight, quivering tail, he applied his sensitive nostrils to the examination.

Tscholens with gratification noted his ab sorption. This was indeed well. The animal's persistent following further might have ham pered his plans and revealed his intrusion. The next moment, as the illau turned to his purpose, densest night seemed to have en compassed him. The shadows cloaked all, save only the blank wall of clay and, down close to the ground, an arched opening into the sanctum sanctorum, — an opening so limited that it might barely suffice to admit a man's body, creeping prone upon the earth, and so whelmed in night that it seemed to give a new and adequate inter pretation of the idea of darkness. Could he hope, all unaccustomed here, to turn in that restricted space to retrace the way? Could a ray of guiding light be caught

from without across this high, guarding bar rier of tiers of seats ? And what perchance might lurk within instead of the object of this search ?

At the mere thought of this object of search all fear, all vestige of anxiety van ished. Tscholens felt his heart beat fast. His blood throbbed in his temples. He dropped upon his knees—a sinuous, supple motion, a vague rustle, and he had passed into the unimagined dark precincts beyond the aperture.

Absolute quietude now reigned in the t(holy cabin." The darkness filled it with a solemnity and awe that made a compact with silence and accounted the slightest sound, the softest stir, as a sacrilege.

When an owl — a tiny thing, the fa miliar little " wahuhu " of the Cherokees — flitted down with its noiseless wings from out the sky and sat, a mere tuft of feathers and big round eyes, on one of the eaves, its shrill cry and convulsive chatter smote the night with a sudden affright — ah 1 the breath less listening spaces of the " beloved square" seemed to shiver at the sound, and the keen sleety lines of snow were tremulously vibrant

with it as the flakes came slanting down once more from the north.

For as Tscholens plunged out from the sanctuary his first consciousness of the world without was the chill touch of the falling snow on his cheek, its moist, icy breath on his lips beating back his own quick, agitated respiration. The little " wa-huhu," all startled by his sudden exit, rose with a sharp, cat-like mew from the eaves above his head, dislodging a drift upon his hair, and fluttered away to a branch of a tree, still gazing after him as he sped swiftly, joyously, to the winter house where he lodged, — the descending snow would soon fill the trace of his light footsteps and none be the wiser.

All danger of discovery, however, was not overpast. One of the braves in the win ter house experienced a vague intimation of an entrance into the building, that peculiar chill which accompanies even to the warmest fireside an intruder from the outer air. It seemed explained when he roused himself and saw standing by the fire the French officer's dog, now gazing at the glow with meditative eyes, now diverted to industri-

ously licking his sides. As the long cane of the waking Indian threw off the summit of the ashes and touched up the embers to a more cordial warmth, the dog, always rel ishing companionship, repaired to the side of the divan, and the young Cherokee, push ing him off, noticed the dripping sides of the animal where the snow had melted on the hair.

" It must be raining," he said to himself, all unaware that aught had entered except the dog, coming and going after the man ner of his restless kind. The incident re curred no more to his mind save for a vague recollection of his error when he perceived in the morning that it was snow that had fallen in the night and not rain.

A new sensation pervaded the town upon its awakening. The " grandfather" an nounced the termination of his visit.

"JVmatschif" (I shall go home) he said. And in explanation of this sudden resolution, " JV'matunguam." (I have had a bad dream.)

Now a dream among the Indians was of hardly less significance than among the He brews of old. It was sufficient justification

for the undertaking of any enterprise or for any change of intention. Thus the depar ture of the Delaware delegation was shorn of all surprise or imputation of discourtesy. The head-men among the Cherokees felt it very definitely a relief to be freed from the importunities of their " grandfather."

" Good speed to the journey of the illau Tscholens ! " Atta - Kulla - Kulla said that evening after the departure, as the head men of several towns sat discussing the matter around the council-fire in the great state-house of Citico.

" A turbulent ' grandfather ' has a stormy voice and makes the heart of a young man like me very poor for fear ! " the aged Tsiskwa coughed out, and they all greeted the great man's jest with a laugh of appre ciation, and felt it was well that one so old could at once be so sage and so merry. But there came a time when they were of a different mind.

A most important crisis had supervened in the policy of the Cherokee Indians toward the British government when their attention was diverted from their projected demonstra tion against the South Carolina colonists by

a sudden attack from their ancient enemy, the Mengwe (the Iroquois, as the colonists called them). It was an altogether unpro voked attack, it seemed. The martial Cher-okees, however, always eager to fight, de manded no explanations, but at once took the war-path with a great array of their brisk young braves, and because of this interrup tion, it was said, the war of the Cherokees against the British was long delayed.

When at last the casus belli of the Iro quois was disclosed it struck the Cherokees of Citico Town like a thunderbolt. The Cherokee nation, said the Mengwe, had pre sumed to recognize the independence of the Lenni Lenape, whom they knew to have been conquered by the Mengwe more than a century earlier.

This, of course, elicited from the Cher okees a denial of any such recognition. Whereupon the Lenni Lenape themselves produced in counter-asseveration the official belt of the Cherokees, given in exchange for their own, and brought to the hand of their chief sachem by their young illau Tscholens, from Citico Town, the residence of the Chief Tsiskwa.

A deep amazement fell upon the Chero-kees of Citico — the sort of superstitious consternation that a somnambulist might feel in contemplating in broad daylight the deeds he had wrought in sleep-walking. As to the rest of the nation, it was in vain that Tsiskwa denied ; for there were many con firmatory details in support of the incontest able fact of the official belt openly shown in the possession of the Lenni Lenape. The gossips recapitulated the long and solitary audience with Tsiskwa to which Tscholens had been admitted — that strange wild cry with which it had terminated seeming now a cry of joy, not pain ; and this interpre tation was borne out by the obvious affecta tion of illness by which he had sought to hide the true import of the interview. More than all, the matter was put beyond reason able doubt by the discovery of the official belt of the Delawares in the sanctum sanc torum of the " holy cabin " in the " beloved square " among the treasures of the blended religion and statecraft which pertained to the government of the Cherokees. That Tscholens could have surreptitiously ex changed the belts, as Tsiskwa of Citico,

dismayed, overwhelmed, yet blusteringly contended, was held to be preposterous ; for there was not a moment, sleeping or waking, when the Delawares were not in the com pany and close charge of the Cherokees, who must needs have been cognizant of any such demonstration.

Only one explanation was deemed plausi ble : the old man, doubtless in his dotage despite his seeming mental poise, had lost sight of the political significance of the bauble; he had bestowed it after the man ner of the presents that all were unofficially heaping upon the " grandfather," and had mechanically, unthinkingly, received in ex change the Delaware belt.

After one reeling moment of doubt the town of Citico recovered its balance and loyally supported its prince, but the rest of the nation was unanimous in the acceptance of the popular interpretation.

How far extended the influence of this recognition by the Cherokees of the inde pendence of the Lenni Lenape it is impossi ble to say, but it is well known that they acted independently in the American phase of the Seven Years' War and fought on

behalf of the French, and in the Revolu tion they took the part of the Americans against the British, contrary to the policy of the Mengwe. About the time of the treaty of the United States with the In dians in 1795, the Mengwe, who had been greatly cast down by the defeat of their allies, the British, came forward of their own accord and desired publicly to ac knowledge the independence of the Lenni Lenape.

The masterly political machinations of Tscholens and the mystery in which they were enveloped did not permanently impair the cordial relations existing between his tribe and the Cherokees, for so late as 1779 a delegation of fourteen Cherokees is chron icled as appearing in the country of the Lenni Lenape at their council-fire, to con dole with them on the death of their head-chief ; but neither before nor since is there any record of another visit of the turbulent " grandfather " to the banks of the Tennes see Kiver.

NOTES

NOTES

1. Page 6. The annals of the southwestern settle ments commemorate many instances of daring hearts in delicate frames, and the pioneer woman who per haps under softer and safer circumstances would have screamed at a mouse often shouldered a rifle and bravely joined the frontiersmen in the defense of the stockade against the most cruel, most wily, most warlike savage foe that ever a civilized force en countered. Courage, of all the qualities of the moral panoply, is the least to be reckoned with by logic. Perhaps after all it is not inherent, even in the no bler organisms, but evolved by a conscientious sense of responsibility and the dynamic potencies of emer gency. La Bruyere says: " Jetez-moi dans les troupes comme un simple soldat, je suis Thersite: mettez-moi a la tete d'une armee dont j'aie a repondre a toute VEurope, je suis Achille ! "

2. Page 114. The chungke stone of this favorite game of the southern Indians bears a certain resem blance to the ancient discus of the Greek athlete. This, it will be remembered,

fashioned of metal or stone, circular, almost flat, was clasped by the fingers of one hand and held in the bend of the forearm, extending almost to the elbow. The genuine chungke stone is solid and discoidal in shape, beautifully pol ished, wrought of quartz, or agate, the most distinc-

tive being concave on both sides, beveled toward the flat outer edge, and having a depression in the centre of both surfaces for the convenience of holding it with the second finger and thumb, the first finger clasping the periphery. Its usual dimensions are about six or eight inches in diameter. There are several varieties of these archaic relics, some flat, others lenticular or of a wedge-shell shape, and others, still, concave on one side and convex on the other. An absolutely spherical stone, bearing the extraordinarily high pol ish that distinguishes these unique objects, found in an ancient mound and supposed to have relation to the same or a similar game, calls to mind the globular quoit of the classical athletes and that "enormous round " described by Homer, "Action's quoit" — to hurl which bowl they vie, " who teach the disk to sound along the sky."

The exquisite finish of the chungke stone was com passed without the aid of a single tool, merely by the attrition of one stone upon another, " from time im memorial rubbed smooth upon the rocks, with prodi gious labor," resulting in an object of such symmetri cal beauty that even in the museums of the present day, out of which it is rarely seen, it challenges ad miration. Antiquaries variously contend that it was hurled through the air and that it was bowled on the edge along the ground, its equilibrium being so per fect that on a level space it will roll a great distance, falling only when its impetus is expended.

The chungke stone is often confounded with the In dian quoit, likewise circular and fashioned of smoothly wrought stone, but with an orifice in the centre, ren-

dering it in effect a ring to be flung over a stake at a distance, or to be caught on the point of a lance.

It has been inferred that Adair is mistaken in his assertion that by the Indian law the chungke stones were exempt from burial with the effects of the dead, since certain of the most perfect specimens known to modern archaeological collections were found in the exploration of mounds in the valley of the Tennessee River. By many these mounds are supposed to be prehistoric, and the game is doubtless of an unima ginable antiquity. As late as his day, among the Cher-okees, 1736, the stones were kept with the " strictest religious care," and were the property of the town where the game was played.

Adair, despite his roving life, had evidently scant sympathy with athletics. He may have been grow ing old and indolent when he speaks of the game as a " task of stupid drudgery " and opines that in stead of a sport it might " with propriety of lan guage " be described as " running hard labor." Other eye-witnesses, however, vaunt the great beauty and grace of the game. Captain Bernard Romans chron icles with relish the dexterity requisite, the great strength and skill displayed by the participants in the violent exercise, although demurely moralizing the while on its perilous fascination to both players and spectators, by reason of the inordinate temptation pre sented by its doubtful chances to the reckless gambler. Lieutenant Timberlake alone calls it " nettecawaw."

As there are moot points concerning the stones them selves and the conduct of the sport, so the chungke spears differ in the accounts of the early adventurers

in this region. The length is variously given as eight, ten, twelve feet. The shape is sometimes represented as a lance or pole heavy in the centre and tapering at both ends to a blunt point, and others describe an implement resembling a magnified golf club of the present day.

3. Page 114. This choice decoration, popular though it was, could not be attained without

a penalty commensurate with its valuation. It is stated by early travelers among the Indian tribes that thirty days were required to properly heal an ear thus dis tended a la mode. The patient, if one so prideful might be so called, could only have one ear in the painful process at a time, in order that he might be able to lie in sleeping on the other side until such time as his embellished ear should be again service able for this prosaic purpose, and permit the like de coration of the opposite member.

4. Page 142. An illustration of how the Choc-taws profited by these earnest labors may be given in the fate of a chapel erected for their benefit at Chick-asaha by the French and placed in charge of a Jesuit missionary. The Choctaws so far accepted Christian ity as to be able to travesty the services and mimic the priest with surprising humor and verisimilitude when the English came in, and were wont to go to the old chapel for this profane exhibition to the mingled delight and reprobation of the military newcomers. The chapel was soon afterward destroyed, but Captain Romans records that in 1771 he saw the cross still standing on the site, a melancholy memorial of futile missionary endeavor.

All the Indians, however, were temperamentally averse to the services and tenets of the Christian reli gion, and Timberlake gives an instance among the Cherokees in 1760 in which a missionary was balked by a unique interruption. " Mr. Martin, who having preached Scripture till both he and his audience were heartily tired, was told at last that they knew very well that if they were good they would go up ; if bad, down; that he could tell no more; that he had long plagued them with what they no ways understood, and they desired that he would depart the country."

The epitome of theology thus deduced was so far a just conclusion. But doubtless the Indians labored greatly with imperfect comprehension. Humboldt describes a service among a South American tribe, in which a missionary preaching in Spanish was at his wits' end to make his audience differentiate between infierno and invierno. They persisted in shivering with horror at the picture of the hell of his warnings in which the wicked were supposed to be subjected to everlasting winter. One is tempted to think that the end might have justified the means if the good padre had fallen in with the prejudice against the rainy season and adopted, in lieu of the fire-and-brim-stone of Scripture, as a future state of punishment, the icy Ninth Circle of Dante's Inferno, where

" Eran V ombre dolenti nella ghiaccia, Mettendo i denti in nota di cicogna"

5. Page 151. The cultivation of personal pride was an essential element of training among the In dians. They held the lower ranks of white people in

great contempt, and Timberlake records that in some athletic diversions at which he and other members of the Virginia regiment were present they refused to play or to hold conference with any of the troops except the officers.

6. Page 179. The primary and somewhat com plex significance of the word ada-wehi is suggested by the idea of sorcery, — a man, or animal, or even element endowed with uncontrolled superlative and supernatural powers. It has been stated that since the introduction of Christianity and the printing of the New Testament in the Cherokee typographical character the word has been utilized with its subtle ties of signification to express spirit or angel. In this story, however, the scene of which is laid in a period long previous to the conversion of the tribe, or even the accepted date of the invention of the Cherokee alphabet, the word is used in its early and original sense to denote a magician of special and expansive gifts of sorcery.

7. Page 186. Although this officer's name was regularly incorporated into the Cherokee vocabulary as a synonym of disaster, he seemed to revolt at the unhappy plight of the people whom in the discharge of his duty he had succeeded in reducing to so abject a condition of

despair and woe, and has left on record expressions of compassion incongruous with his deeds and his position as a professed soldier of long experi ence. He had served in Flanders and Ireland in his youth as captain in the Royal Scots before he first came to America as major in Montgomerie's regiment of Highlanders.

Some adequate idea of the desolation and destitu tion of the Indians may be gleaned from the reports to the British government: " The Cherokees must certainly starve or come into terms, and even in that case Colonel Grant thinks it is hardly in the power of the provincials to save them. He proposed in a few days to send for The Great Warrior (Oconostota) and The Little Carpenter (Atta-Kulla-Kulla) to come and treat for peace, if they choose to save their nation from destruction. Till he receives their answer he will endeavor to save the small remains of the Lower Towns. In the mean time Colonel Grant intends to put Fort Prince George into repair, and to wait there or at Ninety-Six till he receives orders from Sir Jeffrey Amherst."

The idea of the pangs of hunger and the sight of starvation and deprivation may have been the more repugnant to Colonel Grant since he was himself famous as a bon vivant and gourmet. Indeed, even yet, in turning old pages we come upon records of his dinners. Bartram, the Philadelphia botanist, whom the Muscogee Indians quaintly called Puc-Puggy (the Flower Hunter) details the great size of a rattlesnake, " six feet long and as thick as the leg of an ordinary man " which he chanced to kill in his bosky researches near Fort Picolata in Florida, and not the least surprising feature of the incident was a message from the commandant inviting both com batants to dinner, " Governor Grant being very fond of rattlesnake flesh." This officer, at that time Royal Governor of East Florida, was holding a congress with the Creek Indians hard by the fort, having come

from St. Augustine with a detachment of its gar rison for the purpose. Bartram, dining in company with Grant that day, saw his enemy served up in sev eral different styles, — and he, too, must turn soft hearted ! — he could not partake of the dish, — and " was sorry after killing the serpent, when coolly re collecting every circumstance of it." However, neither the rattlesnake nor the Cherokees were in condition to profit by these belated graces of magnanimity.

Through Grant's scattered correspondence there is a flavor of "vivers." Frederick George Mulcaster, still with the garrison of St. Augustine, in a letter ad dressed to Grant, then in Boston, laughingly alludes to his constant good cheer. "Captain Urquhart writes to his brother officers here that' General Grant lives like a General!'" And later, in piteous con trast, "His Excellency (the new Royal Governor) gave a dinner yesterday to the officers of the Four teenth and some others. It is the only dinner he has given since the one he gave to John Stuart (famous as the survivor of Fort Loudon) upon his arrival here," — a matter of two months. He further notes as a point of interest, " Your black man, Alexander, was with me this instant to inquire after your health, and has loaded me with beaucoup de complimens. He wishes much to come to make your bread." Doubtless it was well made, for Grant, prospering, went on from dinner to dinner, from promotion to promotion, attaining the rank of General in the army and great corpulency, representing Sutherlandshire in the British Parliament many years, and dying at the age of eighty-six at his birthplace, Ballindalloch, in the north of Scotland.

8. Page 212. The " Annual Register " in giving among State Papers the text of a treaty between Governor Lyttleton of South Carolina, Captain-Gen eral, etc., and Atta-Kulla-Kulla, "deputy for the whole Cherokee Nation," dated at Fort Prince George, Dec. 26, 1759, adds in a note: " Atta-Kulla-Kulla, the Little Carpenter, who concluded this treaty in behalf of the Cherokee Indians, was in England and at court several times in the year 1730."

9. Page 215. The oratorical gifts of this Indian (under the name Chollochcullah, supposed

to be a phonetic variant of Atta-Kulla-Kulla) are thus de scribed in The Gentleman's Magazine for October, 1755, chronicling the details of an earlier diplomatic occasion: " The speaker rose up, and holding a bow in one hand and a sheaf of arrows in the other, he delivered himself in the following words, with all the distinctness imaginable, with the dignity and graceful action of a Roman or Grecian orator, and with all their ease and eloquence."

10. Page 231. Their tribal name, " men of fire," and their great veneration for that element have given rise to the conjecture that the Cherokees were originally fire-worshipers, as well as polytheistic. The interpolation of the intensative syllable " ta" is, ac cording to Adair, a " note of magnitude," and the title of their prophets, whose functions are blended as priests, conjurers, physicians, and councilors, — the cheera-taghe, — signifies " men of divine fire." But Adair protests that the theistic ideals of the Indians were wholly spiritual, and that they had no plurality of gods. They paid their devotions merely to the

" great beneficent supreme holy spirit of fire, who resides as they think above the clouds," and he argues plausibly that if they worshiped fire itself they would not have willfully extinguished the sanctified element annually on the last day of the old year throughout the nation, the invariable custom, before the cheera-taghe of each town kindled the " holy fire " anew, this being one of their exclusive functions. It may be that in their ancient rhapsodies (many of which Mr. James Mooney has collected for the Smithsonian Institu tion) addressed to bird or flame or beast the Indians adopted a poetic license no more significant of poly theism than the flights of fancy of many Christian poets in odes to the moon, to Fate, " to the red planet Mars," to the "wild west wind." Mere impersona tion and invocation in apostrophe and paeans are not necessarily worship. Doubtless these spells and charms often arose from a superstitious half-belief, an ima ginative freak, such as possesses the civilized visionary who shows a coin to the new moon to propitiate its fancied waxing influence in behalf of a balance at the banker's, or the Christianized Scotch Highlander of even the early nineteenth century who threw a piece of hasty pudding over the left shoulder on the an niversary of Beoildin (the Gaelic for no other than Baal) to appease the spirits of the mists, the winds, the ravens, the eagles, and thus protect the crops and flocks. There is a thin boundary line as difficult to define as " to distinguish and divide a hair 'twixt south and southwest side," between true belief and feigned credence.

The veneration of the ancient Cherokees for the

element of fire, in addition to their name, its care ful conservation throughout the year, their addresses to its spirit, Higayuli Tsunega, hatu ganiga (O Ancient White, you have drawn near to listen), is further manifested by its traces found in the explo ration of burial mounds, intimating a ceremonial in troduction of the element at the remote period of interment, — if, indeed, the construction of these mounds can be ascribed to the Cherokees. Those on which their town houses were erected at a later date, the clay-covered rotunda forming a superstructure look ing like a small mountain at a little distance, accord ing to Timberlake, wherein were held the assemblies, whether for amusement or council or religious observ ances, served also as a substitute for the modern bulletin-board. Two stands of colors were flying, one from the top of the town house, the other at the door. These ensigns were white for peace, and exchanged for red when war impended. " The news hollow," as Timberlake phrases the cry, sounded from the summit of the mound, would occasion the assembling of all the community in the rotunda to hear the details from the lips of the chief. How much more the "death hollow," harbinger of woe !

11. Page 323. They are hardly to be regarded as myths perhaps, rather as dislocated relics of fact. In treating of the "Origin of American Nations," Dr. Barton says: " These traditions are entitled to much consideration, for, notwithstanding the rude condition of most of the tribes, they

are often per petuated in great purity, as I have discovered by much attention to their history." It is generally ac-

cepted that the first historical mention of the Cher-okees occurs under the name of Chelaque in the chronicles of De Soto's expedition in 1540 when they already occupied the Great Smoky Mountains and the contiguous region, but the Indians themselves had a tradition, according to Haywood's Natural and Abo riginal History of Tennessee, which was recited an nually at the Green Corn Dance, in which they claimed that they were the earlier mound builders on the upper Ohio, whence they had migrated at a re mote date. They can be identified with the ancient Talega or Tallegwi if the records of the Walam Olum (painted sticks) may be believed, the wooden originals of which are said to have been preserved till 1822 and considered inexplicable, till their mnemonic signs and a manuscript song in the Lenni Lenape language, obtained from a remnant of the Delaware Indians, were translated by Professor C. S. Rafinesque " with deep study of the Delaware and the aid of Zeisberger's manuscript Dictionary in the library of the Philo sophical Society."

In this, a dynasty of Lenni Lenape chiefs and the events of their reigns are successively named, and from the first mention of their encounter with the warlike Tallegwi or Cherokee to the discovery of Co lumbus there is necessarily implied the passage of many centuries. Even the time that has elapsed since the Tallegwi were overthrown by them is estimated as somewhat more than a thousand years, thus placing this defeat in the ninth century. Professor Cyrus Thomas in "The Cherokees of Pre-Columbian Times " states that he thinks it would be more nearly correct to

credit the event to the eleventh or twelfth century. He quotes in support of his theory from the Walam-Olum as translated by Dr. Brinton, who giving the original in parallel pages, with the mnemonic signs, does not use in the English version the Indian names of the chiefs.

This record of the Walam-Olum is really very curi ous. After passing the account of the Creation, the Flood, the Migrations, and entering upon the Chron icles, the Walam-Olum reads much like a Biblical genealogy, save that in lieu of scions of a parent tree these are military successors, war-captains. The follow ing quotations are from the version given by Squier:

" 47. Opekasit (East-looking) being next chief, was sad because of so much warfare.

48. Said let us go to the Sun-rising (Wapagishek) and many went east together.

49. The Great River (Messussipu) divided the land and being tired they tarried there.

50. Yagawanend (Hut-Maker) was next sakimau, and then the Tallegwi were found possessing the east.

51. Followed Chitanitis (Strong Friend), who longed for the rich east land.

52. Some went to the east but the Tallegwi killed a portion.

53. Then all of one mind exclaimed war, war !

54. The Talamatan (Not-of-themselves) and the Nitilowan all united (to the war).

55. Kinnehepend (Sharp-looking) was their leader, and they went over the river.

56. And they took all that was there and despoiled and slew the Tallegwi.

57. Pimokhasuwi (Stirring About) was next chief, and then the Tallegwi were much too strong.

58. Tenchekensit (Open Path) followed and many towns were given up to him.

59. Paganchihilla was chief, — and the Tallegwi all went southward."

After the earliest mention of the Tallegwi in verse 50 of the First Chronicle there are about fifty chief tains enumerated, and characterized with their suc cessive reigns before the entrance of the white dis coverers of the continent at the end of the Second Chronicle. In this it is stated at verse —

" 56. Nenachipat was chief toward the sea.

57. Now from north and south came the Wapaga-chik (white comers).

58. Professing to be friends, in big birds (ships). Who are they ? "

And with this dramatic climax the ancient picture record closes.

What is known as the Modern Chronicle, a frag ment, begins with the answer, " Alas ! Alas ! we know now who they are, these Wapinsis (East People) who came out of the sea to rob us of our lands."

And that the modern chronicle shall be certainly correct the successor of Lekhibit (the compiler of the ancient story) is assisted by critical philologists, and Rafinesque takes issue with Holm touching a Swedish suffix in an Indian name. " Mattanikum was chief in 1645. He is called ' Mattahorn' by Holm, and «horn' is not Lenapi! "

It is difficult to adjust one's credulity to accept as history this singular Indian picture-record. Its au-

thenticity is supported by the great scope of the sys tem and the reputed subtlety and close accuracy by which abstract ideas, the origin of things, the powers of nature, the elements of religion, could be expressed and read by those conversant with the mnemonic signs, — as easily, Heckewelder says, as a piece of writing. The noted antiquary Squier, however, who in this con nection has lauded Rafinesque's industry, scientific attainments, and eager researches, states that since writing in this vein he has seen fit to read this au thor's American Nations and finds it " a singular jumble of facts and fancies," and adds that it is un fortunate that the manuscript in question should fall in this category. To praise, even with qualifications, the author without reading all his work on the sub ject, while certainly more amiable, is hardly more conducive to an impartial estimate than to disparage on hearsay, according to that travesty of critical judgment: "' Que dites-vous du livre d'Hermodore ?' * Qu'il est mauvais,' repond Anthime . . . ' Mais Vavez-vouslu?" NonJdit Anthime. Quen'ajoute-t-il qiie Fulvie et Melanie Vont condamne sans Vavoir lu, et qu'il est ami de Fulvie et de Melanie ? "

In contrast with this method the caution and criti cal scrutiny with which Dr. Brinton, in his work on " The Lenape," deliberates upon the question of the authenticity of the Walam Olum are indeed marked. He carefully examines all the details both favorable and adverse, and finally adduces the evidence of the text itself. The manuscript submitted by him to edu cated Indians of the Lenni Lenape is pronounced to be a genuine oral composition of a Delaware Indian

in an ancient dialect, evidently dictated to one not wholly conversant with all the terminal inflections of the words, which occasional omissions form the chief defect of the curious " Red Score."

12. Page 324. Some authorities hold that the Talamatan (Not-of-themselves) mentioned by the Walam-Olum were the Hurons who allied them selves with the Delawares against the Tallegwi, and that Heckewelder is mistaken in stating that these confederates were the Mengwe. This story, however, follows the account of the war and the subsequent sub jection of the Delawares as given by Heckewelder.

THE END